REBEL WITHOUT A CLAUS

MOVIE CLUB MYSTERIES, BOOK 5

ZARA KEANE

BEAVERSTONE PRESS

REBEL WITHOUT A CLAUS
(Movie Club Mysteries, Book 5)

Makeup. Mannequins. Murder.

When ex-cop-turned-P.I. Maggie Doyle scores a lucrative undercover job at the makeup counter at a fashionable Galway department store, she expects discounted lipstick and an easy paycheck.

After an altercation with a customer leads to a dead body in Maggie's bathtub, she and her assistant realize there's more to the department store case than missing cash. Can they catch the killer before the holidays? Or will the festive season end in an explosion of tinsel and turmoil?

NOTE ON GAELIC TERMS

Certain Gaelic terms appear in this book. I have tried to use them sparingly and in contexts that should make their meaning clear to international readers. However, a couple of words require clarification.

The official name for the Irish police force is *An Garda Síochána* ("the Guardian of the Peace"). Police are *Gardaí* (plural) and *Garda* (singular). Irish police are commonly referred to as "the guards".

The official rank of a police officer such as Sergeant Reynolds is Garda Sergeant Reynolds. As the Irish frequently shorten this to Sergeant, I've chosen to use this version for all but the initial introduction to the character.

The official name for the Whisper Island police station would be Whisper Island Garda Station, but Maggie, being American, rarely thinks of it as such.

The Irish police do not, as a rule, carry firearms. Permission to carry a gun is reserved to detectives and specialist units, such as the Emergency Response Unit. The police on Whisper Island would not have been issued with firearms.

Although this book follows American spelling conventions, I've chosen to use the common Irish spelling for proper names such as Carraig Harbour and the Whisper Island Medical Centre. An exception is the Movie Theater Café, which was named by Maggie's American mother.

1

When I'd ditched my cheating husband and stagnant career in the San Francisco PD to open a private investigation agency in Ireland, I hadn't envisioned "purveyor of butt bleach" being part of my job description.

Buoyed with enthusiasm after several successful cases, and flush with cash after my divorce, I'd taken out an ad in *The Galway Herald*. The ad had scored Movie Reel Investigations its first two jobs away from Whisper Island—investigating a series of thefts at a high-end store, and a case of suspected embezzlement at a costume manufacturer. While Lenny, my childhood-friend-turned-assistant-P.I., used his computer ninja skills at the costume company, I was stuck behind the cosmetics counter at Dennehy's. Three days into my stint undercover at Galway's most exclusive department store, I was ready to book a one-way ticket to Mars.

"Your incompetence caused me a serious injury," the woman on the opposite side of the cosmetics counter said to me. "I expect to be compensated for my suffering."

I checked the irate customer for obvious signs of crazy-pants. On first inspection, she looked like any other aging trophy wife: caramel highlights, layers of expensive makeup, and mad eyes thanks to an overly enthusiastic facelift.

"Let me get this straight," I said. "You wanted over-the-counter *butt bleach*?"

My coworker, Tracey, stifled a snort and shoved her head into a drawer of lipsticks to drown out her laughter.

"I specifically asked for *intimate* bleach," the customer snapped, her cheeks turning scarlet. "The stuff you gave me is for facial hair."

I blew out my cheeks and counted to five before answering. "You asked for a formula that was suitable for bleaching sensitive skin. I assumed you meant your face."

"I said *sensitive areas*," she hissed. "Surely you knew what I meant without me spelling it out for you."

"You're walking like a gorilla in heat, so it's a safe bet I didn't get the part about you wanting to bleach your butt and pubes."

Oops. Had I said that out loud? From the gaping expression on the woman's face and Tracey's attack of the giggles, that would be a "Yes."

The customer's mouth opened and closed, fishlike.

"This is outrageous," she spluttered. "I want to speak to your supervisor at once."

As if on cue, Nuala Kearns, head of Dennehy's cosmetics department, slithered into sight. She had the emaciated look of a woman who substituted cigarettes for food—cavernous features, sunken eyes, and lines around her mouth that no amount of expensive makeup could hide.

Nuala's raisin eyes bored into me before she pulled her thin lips into a smile and addressed the customer. "How may I help you?"

My accuser wasted no time in launching into her litany of complaints. "Your assistant sold me facial hair lightener instead of intimate bleach. The error left me in considerable discomfort. When I complained about her mistake, she called me an ape."

"Not an ape. I said you were walking like a gorilla in heat." Nuala cast me a quelling look. Okay, so maybe repeating that last sentence hadn't been the smartest move, however apt the description. "Hey, it was an honest mistake to make. I thought she wanted to lighten her mustache."

"How dare you?" The customer quivered with indignation. "I don't have a mustache. How can—"

"I'm *so* sorry about this unfortunate chain of events," Nuala cut in. "On behalf of Dennehy's department store, I'd like to offer you a store credit for one hundred euros."

The customer gave a dramatic sob. "I'm in agony. I hardly think one hundred euros is enough to compensate me for the humiliation and pain I've endured."

I rolled my eyes. Talk about overacting. This lady was milking the situation for all she could get.

"Why don't I speak to the store manager?" Nuala offered in a soothing tone. "I'm sure we'll be able to come to a satisfactory agreement."

The customer regarded me with contempt. "As long as the agreement includes firing this fool."

Whoa. Talk about unfair. "Why should I be blamed for your mistake?" I demanded. "I sold you the product, but it was your responsibility to check it was the item you'd asked for. And you definitely should have read the instructions before you applied it to your private parts."

Nuala's reptilian gaze pinned me in place. "That's enough, Maggie. Go upstairs and wait outside Mr. Dennehy's office. I'll be up in a moment."

I suppressed a groan. I was supposed to work here for at least another week, or for however long it took me to discover which member of staff was systematically stealing from the cash registers.

Ms. Butt Bleach smirked. "Good luck with getting a reference now."

Her words hit a nerve. I'd recently forked out for a private investigator's course for Lenny and increased his hours to full-time. My goal with the Dennehy's job was to use it as a springboard to gain more clients on the mainland—clients who paid better than the average islander.

I unclenched my fists and drew in a deep, calming breath. Without a backward glance at my accuser, I stomped off in the direction of the manager's office. If I got to him before Nuala did, I might be able to talk myself out of the situation.

WHEN I REACHED the fourth floor, I marched through the door marked "Staff Only" and into the reception area of the department store's administration offices. In stark contrast to the opulence of the rest of the store, the walls here were painted anemic beige. The cork-tile flooring had last been fashionable in the Seventies, and the bland choice of framed landscapes reinforced my impression that the place received little love.

Wedged between two leafy plants—the only splash of greenery in the place—was a single-serve coffee machine. Tom Dennehy, a.k.a. Mr. Comb-Over, stood before it, cup in hand. He was a tall, wiry man with sparse brown hair dragged across his scalp in an ineffectual attempt to disguise his bald patch. As soon as he caught sight of my thunderous expression, he reared back in alarm, almost spilling his coffee. "Hi, Maggie. How's it going?"

"Badly." I slid a look at the receptionist, a bouffant blonde in her mid-twenties who'd taken a break from the arduous task of filing her nails to eavesdrop. "Can we talk in private?"

"Sure." He gestured to the coffee machine. "Want a cup?"

"I'm good, thanks." I'd have liked a caffeine hit, but I wanted us to get our story straight before Nuala showed her gaunt face and demanded he fire me. I followed the manager into his office and slumped into the leather chair opposite his desk. "Ms. Kearns is going to ask you to get rid of me."

Tom winced and ran a palm over his scalp, mussing his comb-over. "I warned you Nuala was difficult. What happened?"

"I sold some chick facial hair remover instead of butt bleach."

The man recoiled, his face a tableau of horror. "Is she planning to sue?"

I shrugged. "Ms. Kearns is trying to persuade her to accept a hundred-euro store credit."

The store manager pulled a cloth handkerchief from his breast pocket and dabbed at his sweaty brow. "That's…not good. My father will have a fit. We're already losing money to the store thief."

Tom's father, Seamus Dennehy, was the owner of the department store and the man who'd hired me to catch the thief. Ostensibly retired, Seamus kept a close eye on the business from the confines of his wheel-chair. During my short acquaintance with the Dennehy men, I'd learned that while Seamus spent his days at home in his house in Loughrea, he was still the driving force behind the business.

"We need to come up with a convincing story for

why you're keeping me on staff," I said. "Everyone who witnessed today's drama knows Ms. Kearns wants me gone, and I understand you'd usually defer to her wishes."

Tom drew his bushy eyebrows together and took a sip from his coffee cup. "I suppose I could take her into my confidence and tell her you're an undercover P.I. Nuala's been with us for over twenty years. I can't imagine she's the thief."

Neither could I. Nuala Kearns was a pain in the rear, but she had a loyalty to the store that bordered on fanatical. "Confiding in her might be the cleverest thing to do at this stage. I'm sorry it had to come to this, but I honestly thought the customer wanted facial hair lightener, and she didn't correct my assumption when I handed her the package."

"Some of our wealthier clientele can be prickly. We'll fob her off with the store credit and hope for the best. I need you here to find the thief." Tom regarded me over the rim of his cup. "Apart from causing our customers grievous bodily harm, how's the investigation going?"

I schooled my features into a neutral expression. "I've narrowed down my list of suspects to a few likely contenders."

I didn't add that by "a few," I meant ten-plus. In truth, the investigation was progressing at a snail's pace. Any of the store's employees could be responsible for the missing cash.

"When can I expect a result?" The man's white-knuckled grip on his cup indicated the stress he was under.

"I've only been here three days, and that's counting the half-day shift yesterday when I had no excuse to have lunch with the other staff."

Tom pulled a face. "Sorry about that. I'd have let you work the whole day, but no one from your department had called in sick. Giving you a double shift would have aroused suspicion. The deal we have with our full-time staff is that they're only expected to be here for few hours if they're scheduled to work on a Sunday."

"That makes sense, but I rely on opportunities to mingle with my coworkers to glean info about the missing cash. As soon as I have concrete evidence, I'll let you know." I settled back in my chair, confident that I had the manager on my side. "My assistant and I might need access to the store after hours. Can that be arranged?"

He raised an eyebrow. "Are you planning to catch the person in the act?"

"It's worth a shot. Money is going missing every day, and all members of staff are being searched before they leave the premises. That tells me we're looking at one of two possibilities. Either the thief is passing the money on to an accomplice during opening hours, or they're hiding the cash and collecting it at a time they know they won't be searched."

"But we have a security system and surveillance

cameras," Tom protested. "How can the thief get into the building without setting off the alarm *and* without being caught on camera?"

"You're assuming the thief doesn't know how to disable the alarm. And as your security guards have already told you, the surveillance cameras don't cover every inch of the store." I shifted position in the stiff leather chair. "I'd like to have a copy of the last seventy-two hours of surveillance footage."

Tom frowned. "Your assistant already looked through our recordings from last week. You told me he found nothing."

"Yeah, but I want to have another try. The money isn't vanishing by magic. Someone, most likely a member of staff, is skimming cash from the cash registers and sneaking it out of the store. All the cash registers are covered by cameras. There's got to be a clue somewhere on that footage."

"If you think it'll help, be my guest. I'll make you a copy of the last couple of days of footage."

"Thank you." I flashed him a wry smile. "What are we going to do about Nuala? She'll be furious when she finds out you haven't fired me, and I don't think the news that I'm a private investigator will soothe her."

Tom grimaced. "Leave Nuala to me. I'm not thrilled about having to tell her why you're really here, but it might be handy to have another set of eyes watching for unusual behavior. The sooner we catch the thief…" He trailed off and looked at me sheepishly.

I smiled. "The sooner you can dispense with my expensive services. I understand, Tom. I want to wrap up this case as quickly as I can."

He glanced at his watch. "It's five to six. Your shift is almost over. Why don't you call it a day and go home with the surveillance footage? That'll give me a chance to speak to Nuala before tomorrow."

"Okay. I'll let you know if I find anything useful on it. What about gaining access to the store after closing? Ideally, I'd like to try tomorrow night."

"I'll give you a key card for the admin staff entrance and write down the security code." He opened a desk drawer and located a key card. He scribbled a code on a sticky note and gave it to me, along with the key card.

"Thanks." I slipped them into my pocket. "What about the surveillance footage?"

"I'll get that for you now." Tom rooted around in another drawer and withdrew a flash drive. He stuck it into his laptop and pressed a few keys. "I have access to the last seventy-two hours of surveillance footage ending at six o'clock this morning. That's when the recordings are backed up to our cloud storage."

"That's okay. They'll give me a good overview of what goes on after hours."

After he'd handed me the flash drive, Tom stood, indicating our meeting was at an end. "Good luck,

Maggie. I'd like to get this problem solved before Christmas."

I extended a hand and shook his in a firm handshake. "I'll give it my best shot."

Back out in the reception area, the nosy receptionist glanced up from her computer screen, and then looked sharply to her left. I followed the direction of her gaze and swallowed a groan. Sitting ramrod straight on a chair was Nuala Kearns, evidently fuming at being forced to cool her heels while I spoke to her boss.

"I told you to wait for me," she snapped, her eyes flashing.

"Yeah, you did. I didn't listen."

Her thin lips pressed into a line. "Well?" she demanded through gritted teeth. "Did Mr. Dennehy fire you?"

"You'll have to ask him that question. Have a nice evening, Ms. Kearns." I sauntered out the door, aware of her eyes boring holes into my back.

She'd make my life a misery tomorrow, but I'd deal with that when the time came. Right now, all I wanted was to get out of this place and have a boring, drama-free evening. My lips stretched into a smile. Okay, maybe not entirely boring—I was due to see my boyfriend for the first time in a couple of weeks. After dinner with Liam, I'd head back to my apartment and have a long soak in the bath before tackling the surveillance footage. *Bliss.*

2

I took the stairs down to the basement, where the retail staff lockers were located. The sharp edges of the flash drive bit into the palm of my hand. I'd split the work with Lenny and watch the recordings on high speed, but it would make for a long and tedious night. Still, I hadn't gone into the private investigation business expecting glamor.

In one of the staff changing cubicles, I swapped my uniform for my street clothes. I was back at my locker and lacing up my sneakers when four employees burst in, chattering loudly. Tracey, my coworker from the cosmetics department, gasped when she saw me. "You're still here?"

"Guilty as charged." I grinned. "I noticed you disappeared the instant the trouble started."

The young woman laughed. "Can you blame me? Nuala's a tyrant. I had no desire to get dragged into that mess. What did Dennehy say to you, anyway? I've been dying of curiosity."

"He's not happy, but I'm not fired. Yet."

Siobhan, a hard-faced woman who worked in the household appliances section, stared at me accusingly and slammed open her locker. "Why didn't he sack you? If *my* mistake burned the behind off a customer, I'd be gone with no notice and no reference."

"Me, too." Jasper, a weedy guy from the men's fashion department, had a permanent droop to his mouth and the mood to match. "I wouldn't be surprised if we're all fired before the new year."

I caught Barry's eye and grinned. A Ken-doll looka-like who worked in the toy department, Barry had given me the grand tour of the department store on my first day. We'd hit it off immediately. He'd filled me in on all the full-time staff's idiosyncrasies, including Siobhan's prickly attitude and Jasper's paranoia, and had proved to be my best source of info on the robberies so far.

"Maybe Mr. Dennehy is in a good mood," I said breezily. "Or maybe he has enough sense to realize that I gave the customer exactly what she'd asked for. It's not my fault she was too embarrassed to use direct language and too careless to check that the product I gave her was the one she wanted."

"I can't believe she came back to complain," Barry said with a shudder. "If I'd been stupid enough to burn my behind, I wouldn't limp back to the beauty counter where I'd bought the wrong product."

Tracey pulled a pink cashmere sweater over her uniform and checked her lipstick in the locker mirror. "Nuala won't like the idea of you getting a second chance, Maggie. She's been itching to get rid of you since you refused to get her coffee on your first morning."

"There's nothing in our job description about slaving for Nuala Kearns," I said. "If she'd asked politely, I'd have gotten her the coffee."

"She's always been difficult, but she's been particularly prickly recently." Tracey opened her makeup bag and touched up her lips. "She demanded I tidy the entire Foxy Looks display yesterday and made me late for my acting class. And we were expecting a producer to visit us. I'd hoped to pitch him my idea for *Roisin Takes Hollywood*."

I exchanged an amused look with Barry. Tracey, an aspiring actress and director, tended to drone on about her drama group and her ideas for movies that were destined to conquer the box office. I'd learned to tune her out when she got on a roll.

"Everyone's on edge these days," Barry said before Tracey had the chance to rant about her movie project's financial woes. "It's the disappearing money and the searching staff before we leave the building. It doesn't exactly make for a pleasant working atmosphere."

"Once word gets out about a thief on the loose, no one will want to shop at Dennehy's." The combination of Jasper's distraught expression and monotonous delivery brought a bubble of laughter to my throat. "The place will go bust, and we'll have no jobs."

Tracey rolled her eyes. "Always the optimist, Jasper. Dennehy's has been around for decades. They're not going anywhere."

"If Mr. Dennehy doesn't catch whoever is stealing from the tills, he might carry through with his threat to fire all of us," Siobhan warned. "I can't afford to lose this job."

"I bet he said that in the heat of the moment. He can't replace everyone overnight." I seized on the opportunity for behind-the-scenes gossip. "Do you have any idea who's responsible?"

They all shook their heads. "Not a clue," Barry said, "but I have plenty of people I'd happily cast in the role of the thief if it meant I didn't have to work with them anymore."

Tracey tugged a brush through her long, dark hair and pulled it into a ponytail. "I'd love it if Nuala were the thief, but I don't think she's got it in her."

"It's bizarre." I adopted an incredulous expression. "How can someone steal from the cash registers every day and no one notice?"

"I don't want to think about it," Siobhan muttered. "The whole situation creeps me out. Derek thinks I should look for a new job before Dennehy goes on a firing spree." Over our canteen lunch, I'd been subjected to Siobhan's vacation snapshots. Like her, Derek was a bulky, tattooed biker type and exuded the same pervading air of menace.

"Why don't we head to the pub and forget about this place?" Barry suggested.

"Definitely," Tracey and Siobhan said in unison.

Jasper shrugged his slumped shoulders. "I guess."

Barry looked at me. "What about you, Maggie? Want to help us drown the day's sorrows?"

A hard ball of regret formed in my chest. It was the first time my coworkers had asked me to hang out with them after work. I was loath to turn down the opportunity to pump them for more info, but I had plans. "I'd love to, but I'm meeting my boyfriend for dinner."

"Ooh." Barry grinned. "Is this the sexy police officer you mentioned?"

The butterflies in my stomach took flight at the mere thought of seeing Liam. "I don't think I mentioned the 'sexy' part, but yeah. He's the one."

Barry winked. "He can help you take your mind off a bad day at work."

"I hope so." I pulled on my jacket, hat, scarf, and gloves. "I'll see you guys tomorrow. Enjoy your drinks."

"Have fun with your man," Barry called. "Don't do anything I wouldn't do."

I winked at him. "That doesn't leave many items on the Don't-Do list."

At the staff exit, the security guard took a painful amount of time to search my bags before letting me leave. I understood why I had to submit to the search as part of my undercover persona, but I was cutting it close to meet Liam.

When the guy grunted and gestured for me to go, I speed-walked to Eyre Square, ignoring the icy drizzle that began the instant I stepped onto the sidewalk. I'd taken advantage of my forced half-day yesterday to explore the city, including a historic bus tour. Galway began life as a fishing village. Due to its strategic position where the River Corrib meets Galway Bay, it grew in importance and size. Today, it was a wonderful blend of old and new: cobbled streets and stone arches combined with a vibrant, modern atmosphere. Although I'd visited the city on several occasions since I'd moved to Whisper Island, this was the first time I'd had the opportunity to explore it in detail. This evening, I planned to visit the northern part of the city with my boyfriend, stopping for dinner at a restaurant he'd recommended.

I glanced at my watch and increased my pace to a jog, deftly navigating the hoards of holiday shoppers and their enormous bags. I'd told Liam I'd meet him at six-ten, and it was nearly six-fifteen. I hated being late, especially when I hadn't seen him in over two weeks. First, he'd been away on a training course, and then I'd left for Galway the day before he'd returned to Whisper Island.

Liam and I had been dating for six months. I'd only recently managed to wean myself off thinking of him as Reynolds—the former cop in me automatically slotted fellow police officers into the surnames-or-nicknames category, and my recently bruised heart liked the layer of distance. Taking the step to pull down my emotional barriers was a big deal, and I was still getting used to this new phase in our relationship.

Five minutes later, I reached Eyre Square. Although it had been officially renamed John F. Kennedy Memorial Park in 1965, the locals had never fully adopted the new name. Moving as fast as I could, I made a beeline for the famous Galway Hookers fountain—named for a type of boat, not a lady of the night. When I reached the fountain, I slowed my pace and scanned my surroundings. Crowds of people bustled past, but there was no sign of Liam. I frowned. It wasn't like him to be late.

I slipped my phone out of my coat pocket, and my stomach slumped when I saw the two missed calls and a voicemail message from Liam's number. I pressed play on the message.

"Hey, Maggie. I'm sorry, but I have to cancel our dinner tonight. Something's come up, and I can't make it. I'm going to be incommunicado for the next couple of days, but I'll try to call you as soon as I can." A slight pause. *"I love you."*

And then he was gone. I kept the phone pressed to my ear for several seconds after the message ended.

All the weirdness of our last few phone calls came crashing down on me. I hadn't imagined my boyfriend's distraction when we'd spoken yesterday. He'd seemed anxious to end the call and had barely listened to my funny anecdotes about the store's employees.

I stared blindly into space. I could call Tracey and find out which pub they'd chosen for their drinks, but I didn't feel like socializing, not even if it meant the chance to question the staff about the store thefts. While my insecure side ascribed Liam's strange message to him pulling away, my cop-turned-private-investigator side picked up on the anxiety in his tone.

I replayed the message twice. Sure enough, something—or someone—had rattled him. Was it a new investigation on Whisper Island? If there'd been a sudden crime spree, my aunts or cousin would have sent me a message. And if Hannah, Liam's daughter, were sick, he'd have told me straight up.

Even though he'd said he'd be unavailable, I hit his number. It went straight to voicemail. With a prickling sensation on the nape of my neck, I disconnected without leaving a message.

I took a deep breath. If I couldn't get through to Liam, I'd have to be patient and trust that he'd call me when he had a chance. In the meantime, I'd grab groceries and head back to the apartment Lenny and I were staying in while we were working in Galway. A long soak in the bath would ease away the stresses of the day. I sent my assistant a quick message to say I'd be home early after all and then walked across Eyre Square in the direction of a grocery store.

As if to mirror my mood, the drizzle had turned into a deluge. Thanks to the strong Atlantic wind that blew in from the coast, my umbrella was useless. I pulled up the hood on my jacket and ran all the way to the store.

The place was packed with both shoppers and loiterers hoping to buy a few minutes out of the rain. I battled my way through the aisles and stocked up on a few essentials. As I was leaving the store, I paused at a rack of newspapers and scanned the headlines.

Neighbours Come to Blows Over Wheelie Bins. Gang Dressed in Santa Costumes Terrorizes Galway. Beauty Blogger Eliza Donati Visits Dublin.

My limbs grew numb as I studied the photograph of the beautiful woman staring back at me. Years of jealousy and resentment brought bile to my throat. Eliza Donati, born Elizabeth Doyle, was my sister.

How long had she been in the same country as me? Did she intend to contact me while she was here? Why hadn't Dad mentioned my sister was traveling to Ireland? Mom and I weren't on the best of terms since my divorce, but Dad checked in with me every couple weeks, even it was just a short email. Dublin was less than three hours from Galway by car. Had I known to expect her, I could have met Beth at the airport, maybe even sprung for dinner.

Not that Beth was likely to want to hang out with me. This sobering reminder sent my bad mood into a tailspin. My grip on my grocery bags tightened, and I marched past the newspaper rack and out of the store, no longer caring how wet and bedraggled the rain and wind made me. On the twenty-minute walk to the apartment, I dodged puddles and brooded over my lousy relationship with my sister.

Beth was ten months younger than me. We'd suffered the indignity of being in the same year in school. Our closeness in age had become a running joke among our classmates, who'd never tired of calling us Irish twins. Despite the twin moniker, being sisters was the only thing we had common. While I'd scored honor grades that had never been good enough for our parents, my beautiful sister had barely passed her classes, yet had received praise and encouragement.

Like our older brothers, I'd been expected to follow our parents' footsteps and join the San Francisco PD. My sister, in contrast, was an aspiring model and actress. In between stints as an extra on a sitcom, and a few minor modeling jobs, Beth had trained to be a cosmetologist. When she'd started a makeup channel on YouTube three years ago, our mother had been inexplicably thrilled. I'd never paid attention to my sister's channel until a few months ago when a successful collaboration with a well-known makeup brand gained her media attention. It seemed my little sister had turned her hobby into a lucrative career.

I stomped onto Snipe Avenue, blinking at the harsh reflected streetlight on the puddles. Lenny's brother, Jake, was on sabbatical from his job as a geology professor at NUI Galway. He'd allowed us to stay at his apartment whenever we had work in the city.

As I approached Jake's apartment building, I fumbled for my key, my thoughts still preoccupied with Liam's strange behavior and my sister's sudden fame. In the distance, church bells chimed the hour. Seven o'clock. A long night of surveillance tapes loomed before me. I stretched my stiff neck, already anticipating sinking into the warm bubble bath I'd have before tackling the footage.

I climbed the short flight of steps to the front door and raised my hand to put the key in the lock. Before I could do so, an apparition appeared on the other side of the glass door. I screamed and took a step back, stumbled, and dropped the grocery bags.

The door swung open, and a man dressed in a clown costume leaped in front of me, grinning widely. "Yo, Maggie. Wazzup?"

3

"**L**enny?" My heart rate slowly returned to normal. "Jeez, man. You scared me. Why are you dressed like a clown?"

My friend, and assistant in my private investigation business, beamed. "I got my outfit discounted at the costume factory. Isn't it awesome?"

"I'd find it more awesome if the sight of it hadn't caused me to drop my groceries."

"Yeah... Sorry about that." He leaped down the steps and shoved stray yogurt containers back into the bags.

"Aren't you a little late for Halloween?" I asked as we crossed the black-tiled lobby of the apartment building.

"They have a ton of scary stuff left over from Halloween, and I get a staff discount. I'm going to stock up for the business."

The building's clanky elevator was in motion. In

deference to my dislike of small, enclosed spaces, we didn't wait for it to return to our level and opted instead for the stairs. "Seeing you in that outfit is like a flashback to our misspent youth," I said. "Remember the time you showed up to a picnic dressed in a cowboy costume, complete with holster and toy gun?"

"Dude, I was prepared. Who knew what perils we might have encountered on the hills of Whisper Island?"

"As I recall, the only danger was you straying onto Paddy Driscoll's farm and getting chased by a bull."

Lenny grinned. "What can I say? The bull took exception to my costume."

My heart swelled at the memories of happy childhood summers spent on the remote Irish island where my father had grown up. Lenny and my cousin Julie featured in most of those memories. Reconnecting with them over the last year had been an unexpected joy in the middle of the turmoil of my divorce.

We trudged upstairs and hung a left when we reached the second floor. "I'm delighted you're having fun working on your case," I said, "but I seriously don't think Movie Reel Investigations needs a closet full of crazy costumes."

Lenny, unperturbed by my lack of enthusiasm for his buying spree, laughed off my objections and threw open the door to his brother's apartment. "Now that we're in the private investigation trade, we've gotta get a few disguises."

I regarded my friend's colorful clown costume and

suppressed a grin. "Unless we're planning to disguise ourselves as Pennywise from Stephen King's *IT*, I don't think that outfit will be useful."

Lenny followed me into the apartment and put the grocery bags on the kitchen counter. "Okay. Maybe the clown costume isn't an ideal disguise for a private investigator, but get a load of these." With a wide grin, he unzipped the large wheelie suitcase I'd failed to spot behind the apartment door. A pile of costumes tumbled onto the floor. "I've got a Charlie Chaplin outfit for me, and a naughty nurse for you."

"That'll come in useful while tailing cheating spouses."

He appeared not to notice my sarcasm and continued to trawl through his loot. "Isn't this stuff fantastic? I got us a bunch of wigs, fake beards, ears, and noses."

I picked up a hot pink mullet wig and tried it on, checking my reflection in the hall mirror. "If anyone sees two freaks following them down the street wearing a wig like this one, they'll call the cops. I know I would."

"You haven't seen my best find of the day." Lenny rubbed his hands with glee before unzipping a compartment in the suitcase. "Check these out."

Two padded suits rolled onto the floor, followed by cheek stuffers and fake double chins.

I raised an eyebrow. "Have you ever tried on a padded suit? I wore one to a costume party where I dressed up as the Pillsbury Doughboy. Trust me, it wasn't fun. I sweated like a pig. I wouldn't want to have to tail a mark for hours on end while wearing one."

Lenny waved a hand, unconcerned by my objections. "We'll get used to them. The fantastic part about the padded suits is that we can wear them under a bunch of disguises. We can't make ourselves skinnier, but we can totally add a few kilos."

While he prattled on about his fabulous costume finds, I went into the kitchen, unpacked the groceries, and fixed us sandwiches. Lenny and I ate a hot lunch in our respective lunchrooms to have the chance to talk to the staff, so we tended to eat something small in the evenings.

When we were seated at the table, Lenny filled me in on his case. "It's definitely embezzlement. The CFO's been engaging in creative accounting to hide the fact that he's transferring company money to an offshore account in his wife's name."

"Ouch. Sounds like he didn't do a great job at burying his tracks."

"Nope. Once I've followed all possible trails, I can wrap up this case and hand over my results to the CEO."

I nodded in approval. "Well done. I'm impressed."

Now that Lenny was a fully licensed private investigator, he was able to take on his own cases, and this job for The Costume Emporium was his first big solo job.

He stuffed the remainder of his salad sandwich

into his mouth. "I've probably spent most of what I earned on costumes," he said between chews, "but it'll be worth the investment."

I stifled a smile. "Whatever you say."

"Thanks for the sandwiches, Maggie. I expected to be eating beans on toast this evening while you dined out in style with Reynolds. Why did he bail on you, anyway? Is a serial killer on the loose on Whisper Island?"

The reminder of my canceled date put a damper on my relaxed frame of mind. "Not as far as I know. Liam left a voicemail, saying he'd be unavailable for a couple of days."

Lenny frowned. "That's not like Reynolds."

"No." I stared at my fingernails. "I can't help worrying he's having doubts about us."

Under his thick clown makeup, my friend's eyebrows shot up. "Are you mad? Reynolds adores you. Anyone who sees you two together knows that."

"Yeah." I shoved a stray curl behind my ear. "I'm probably feeling rough today because of what happened at the department store."

Lenny perked up at this revelation. "Drama at Dennehy's? Don't leave me in suspense."

"Put it this way—I better find the thief soon, or Movie Reel Investigation's reputation will be mud all over Galway. I almost got fired today. If the cosmetics department supervisor had gotten her way, I would have been."

"Wow, Maggie. What did you do?"

"As far as I'm concerned, I did nothing wrong. A crazy chick came into the store and accused me of burning her butt off."

Lenny blinked. "That's wild, even by your standards."

"Jeez, thanks. Your faith in me is touching."

He waved a hand in a vague gesture. "You always get the job done in the end. Why did this chick think you were responsible for her predicament?"

"Because I sold her facial hair lightener instead of the product she claims she asked for. But she was too embarrassed to spell it out for me, and I assumed that bleach for sensitive areas meant for the face."

Lenny roared with laughter. "I wish my job was as exciting as yours. All I've been doing is staring at spreadsheets."

"And blowing your salary on discount costumes," I reminded him with a grin.

"That's the upside of the job."

"As for excitement, Tom Dennehy gave me seventy-two hours' worth of surveillance footage to look through. I'm going to tackle it this evening. I'd appreciate your help."

"Sure thing." Lenny's grin faded. "By the way, I saw your sister on the front page of the newspaper when I was walking home."

My stomach clenched at the mention of Beth. "Yeah. I saw that, too. I guess she's in Dublin for something. I just glanced at the headline."

"She's rumored to be shooting a film in Ireland next year. Have you heard about that?"

"My sister doesn't keep in touch." I failed to keep the edge out of my voice. "Apart from her beauty channel, I have no idea what she's working on at the moment."

"Yeah. Even my mother watches Beth's makeup tutorials. Her channel's become something like an overnight success, right?"

I shrugged. "I don't know. I guess so. Before last summer, I don't recall seeing her videos mentioned everywhere like they are now. It's not like I watch them."

The words slipped out before I could filter them, defensive and tinged by the bitterness and jealousy I was ashamed of feeling. Beth was my only sister. Even if we weren't close, I should be glad for her success.

"I recall Beth being a right pain when we were kids. Good-looking but knew it," Lenny said. "How's she as an adult?"

In spite of Lenny's eccentricities, he was a more astute judge of character than most people gave him credit for.

"She's even worse," I admitted. "Mom and Dad think Beth walks on water, and she dominates every family get-together."

"Does she still put you down all the time? I remember her shooting nasty comments in your direction. That's why we always ditched her and did our own thing."

"Yeah. She was catty last Christmas after I split with Joe. On the positive side, her constant digs proved to be the catalyst I needed to accept my aunt's offer of a job on Whisper Island."

"I'm glad you moved to Ireland, but I'm sorry for the reasons it happened. Families can be complicated."

"Yeah, they can." I cleared my throat and forced a smile. "Is it okay if I have a bath before we tackle the surveillance footage? I could do with a relaxing soak."

"Go for it. I'll load the dishwasher and make a start on that footage."

I stood and stretched my stiff neck from side to side. "Thanks, Lenny."

My friend grabbed our plates from the table. "No problem. Enjoy your soak."

I went into my bedroom and got a fresh pair of pajamas and clean underwear out of my suitcase. From my selection of toiletries, I chose a lemon bath bomb. I figured it was a compromise between relaxing warm water and a scent that would invigorate me. I needed to be able to concentrate on the surveillance footage.

When I returned to the living room, Lenny was absorbed in front of his laptop, looking through the surveillance footage on fast-forward.

I left him to it and crossed the room to the bathroom. The door was closed. I frowned. I'd been the last to leave this morning, and I'd swear I'd left the door open. Maybe Lenny had used it when he'd come up to change into the clown costume before scaring me. Balancing my clothes and toiletries in one arm, I turned the handle with my free hand.

A sense of foreboding hit me the instant I stepped inside. It took me a moment to register what I was seeing, and even longer to realize that the piercing scream echoing through the apartment was coming from me. A woman lay in the bathtub, fully clothed and very dead. I recognized her instantly. It was Ms. Butt Bleach.

4

At the sound of my scream, Lenny shouted. "What's the matter? Is there a spider in the bathroom?"

"Have you ever known me to scream about a spider?" I yelled in response. "There's a dead body in the tub."

There was the sound of running feet, and my friend burst into the bathroom. Even though I knew it was futile, I was in the process of searching for a non-existent pulse.

"What the—?" Lenny reared back, eyes bulging. "You weren't joking."

"Nope. Looks like she's been strangled." I got to my feet. "Do you have your phone with you?"

"Yeah." Shaking his head, he slipped his phone out of his pocket. "Man, life with you is never boring."

While Lenny contacted emergency services, I took another look at the corpse in the bathtub, examining the body from every angle but careful not to move her.

Lenny ended his call and came to join me by the side of the tub. "Was she killed here?"

"Hard to tell. Wherever she was killed, the body was placed in the tub after death."

"How do you know that?" My friend leaned over the corpse, staring at the dead woman with a mixture of horror and fascination. "I can't tell that just by looking at her."

"See the pattern of the marks on her neck? They indicate she was strangled from behind, possibly by something soft like a scarf." I pointed to the side of the tub. "The inside of the bath is dry to the touch, and the victim is fully dressed. Unless she climbed in with her clothes on, my guess is that she was killed elsewhere and placed here after death."

"I'm not sure if your knowledge of murder methods is awesome or revolting."

"Let's roll with both," I said with a wry smile. "I saw plenty of strangled bodies during my time at the San Francisco PD. I can recognize the difference between a strangulation by rope or wire, and one using a softer material.

"I don't see any sign of a scarf now," my friend said, looking around the bathroom.

"Neither do I, and a scarf as the weapon is just a guess. We'll check the apartment, but I'd say the murderer took whatever he used to kill her with him when he left."

"If the woman was killed somewhere else, the weapon mightn't have been in our apartment."

"Exactly." I straightened my back. "Or he killed her here, but not in the bathtub. Either way, I'm going to get my camera and take photos."

"The ambulance will be here in ten," Lenny said. "You'd better hurry."

I jogged to my bedroom and grabbed my digital camera. Back in the bathroom, I photographed the scene from every angle.

"Doesn't look like she was killed for money," my friend mused as I snapped more shots. "Her watch and jewelry look expensive. I wonder who she was."

I blew out my cheeks. "No clue. What I do know is that this woman is the chick I was telling you about. The one who tried to get me fired."

"The butt bleach lady?" Lenny stared at me, aghast. "Why'd she go and get dumped in our joint?"

"I have no idea, but it makes me think the scene at the cosmetics counter today was no accident. I got the impression she was overdoing her act. What if my subconscious was telling me the scene was staged?"

Lenny's eyes widened. "Are you saying she deliberately created a fuss?"

"She was very quick to demand I be fired. Why do that right after she'd been offered store credit for one hundred euros?" I closed my eyes and ran through the events of the day. "I'm pretty sure I saw her browsing in the store before she came over to the cosmetics department."

"You mean she waited until she could make sure you served her?"

My gaze met Lenny's. "I'm not sure. Tracey was with me, but she was bending down and tidying the extra stock in one of our cabinets. It might have looked like I was alone."

"If her goal was to get you fired, she must have known you're a private detective."

"Yeah. That's what I suspect. And if my being a P.I. was the reason she wanted me fired, she had to have been in league with whoever is taking cash from the store." We regarded the dead woman in the tub. "Why kill her?" I wondered aloud. "And why leave her in our apartment? To send me a message?" The idea sent a shiver of fear down my spine.

"There's another possibility," my friend said gravely. "What if the killer wanted to frame you for the murder? It sounds farfetched, sure, but it's the only thing that makes sense. Why else leave her body here?"

At the sound of approaching sirens, I spoke fast. "Tom Dennehy estimates the store's lost almost ten thousand euros to the thief over the last couple of months. That's a lot of cash, but is it enough to kill for?"

"Unless there's more to the missing cash business than we're seeing." Lenny's mouth settled into a grim line. "Did you ask Dennehy about us staking out the place one night?"

"Yeah. He's okay with the idea. Want to shoot for tomorrow?"

"Sounds good. Whatever's going on at the store has to be connected to the dead woman."

The doorbell reverberated through the apartment. My attention shifted to the camera in my hands. "I need to get rid of this. The cops won't like me taking pictures of the crime scene."

"Go. I'll answer the door."

I darted into my bedroom and put my camera back in its case. When I reemerged into the living room, Lenny was ushering the paramedics into the bathroom. A moment later, two uniformed police officers trooped into the apartment. When they turned around to look at me, I groaned.

Gavin Reynolds, Liam's brother, grinned at the sight of me. "Hey, Maggie. Liam said you were in Galway. When the call came in, I should have guessed the dead body would be in your apartment."

Fantastic. I'd promised Liam I wouldn't get involved in any more murders, and here I was with a dead woman in my bathroom. From Gavin's bemused expression, I judged it unlikely that he wouldn't share this information with his brother.

Gavin's fellow officer, a dark-haired man of around forty-five, eyed me with suspicion. "You two know each other?"

"Maggie, this is Inspector Craddock. Sir, Ms.

Doyle is my brother's girlfriend." Gavin was either oblivious to his partner's hostile tone or willfully ignoring it. "She has a habit of finding murder victims."

I sighed and blew out my cheeks. "As I've said to Liam many times, it's not like I go *looking* for dead bodies."

Craddock's lip curled. "From my understanding, you didn't have to *go looking* for this particular dead body."

I chose to ignore his sarcasm. "Why is an inspector responding to the initial callout? Isn't this below your pay grade?"

Craddock's gaze flitted toward Gavin and then back to me. "We were in the area."

"Has there been another murder?" I demanded. "Also strangulation?"

The inspector glared at me. "Leave the questions to us, Ms. Doyle. The only alleged murder victim we're interested in right now is the woman in your bathtub."

"Strictly speaking, it's not my bathtub. The apartment belongs to my assistant's brother. We're staying here for a couple of weeks."

As if on cue, Lenny lumbered back into the living room, still wearing his clown costume. Gavin and Inspector Craddock reared back in alarm. Lenny grinned when he saw my boyfriend's brother, recognizing him from one of our previous investigations. "Yo, dude. How's it hanging?"

"If you're referring to my jaw, it's hanging open." Gavin scanned Lenny from head to toe. "Are you on your way to a costume party?"

I rolled my eyes. "Nope. Lenny's choice of outfit involves discount costumes and a desire to scare the life out of me."

"Isn't it awesome?" Lenny shook a multicolored leg for our inspection. "I picked up this beauty for just ten euros."

"A bargain," Gavin said dryly. "Lenny, this is Inspector Craddock. Sir, this is Lenny Logan."

Craddock regarded Lenny with a hostile expression. "Care to share how the clown costume ties in with the woman in the bathroom?"

"Well, it doesn't." My friend's expression turned sheepish. "When Maggie texted me to say her boyfriend had bailed on their dinner date, I figured she'd need cheering up."

My cheeks burned at the mention of my canceled date, but Gavin's attention remained fixed on Lenny. "Your idea of cheering up Maggie was dressing like a clown?"

"Nope. I thought it'd be fun to give her a fright. So I hid in the lobby until she got home, and then I leaped out at her."

"*Right.*" Having been subjected to Lenny's brand of humor before, Gavin took this revelation in his stride.

Inspector Craddock was less understanding. "Do

you mean to tell me you two were playing practical jokes while a dead woman lay in your flat?"

Seriously, this guy. We'd have to watch our tongues around him. Craddock was the type to take everything literally. "We didn't know she was there when Lenny pranked me."

The two paramedics emerged from the bathroom. At Craddock's raised eyebrow, the taller paramedic shook his head. "Nothing we can do for her. This is a case for forensics."

Displaying no flicker of emotion at this revelation, Craddock shifted his attention to Gavin. "You call it in, Sergeant. I'll take a look at the body."

"Yes, sir." Gavin grimaced and extracted his phone from his jacket pocket.

After Lenny and I had seen the paramedics out, we waited in awkward silence, anticipating the inevitable barrage of questions. We didn't have to wait long.

Craddock stuck his head out of the bathroom and fixed us with his hard stare. "You two. Come here a sec."

"Why is he treating us like criminals?" Lenny muttered. "We didn't kill her."

"We found the body in our apartment. If I were Craddock, I'd put us at the top of the suspect list." Annoying, but true. I didn't like the guy, but he was right to be suspicious. He'd bust a gut once I revealed my prior acquaintance with Ms. Butt Bleach.

5

Lenny and I approached the bathroom with obvious reluctance and stopped outside the door. Craddock stood aside to give us a better view. The bathroom was unchanged from the last time I'd seen it. The paramedics must have recognized they were dealing with a murder victim right off the bat and had taken care not to disturb the crime scene any more than necessary.

"The woman has no handbag and no I.D. on her," the inspector said. "Have you seen a purse or bag that doesn't belong to you anywhere in the flat?"

Lenny and I shook our heads.

The inspector stared at us through narrowed eyes. Being the prime suspects sucked, but we were the only people staying in an apartment where a murder victim had been discovered. "Wait outside, Mr. Logan. I want to talk to you and Ms. Doyle separately."

My friend darted a look at me and then shrugged. "Okay. I'll see if I can scare a few neighbors."

After Lenny left, Craddock rounded on me, his hard stare pinning me in place. "What time did you discover the corpse?"

"I didn't have a watch or a phone with me, so I can't be precise, but it must have been around seven-thirty. Lenny called emergency services shortly after I found her. The time he made the call will be on his phone."

Craddock's accusatory stare didn't waver. "Tell me exactly what happened from the time you arrived at the flat this evening to the point you found the body."

"After Lenny scared me downstairs, we came up to the apartment. I unpacked groceries and made sandwiches. While we ate, we filled each other in on our respective days. Clown costumes aside, we're both working on undercover jobs."

Craddock's bushy eyebrows shot up. "Undercover?"

"We're private investigators. Lenny is currently working at The Costume Emporium, a costume manufacturer with an online store. I'm at Dennehy's department store."

The inspector's grunt could have been an expression of disdain, disapproval, or both. "What happened after you had your sandwiches?"

"Lenny tidied up and started viewing surveillance footage for one of our cases. I decided to take a bath. I got my clothes from my bedroom and went to the bathroom. I noticed the door was closed, and that struck me as odd. I was the last to leave the apartment this morning, and I'm sure I left it open. I turned the handle and opened the door. That's when I saw her." I nodded at the body.

Gavin joined us, shoving his phone back in his pocket. "Forensics will be here in fifteen minutes, sir. Want me to question Lenny?"

Craddock grunted. "Let the clown stew for a while. Take over taking notes, Sergeant. I'll ask the questions."

Without demur, Gavin took out a notebook and pen and waited expectantly for his superior officer to continue questioning me.

"Was it immediately apparent to you that the woman was dead?" Craddock asked.

"Yeah. And I saw right away she'd been strangled. Probably from behind with a soft object like a scarf."

Craddock's eyes narrowed. "You know a lot about strangulation victims for a private investigator. Don't you people specialize in cheating spouses and missing cats?"

"Before I opened Movie Reel Investigations, I was a police officer for the San Francisco Police Department," I explained, jutting my jaw in defiance. "I've seen plenty of murder victims in my time."

From the way his nostrils flared, this explanation didn't please Inspector Craddock. "Did you touch anything in the bathroom? Or disturb the scene in any way?"

I regarded him with ill-disguised distaste. "Lenny and I have been living in this apartment for the last few days. Our fingerprints will be all over the bathroom. And no, I did not tamper with the scene." I skipped the part about quickly taking a few snapshots. No need to give Craddock a heart attack.

"Did you move the body?" the officer demanded.

I resisted the impulse to roll my eyes. "Of course not. I checked her for a pulse. I knew it was hopeless the moment I saw her, but I had to try."

"Of course you did." Gavin's soothing tone was one I recognized from my days on the force. He'd obviously slotted himself into the role of good cop while his pal played bad cop. "We need to ask you these questions, Maggie. As a former police officer, I'm sure you understand."

Oh, I understood all right, but I didn't have to like the situation. I shifted my weight from one foot to the other and regarded my interrogators. "Let's cut to the chase, gentlemen. You want to know if I killed the dead woman, or if I knew her."

"Well?" the older police officer demanded. "Did you kill her?"

"I didn't, but I have seen her before."

Craddock leaped on this revelation. "When and where did you meet her? Do you know her name?"

"No, but the cosmetics department supervisor at Dennehy's will, and possibly the store manager as well. They had to offer her store credit today after an alleged mishap on my part."

The frown lines on the inspector's forehead deepened. "Can you elaborate?"

"The woman approached me at the cosmetics counter in Dennehy's department store around an hour before I clocked off this evening. She'd been to the store yesterday, and I'd served her. She accused me of selling her facial hair lightener instead of the butt bleach she'd asked for, thus causing her to injure herself." I waited for Gavin and Craddock to rearrange their jaws before I continued. "When I disagreed with her assessment of the situation, she demanded to speak to my supervisor. As it happened, Ms. Kearns had just returned from her break. The woman wanted compensation and demanded that I be fired. Ms. Kearns offered the customer store credit to the value of one hundred euros and sent me upstairs to speak to the store manager."

"What time was this?" Gavin asked, forgetting Craddock's command that he be the one to ask the questions.

"The customer approached me a minute or two before five-twenty."

"Are you always such a precise keeper of time, Ms. Doyle?"

Craddock's sneer managed to combine suspicion and derision. "I can be exact because my supervisor, Nuala Kearns, is working the late shift tonight. She timed her last break of the day to be back at the cosmetics section in plenty of time before my coworker and I left for the evening. She started her twenty-minute break at five o'clock, and she's always punctual."

"When did you last see the dead woman alive?" The police inspector drew his bushy eyebrows together to form an uncompromising V.

"Nuala sent me to speak to the store manager. I guess that must have been around five-thirty."

Gavin's pen moved across his notebook in a scratchy motion. "How long did your meeting with the manager last?" he asked, forgetting the inspector's order to keep quiet.

"Around twenty-five minutes."

"Did the manager fire you?" Craddock asked, shooting Gavin a warning look to stay silent.

"No. As I mentioned before, I'm working there undercover. Tom Dennehy and his father, Seamus, hired me to look into a matter that was bothering them. Tom saw no reason to terminate the contract with Movie Reel Investigations." Although he might change his mind once he found out about his customer winding up dead in my apartment...

"Why did the Dennehy's hire you?"

"We have a confidentiality agreement as part of our contract. You'll have to ask Tom or Seamus if I can break it."

Craddock stiffened. "This is a police investigation, Ms. Doyle, and probably a case of murder. Are you refusing to cooperate with us?"

"I'm happy to cooperate with you, Inspector Craddock," I said smoothly. "If the Dennehys don't give me permission to talk about their case, you should have no difficulty getting a court order. Once you do, I'll comply." He opened his mouth to protest further, but I cut him off. "I can, however, tell you my exact movements after I left Tom Dennehy's office this evening. I assume you need me to account for the time between my last seeing the woman alive and finding her in the tub."

Gavin coughed into his fist, possibly to hide a laugh. Craddock glowered at me. "Well? What did you do after your meeting with Dennehy?"

"I took the stairs to the basement, collected my stuff from my locker, and left the building."

"Did anyone see you before you left the department store?"

"Several people. Nuala Kearns, my supervisor, was waiting outside Mr. Dennehy's office to discuss the matter of the store credit and my continued employment. The receptionist was also there. Down in the locker area, four coworkers came in while I was getting ready to leave."

"I need names," Craddock muttered, clearly displeased that I was able to provide alibis.

"I mentioned Nuala Kearns. I don't know the receptionist's name, but Tom Dennehy can tell you that. Two of the coworkers I spoke to by the lockers were Tracey Egan and Barry White. Another was

Jasper Ramsbottom from men's fashion. Siobhan from household appliances was also there, but I don't remember her surname. I can check my case notes for you."

"Anyone else see you?"

"Fred, the security guard outside the staff exit. He searched my bags and coat."

Craddock frowned. "Why do they have a security guard searching staff?"

"I was hired to go undercover at the store. All members of staff are searched before they leave." I flashed him a smile. "You're the police inspector. You figure it out."

The older man's jaw tightened. "The altercation with the dead woman must have made you angry."

"Not angry enough to kill her."

"And yet she wound up dead in your bathroom." Craddock's lips twisted into a cross between a smirk and a snarl. "Where did you go after you left Dennehy's?"

"I walked to Eyre Square to meet my boyfriend. When I realized he couldn't make our dinner date, I texted Lenny to tell him I'd be home early after all."

"What route did you take from Eyre Square to the apartment?"

"I headed to Mainguard Street to buy groceries. After that, I took Bridge Street over the river and walked in the direction of the university campus and on to Snipe Avenue. The store has surveillance cameras, and I assume there are some along the route I took back to the apartment. Church bells were ringing when I reached the apartment, so I know I got here at seven o'clock."

"We can verify your movements from the security cameras along the route you took. I play golf with Tom Dennehy. I'll give him a call now and confirm your undercover story." Craddock's hard eyes turned to Gavin. "I'll leave questioning the clown to you, Reynolds."

After the inspector withdrew to make his call in the hallway outside the apartment, Gavin flipped to a fresh page. "Do you mind swapping places with Lenny, Maggie? You know how this works. I need to talk to him without you present."

"Sure."

Gavin accompanied me out to the corridor, where Lenny was pacing impatiently.

"Your turn," I said. "Have fun."

The door hadn't clicked shut before Lenny launched into a loud account of his movements. "Dude, I didn't kill her. First time I saw the dead chick, she was on a one-way ticket to the morgue. I wouldn't even have come home this early if your brother hadn't bailed on Maggie."

"Liam didn't bail on her," Gavin muttered. "He just won't get to my place until late tonight, after—"

Whatever else Gavin had said wasn't discernible through the closed door. It took a moment for his words to sink in. A cold numbness spread through my limbs. Why was Liam spending the night at Gavin's house if he wasn't meeting me? Why would Liam say he was unavailable for a couple of days, yet come to the same city I was staying in without telling me?

My head was still spinning when Inspector Craddock came up the stairs and handed me his cell phone. "Seamus Dennehy is on the line."

I took it gingerly, my gaze not moving from the inspector. "Hello?"

"Hi, Maggie." Seamus's deep voice boomed into my ear. "This is a dreadful business. Inspector Craddock filled me in. Go ahead and tell him anything he needs to know."

"Thanks, Seamus. I'll call you tomorrow, and we can discuss how I should proceed with my investigation." After I disconnected, I handed the phone back to the inspector. "I was hired to investigate an ongoing series of thefts at the department store. Roughly ten thousand euros has been stolen over the last few weeks. It's disappearing at the rate of two or three hundred a day, taken from different cash registers."

"Dennehy said he'd reported it to the police," Craddock said. "Why did he think you could help?"

"The police can't be at the store all day, every day. Working undercover, I can observe customers and staff. We assume an employee is involved, but it's possible that he or she has an accomplice on the outside."

"Hence the security guard searching the employees before they leave the premises," Craddock added.

"Exactly. But they can hardly pat down the customers, especially during the busiest season of the year. No one would shop at Dennehy's, and the store would lose the lucrative holiday trade."

"How does the dead woman tie in with your investigation?" Craddock asked. "If you didn't kill her, I'm assuming it's no accident that she ended up in your bathroom."

"That's what I'm thinking. She was adamant that I be fired, but I don't know why she was killed, or by whom."

"Have you made any progress in your investigation? Do you have any suspects?"

I rolled my eyes. "I have a long list of suspects. The problem is narrowing it down to just one or two. I can email their names to you later, along with my case notes."

The apartment door opened, and Gavin appeared. "Lenny's story matches Maggie's."

Craddock snorted. "The only good part about that information is we can finally get out of this freezing hallway."

When we trooped back into the apartment, Lenny lounged on the sofa, a subdued expression on his face. Clearly, being questioned by the police had brought home the depressing reality of our surreal situation. I took a seat beside him, and Craddock and Gavin sat on the sofa opposite.

"So neither of you have any idea how this woman ended up in your bathtub?" Craddock muttered. "No idea at all?"

Lenny and I shook our heads.

A van door slammed shut outside. Gavin went over to the window and looked down onto the street. "Forensics just pulled up. Do you have any questions to add, sir? Or will I arrange a time for Maggie and Lenny to make a formal statement at the station?"

Craddock's thunderous expression indicated he'd rather watch us squirm a while longer, but he had no choice but to let us go while forensics did their thing. He pulled a card from his breast pocket. "I want you two to report to this station at nine o'clock tomorrow morning. Please stay in the area."

"We'll try to get rooms in a hotel," I said. "I'll text Gavin the number when I know where we're staying."

Gavin's smile was smooth. "No need for that. I'll hook you up with hotel rooms."

In other words, the police would keep an eye on us. After all, Lenny and I were currently their only suspects. I forced a smile. "Thanks. I guess we'd better pack our stuff."

"I can't allow you to remove anything from the bathroom, and you'll need to leave your phones and computer equipment with us."

I put my hands on my hips and glared at him. "Do you have a warrant to do that? Our business depends on us having access to our files and electronic equipment."

"I don't have a warrant," Gavin said easily, "but I can get one. It'll be a lot faster if you allow us to look through your devices. If we find nothing, you can have them back in a couple of days."

"A couple of days?" Lenny's expression of outrage was comical in combination with his clown costume.

"And to think I said I'd email you my case notes and suspect list," I muttered, a plan forming in my mind. "Fine, take whatever you want. When can we get back into the apartment?"

Gavin shrugged. "A day or two. Possibly longer."

"My brother will freak when he finds out we found a dead body in his flat." Lenny groaned. "How am I going to tell him?"

"We'll figure something out." I looped my arm through his. "We'd better pack. Okay if I use your computer bag? I don't want to have to haul my entire suitcase with me for just a couple of days."

This was a blatant lie. The suitcase I'd brought with me to Galway was the smallest I owned. Thankfully, Lenny was a quick study. With a barely perceptible wink, he said, "Sure. Help yourself."

While Gavin called a hotel, I sauntered over to the table where Lenny had set up his laptop. Keeping half an eye on Gavin, I grabbed my friend's large computer bag and made a great show of emptying its contents onto the table. Using the bag to conceal my hands, I tugged Tom Dennehy's flash drive free from the laptop and slipped it into my pocket.

Breathing a silent sigh of relief, I headed to the bedroom to pack. Lenny and I might not have our full complement of hardware, but at least I'd salvaged the surveillance footage.

6

To my annoyance, Gavin escorted Lenny and me to the accommodation he'd booked for us, a three-star hotel on Eyre Square. The police officer waited while we checked in and then insisted on escorting us up to our rooms.

"I'm taking the stairs," I declared. "I don't like elevators." This was true, but my reluctance to get into an elevator was momentarily trumped by my desire to irritate Gavin. Childish, yes, but as of five-fifteen this evening, various people had manipulated me, and I was done being played.

"Stairs it is." The knowing glint in Gavin's eyes reminded me of his brother and did nothing to stem my rising temper.

Lenny and I followed the police officer up to the third floor—or the second floor, according to the Irish, who insisted on describing the first as the ground floor.

"Are you planning to come in and stand guard all night?" I demanded when we reached the adjoining rooms the receptionist had secured for Lenny and me.

"No, but I'm relying on you not to stray far from the hotel between now and our appointment tomorrow morning."

I slung my bag on the ground and placed my hands on my hips. "Do you seriously believe Lenny and I are killers?"

Gavin flashed me an easy smile. "You know the drill, Maggie. You two are persons of interest in this case. The body was found in your flat."

"Found *by me*," I said in a frosty tone. "And Lenny called it in immediately."

"It wouldn't be the first time a killer has done that to try to cover his or her tracks. I know you don't like being a suspect, but until or unless we find a more likely explanation for why that woman ended up dead in your bath, you two are all we've got. The only reason you're not spending the night at the station is thanks to my intervention. Had it been left to Craddock, he'd have happily let you stew in an interrogation room all night."

He was right, and I knew it. In his position, I'd have acted the same way, even when my gut told me the suspects were innocent.

"I know and thank you. The hotel beds are bound to be better than whatever accommodation your station offers." I took a deep breath. "Do Lenny and I need legal representation tomorrow?"

"At the moment, all we're planning on doing is getting you to sign your statements." Gavin glanced at his watch. "I'd better get going."

"Night," I said. "We'll see you in the morning."

He winked at me. "I'll give your regards to my brother."

The reminder that Liam was in Galway and not with me acted like a bucket of ice water over my already foul mood. I forced a smile. "You do that."

Lenny and I waited until Gavin went down the stairs before turning to one another.

"Good job sneaking out the flash drive," my friend said under his breath. "I hadn't finished copying the footage to the cloud when you started screaming. Now we need a laptop to use the flash drive with."

"I snuck my camera into my bag, too, but I doubt there's anything interesting on those photographs." I checked the time. It was nine-thirty. "If we dump our stuff in our rooms, we should have time to get the shopping center across the square before it closes and buy a computer."

Lenny grinned. "Exactly what I was thinking. Thank goodness it's the week before Christmas. We wouldn't normally find a computer place open this late on a Monday night. Want to meet down in the lobby in five?"

"Sounds good."

I slid the key card into its slot and opened the door to my room. It was small and simply furnished, but spotlessly clean. I threw my bag onto the bed, grabbed my purse, and went back downstairs to the lobby.

Lenny was waiting for me by the exit, and we headed right out onto the square.

"Why don't we divide and conquer?" I suggested. "Give me a list of the toiletries you need, and I'll take care of buying those while you hit up an electronics store."

My friend wrapped his wool scarf around his neck and shivered in the chill evening air. "Okay by me. All I need for tonight is a toothbrush and toothpaste and maybe some shower gel. Oh, and don't forget junk food."

"Apart from the carbs and sugar hits, you should have all of those items in the hotel bathroom, but I'll get toiletries just in case."

We didn't have to walk far before we reached the shopping center, which was still crowded despite the late hour. Lenny and I battled our way through the main entrance, dodging holiday shoppers in various states of sobriety. The building was a modern affair with floor-to-ceiling windows and an airy central section overlooked by three circular floors of stores. At the moment, the entire place was festooned with festive ornaments and twinkling lights. To add to the holiday spirit, Christmas muzak spilled from the loud-speakers in a never-ending loop.

Lenny gestured toward an electronics store to our left. "This is my stop. Do I have a specific budget to work with?"

"Use the company credit card, but don't go wild. We can survive with one laptop until we get our gear back from the police."

"Yes, boss." Lenny gave me a mock salute.

I checked the store guide on one of the large screens suspended from the ceiling and located a grocery store on the next level. Aware of the ticking clock, I took the stairs two at a time and tore through the store, grabbing a few essentials to last Lenny and me through the night. I included two Cadbury chocolate bars and a can of Lenny's favorite sugar-free soda.

As I was paying for my goods, a mad impulse hit me, and I snatched a glossy magazine off a shelf. My sister's beautiful face stared back at me from the cover. The sales assistant had already scanned the barcode before I came to my senses. Feeling like a teenage boy who'd just purchased his first girly magazine, I stuffed it into a bag with the rest of my purchases and hurried back to the electronics store where I'd left Lenny.

My friend was paying when I arrived. "Yo, Maggie. I got an awesome deal," he boomed, much to the amusement of the guy behind the counter. "I can never tell my dad how much the shops in Galway are charging for this stuff."

Lenny's parents ran Whisper Island's one and only electronics store. My friend was vague on how the business was doing, but I could imagine the Logans were feeling the pinch from online shopping and the cheaper stores on the mainland.

"Should we add a couple of burner phones?" I asked. "We can't be without phones for too long."

"Already taken care of." Lenny patted a plastic bag on the counter.

I gave him a high five. "You're brilliant."

He grinned. "I aim to please."

With Lenny lugging our new laptop in its shiny packaging, we left the center and headed back across Eyre Square to our hotel. The chill rain had turned to icy sleet, and I berated myself for forgetting to replace the pair of gloves I'd lost yesterday.

When we reached the hotel, we headed up to Lenny's room to tackle the surveillance tapes.

"I suggest we work in shifts between now and our appointment at the police station," I said. "I'll contact Tom Dennehy to say I'll be late tomorrow, and you do the same for The Costume Emporium."

"Sure. Give me a half hour to set up this beauty, and we'll get started."

While Lenny unpacked the laptop, I took my new phone out of its packaging and went through the motions of setting it up. After I'd dug Tom Dennehy's business card out of my purse, my first move on the new device was to send him a text, informing him of my appointment with the police and giving him my new contact info. Once I'd contacted Tom, I rummaged through the bag of stuff I'd bought at the convenience store and found the notebooks and pens.

"What did Gavin say about Liam getting to his place late tonight?" I tried to make the question casual but failed.

Lenny spun his chair around, a knowing glint in his eyes. "Nothing you didn't overhear. He clammed up tight once he realized you and I didn't know Reynolds was staying with him after all."

A hard lump formed in my throat. "I see. I'd better make a start on my notes on the Dennehy case, especially after we found Ms. Butt Bleach."

"I'm sorry you're hurting, Maggie," Lenny said gently. "I don't know what Reynolds's deal is, but I can't imagine it has anything to do with your relationship. You've been with the guy six months. Don't you think you owe him a little trust?"

"I guess." I put my pen down on the notebook. "Okay, I know I should give Liam the benefit of the doubt, at least until he contacts me and tells me what's going on."

"However much it sucks, there's nothing you can do about it right now. Why don't you have some of that chocolate you bought and distract yourself with making notes? I should have the laptop ready to go pretty soon. The operating system and several apps were pre-installed, so it won't take me long."

Munching on chocolate, I forced myself to concentrate on my notes. I'd type them once I had access to a computer again, but I liked working with pen and paper. They helped me think.

"You ready to get started?" Lenny asked a few minutes later.

His words jolted me out of my intense concentration. "Uh, yeah. Just a sec."

I slid the flash drive out of my pocket and grabbed a seat at the table where my friend was working. He inserted the flash drive into the laptop and clicked on a file. "Why don't I take the first shift, and you can try to get some sleep?"

At the mere mention of sleep, I yawned. "It's not yet nine. I shouldn't be this tired."

"It's been a crazy day. No wonder you're exhausted."

"What time do you want me to take over?" I asked, stifling a second yawn.

He examined the card the police had given us. "Gavin and Craddock's station is a five-minute walk from the hotel. If we work until eight tomorrow morning, we'll have enough time to shower and eat breakfast before our appointment. Why don't you sleep now and take over for me at around three?"

"Sounds good. I've left your toiletries on your bed, plus a chocolate bar if you need a sugar shock later."

He grinned. "Awesome. Thanks, Maggie. Sleep well."

"I will. Feel free to wake me if you strike gold."

"Will do." My friend turned his attention back to the laptop screen.

Using one laptop would make the job longer than if

we'd been able to work on two computers, but working in shifts was a decent compromise. I left Lenny to the tedious job of staring at footage for hours. Unfortunately, we had no choice but to push through and watch the recordings. In spite of my bravado in Tom Dennehy's office, I had no idea who was behind the missing cash. My list of ten main suspects comprised of all the full-time workers who rang up purchases. In other words, I was rolling with the most likely candidates but couldn't narrow my list down further.

I collapsed onto my bed and fell into a surprisingly dreamless slumber. When my alarm went off at three, I groggily rubbed my eyes and hauled myself out of bed. I threw on my clothes and went next door to get the laptop from Lenny.

While my friend slept, I watched the surveillance footage on fast forward and nibbled on a chocolate bar. Dennehy's had cameras placed at the entrances, overlooking the cash registers, and at sporadic points throughout the building. It was a rudimentary setup for an exclusive department store, and I'd shared this opinion with Tom Dennehy at our first meeting. He'd hired a firm to fit a more sophisticated surveillance system after the holidays. In the meantime, he was relying on me to catch the thief.

With limited time, Lenny had opted to concentrate on the footage from the cameras that overlooked the cash registers, and I followed his example. Sipping coffee, I consulted the notes my assistant had made. He'd zoomed in and identified the names of the employee behind each cash register and what time they'd clocked on or off, or gone on a break. The steady stream of people paying for items made for mind-numbingly dull viewing, but I persevered, noting names and times and any instances of customer interaction that went on longer than normal.

During my second hour, I struck gold. My heart pounding in my chest, I scrolled back and rewatched the footage. I leaped to my feet and fist pumped the air. "Bingo."

7

My gait unsteady from exhaustion and excitement, I raced next door and pounded on my assistant's door. A sleepy-looking Lenny answered my impatient knocking.

"You've got to take a look at what I've found," I said breathlessly. "This is major."

My friend rubbed his sleepy eyes. "Okay. Give me a sec to pull on clothes."

He joined me in my room a minute later and leaned over my shoulder to look at the computer screen. "What did you find?"

"Let me rewind this part." I took the recording back a minute. "This footage is from Saturday. There's Ms. Butt Bleach, paying for a man's shirt."

Lenny yawned. "Maybe she wanted to buy something for her husband. So what?"

"Look at her interaction while she's paying. Watch how her eyes dart to the side and observe her mouth movements."

"Can I watch that part again?"

"Sure. I think she's communicating with the guy behind the cash register. Look at this part." I zoomed in on the sales assistant's hands. "Doesn't it look like he's pushing something into an envelope?"

"Yeah, but it could be a gift certificate. People are buying tons of those this time of year, and the fancy envelope fits."

Even though Lenny's dubious tone put a dent in my certainty, the niggling sensation that I was on to something remained. "The envelope is pretty thick for a gift certificate," I said. "It's worth following up on."

Lenny leaned forward and zoomed in. "Who's the dude behind the counter? I don't remember seeing him in the footage I watched."

"Evan Manning. Balding, mid-forties, and lives with his mother." I sighed in relief. "I'm so glad I backed up my case notes to cloud storage."

My friend scrunched up his forehead and scrutinized the screen. "Are you sure? E. Manning was in some of the footage I watched. This guy is balding, yeah, but he looks too young to be in his mid-forties."

"I know Evan from the staff canteen. When he began his shift, I didn't need to check his name tag to be sure it was him."

Lenny zoomed in on the sales assistant's face.

"You sure this is him? I watched footage of Evan for hours. This guy stands differently. He hunches his shoulders."

I stared at the screen and slow-blinked. "You're right. Evan has excellent posture. This man hunches his shoulders and looks away from the camera. That doesn't make sense. Evan was there a minute ago."

My friend scrolled through twenty minutes of footage and played it back in real time. As I'd noted on my sheet, Evan disappeared through a door marked "Staff Only" at 13:15. At 13:20, he reappeared and returned to his position behind the first cash register. Or did he? The man returning from the staff area had his back to the camera. Once he stood at the cash register, his balding head was bowed.

"He doesn't move the same," I said under my breath. "The man who went through the staff door was Evan, but Evan didn't come back out."

Ten minutes went by, and we got to the part where the mysterious sales assistant served Ms. Butt Bleach. I put it on slo-mo and leaned forward to get a better look at the screen.

"See? That envelope is way too thick to be a gift certificate. And look at the furtive way he darts a glance to the—" I gasped and hit pause at the moment when the sales assistant's face was visible. "I need to zoom in."

"Do you recognize him?" Lenny asked after I'd enlarged the man's face. "Because that guy's not Evan."

"Yes," I said, hoarse with excitement. "That's Jasper Ramsbottom."

"Whoa. Poor guy getting saddled with that name."

"This doesn't make sense. Jasper isn't balding. He has dark curly hair. And he doesn't work at the cash registers. He's strictly floor staff only."

"He looks bald to me. Maybe he wears a wig."

I conjured an image of Jasper's wiry dark hair. "I guess. I don't know much about disguises, but I imagine taking off a wig would be a lot quicker than fitting a bald patch over existing hair."

We fell silent and watched as Ms. Butt Bleach disappeared from the screen. Jasper served a couple more customers, and then went back through the staff door. A couple of minutes later, Evan returned and resumed his position behind the cash register.

"Cleverly timed," Lenny said. "The three women serving at the other cash registers didn't even look up when Evan and Jasper traded places. They were too busy serving customers. It's hard to tell, but I'm pretty sure Jasper slipped more than a shirt into her gift box."

For what felt like the hundredth time, we rewatched the segment of footage. "Yeah. I think you're right. It looks like Jasper's maneuvering something under the shirt and into the gift box. Even if her corpse in our bathtub hadn't clued us in, we've got to conclude Ms. Butt Bleach is involved in the store thefts."

"It's one heck of a coincidence if she's not." Lenny leaned forward, now wide awake. "Remember we wondered if a few thousand euro wasn't enough to be an incentive for murder?"

"Yeah. Perhaps whatever old Jasper put in the woman's bag wasn't money," I said. "Maybe there's more going on at the store than Tom Dennehy's missing money."

"Like dealing drugs? We don't know what else Jasper put in Ms. Butt Bleach's shopping bag."

"That's one possibility. Another is stolen luxury goods. I don't know how often Dennehy's does a full stock inventory, but I'd love to see what was on Ms. Butt Bleach's sales receipt."

"We have the time of the transaction, and we know which machine was used. Tom Dennehy should be able to access that information." Lenny whistled softly. "An upscale store like Dennehy's is the last place the police would expect to uncover a criminal operation. Are they paying their accomplices with money stolen from the store?"

"If they are, they're amateurs," I said. "We'd never have looked at the surveillance footage if it hadn't been for the missing cash. Slipping packages of drugs or stolen goods into gift boxes is a pretty ingenious way of distributing a product in small to medium quantities. Screwing that up by stealing from the cash registers seems counterintuitive."

We sat in silence for a moment. Finally, I said,

"Unless *that's* why Ms. Butt Bleach was murdered. Maybe she was killed because she was demanding cash in return for her silence."

Lenny drummed his knuckles on the table, his forehead creased in thought. "The only reason to stick her dead body in our bathtub is if whoever was behind the murder knew you were working under-cover at Dennehy's and wanted to frame you. Getting you fired didn't work. Having you arrested for a crime you didn't commit is a surefire way to get you out of the picture."

"And even if framing me didn't work, they'd have known my being a suspect would hamper my investi-gation. And they're right. Our appointment at the station tomorrow morning will waste a chunk of the day." I sighed and split the last piece of my chocolate bar with my friend. "I'd love to know if Ms. Butt Bleach used hair lightener on her rear end. If she didn't, it would back up my theory that she deliber-ately tried to get me fired."

"Yeah. But unless we break into the morgue and check out her butt, that's not going to happen. Logic says she was involved and that her body ending up in our tub was an attempt to derail your investigation."

"Getting rid of me would have been a temporary solution," I pointed out. "The Dennehys would have hired another P.I."

"Unless she and whoever else was involved in the thefts were planning something big within the next day or two," Lenny said. "How quickly could Dennehy replace you with another undercover private investigator? It was almost closing time when this incident went down, right?"

He had a point. "Yeah. This close to the holidays, he'd struggle to find a replacement quickly, but he'd probably find someone who could start within a couple of days."

"That still leaves a window of at least forty-eight hours," Lenny mused. "If Ms. Butt Bleach knew you were a P.I., who told her? Who else at the store is aware you're there undercover?"

"I have no clue. The Dennehys were adamant no one at the store should find out why I'd been employed. Nuala Kearns must know by now, but Tom planned to tell her this evening, and that was *after* my encounter with Ms. Butt Bleach." A memory stirred in my mind. "I suppose it's possible that Tom's receptionist listened in on our previous conversations. The walls in the admin area are pretty flimsy."

"If she'd passed the info on to someone else, who could it have been?"

"I don't even know the receptionist's name. Tom gave me the personnel files for everyone who has access to the cash registers, and she wasn't on the list." I scrunched my chocolate bar wrapper into a ball and tossed it into the wastepaper basket. "Let's say Jasper and whoever else is in on this money-stealing-and-possibly-more gig have a heist planned. When are they planning on carrying it out? During the day? At night? We've been focused on watching the cash registers, and they're empty at night. Maybe it's time for us to fast forward to the store after closing time."

Lenny stifled a yawn. "We didn't see any nocturnal shenanigans on the last batch of footage Dennehy gave us."

"No, but it's worth a shot. I'll take care of it. Go back to bed and try to catch another couple of hours of sleep."

My friend shook his head. "Nah. I'm up now. Knowing my luck, you'd be pounding on my door again with another discovery as soon as I nod off."

I laughed. "Fingers crossed we're lucky a second time."

Lenny made us another pot of coffee from my room's small machine, and we settled down to watch more footage.

"Want to multitask?" I asked. "I'd like to go over the timeline. I last saw Ms. Butt Bleach alive shortly before six o'clock. Can you remember the exact time I found her?"

"I checked my phone when Gavin questioned me. I made the call at seven thirty-five. You must have discovered the body a couple of minutes before that."

"What time did you get home? You went up to the apartment to change into your costume, right?"

"Right. I probably got there ten minutes before you did. I dumped my suitcase with the costumes in the hallway and got changed there. I debated putting on clown makeup, but there was no time, so I settled for a mask. I can't have been in the lobby more than a couple of minutes before you showed up."

I digested this information for a moment, my mind picturing the various routes from Dennehy's department store to the apartment on Snipe Avenue. "I wish we knew when Ms. Butt Bleach died."

"Unless the police share the pathologist's report with us, we won't know," Lenny said, "but it has to be some time between five-forty and six-fifty."

I shook my head. "The time range is narrower. Presumably, Nuala Kearns was with the woman for a few minutes after I went up to Tom's office, so let's make it around five forty-five when she left the store. You got home at six-fifty. We can presume Ms. Butt Bleach was already dead in our bath by then."

"Yeah. I can't imagine her killer lugged her body through the apartment building during the few minutes I went down to the lobby to scare you."

A memory clicked into place. "We can't rule it out. The elevator was in use when we were about to go upstairs, remember?"

"True, but wouldn't I have seen someone haul a dead body through the lobby?"

"I don't think the killer used the main entrance," I said. "I haven't been down to the basement in your brother's building, but isn't there a door and a flight of steps that lead up to the communal garden?"

"I think so. I'll have to ask Jake to be sure."

I focused on the laptop screen and stifled a yawn. We were an hour into footage filmed after the last workers had left the store, and nothing was happening —literally. I took a sip from my coffee mug, and it went down the wrong pipe. "Look," I wheezed between coughs, pointing at the laptop. "The guy in black."

Lenny pounded me on the back, his eyes never leaving the screen. Shortly after ten o'clock on the footage's timeline, Jasper Ramsbottom had strolled into view, clad entirely in black. Beneath his winter hat, only his face was visible, but I recognized him instantly.

So did Lenny. "There's our boy," he said in excitement.

I took a long drink from my water glass and gave another cough. "Jasper's no master criminal. He's not staying out of view of the cameras."

In the next instant, Jasper's neck jerked to the side, and he addressed a person out of the camera's range. Then he changed position and disappeared from the screen.

"His companion told him to move," I said, leaning forward. "A companion who's more intelligent than he is."

Lenny rubbed his hands together with glee. "You know what this means, Maggie?"

"This job got a whole lot more complicated?" I

sighed. "I wanted to get this case wrapped up before Christmas."

"Complicated means more interesting," Lenny said, his enthusiasm palpable. "Just you wait and see. Tomorrow's stakeout is going to be *awesome*."

At ten-thirty the following night, our stakeout didn't feel awesome. Not even slightly. After a morning of questioning by the police, and then again by Tom Dennehy, I'd spent the afternoon under Nuala Kearns's watchful eye. Far from endearing me to her, the revelation that I was working undercover made her critical of my every move.

The only saving grace was that Nuala didn't yet know of my connection with the dead woman. Until the police could identify the body and inform her next of kin, they were being cagey with the press. Lenny, the Dennehys, and I had been ordered to keep quiet about the incident. While the murder was the talk of the staff room, none of my coworkers had linked the dead woman to me, or to the store.

After a long day fueled by coffee, all I wanted to do was crawl to our hotel and sleep. Unfortunately, last night's discoveries made the stakeout a priority, so

I knocked back another espresso and met Lenny by the staff exit as arranged.

Ninety minutes into our stakeout, we'd scoured the building for clues and intruders, and found neither.

Lenny squelched out of the storerooms in the basement and joined me on the staircase that led to the entry level of the store. "Nothing untoward in there."

I cast him a wry look. "The only untoward thing I've seen tonight is your outfit."

My friend had chosen to wear his latest costume find on our stakeout, a male mannequin outfit, complete with discreet fake crotch area and a blank-expressioned mask.

"Dude, my outfit is the biz." As if to prove his point, Lenny tweaked a piece of the rubbery material between his thumb and forefinger and winced when it snapped back against his skin.

"Whatever you say. I just hope you can run in it if you need to."

"Sure I can. Its one drawback is no pockets for my tissues. I think I'm getting a cold."

I took a step away from him. "Keep your germs to yourself. I can't afford to get sick until I wrap up this case."

When we reached the entry level, we continued up to the next floor, where men's fashion and leather wear made their home. Leaning against a pillar, I yawned into my fist and unscrewed my coffee Thermos. "I feel every second of my thirty years. I remember bouncing into work on two hours of sleep when I was younger."

Beside me, Lenny stretched his shoulders. "I hear you. We're getting old, man."

I took a sip from my flask and surveyed the men's section. "I still think we should stick to the original plan and split up. We're more likely to see an intruder if we're on different floors."

"No way." Lenny's tone was uncharacteristically serious. "There's a killer on the loose. I'm not letting you out of my sight."

I eyed his tight outfit from rubber scalp to latex toe. "The store doesn't generally display naked mannequins."

"Yeah, but the only suit I own is the one Dad wore to his wedding. I didn't think it'd pass muster."

I'd seen the aforementioned suit on several occasions. Plum-colored with navy pinstripes, it was a throwback to the Seventies, right down to the flared pants. "I don't think your suit would pass for anything Dennehy's would stock."

"My point exactly. I've gotta blend in."

I snorted coffee. "Dude, you don't blend in anywhere. If we're attacked, how are you going to defend yourself in that tight outfit?"

"I'll use my newfound ninja skills. Günter is a good teacher."

Günter, my cousin's boyfriend, had recently started a series of self-defense classes on Whisper

Island, and I'd signed Lenny up. "Even Günter's tips can't help if you can't move your limbs. We need this stakeout to go well. No falling into nettles, or any other disasters like we've encountered on previous stakeout missions."

"At the rate tonight is going, our biggest danger is falling asleep. It doesn't look like this Jasper dude is going to show. Did you see him at work today?"

I shook my head. "My shortened workday meant no opportunity to talk to him in the canteen. I looked for Evan—the sales assistant Jasper traded places with on the surveillance footage—but he was home with the flu."

"We don't even know why Jasper was in the store after closing," Lenny said. "Maybe he forgot something, and it had nothing to do with the missing money."

"He'd need a key card that worked 24/7 and the alarm code. That took planning. There's no way he'd go to all that trouble for a forgotten sweater. Besides, he wasn't alone. I want to know who his companion was." I surveyed the empty shop floor. "Okay. Here's our next move. There are two ways into the store. Through the staff entrance in the basement, and through the front doors. We can assume no one is going to be stupid enough to use the front. So that leaves us with the staff entrance, and the elevator leads from the delivery bay up to the admin offices. I suggest we—"

I broke off at the sound of approaching footsteps. "Quick," I said to Lenny. "Hide."

I darted behind a sales rack, neatly adjusting the large discount sign to obscure my head. Lenny dove into position and adopted a still posture in imitation of a genuine mannequin. I bit back a groan. He'd never pull it off, particularly without clothes.

The elevator doors slid open to reveal Jasper and a wheelie suitcase. I sucked in a breath and stayed very still. Jasper gave a cursory look around the store but appeared to be confident that he was unobserved. He skirted the floor via a circuitous route, cementing my suspicion that he knew how to avoid the surveillance cameras.

Jasper strode in the direction of the changing cubicles in men's fashion, dragging the case behind him, and disappeared from view.

I looked at Lenny. *What now?* I mouthed.

He mimed sneaking up behind our target.

I shook my head. For all we knew, the man was armed. Keeping an eye on both the changing area and the elevator, I sidled over to my assistant. "Unless Jasper plans to disable the fire alarm, he can't use the fire exit. He has to come back this way."

"What's in the suitcase?" Lenny whispered. "You said a couple of hundred euro was being stolen each day. It doesn't take a suitcase to transport that amount of cash."

"No, but we suspected he wanted to get rid of me before he and whoever else is involved in the missing cash attempted a bigger job. Maybe that's going down tonight."

"Should we call the cops?" Lenny asked. "We can't let the guy stroll out of here."

I blew out a breath and nodded. "I'll text Gavin and get him to call it in. Even if Jasper isn't carrying wads of cash, there's no way he can justify sneaking into the store at this hour. If he's smart enough to stay out of range of the cameras, it'll be our word against his if we don't have more witnesses." I retrieved my phone from my pocket and typed a quick text. Once I'd sent it, there was nothing left for Lenny and me to do but hunker down and wait.

After five painful minutes, Jasper reemerged from the men's changing rooms. He was now wearing an expensive suit and admiring the fancy watch on his wrist. The breast pockets of his suit bulged. Could this be today's stolen money? Now that Ms. Butt Bleach was dead, he had to be getting the cash out of the building somehow.

I checked the guy for signs of a weapon, but there were none. Either Jasper was cleverer than I'd given him credit for, or he was unarmed. I was inclined to go with the latter. Whatever was going on, he didn't strike me as the brains of this operation. Keeping out of sight of the cameras, the man strode across the store with more confidence than I'd seen him display before. It was amazing what a ten-thousand-euro suit could do for a guy.

Lenny and I exchanged a worried glance. If the

police didn't get here soon, Jasper would be gone. I couldn't let that happen. The man's route grew closer to our position. Buzzing with adrenaline, I stuck my foot out to trip him up but drew it in again the instant the elevator pinged.

Jasper whipped around just as the doors slid open.

Three masked men marched out of the elevator. Ignoring the cameras, they strode across the shop floor toward Jasper.

He paled, and his grip on the suitcase tightened. "What do you want?"

The tallest of the masked men grabbed him by the front of his suit jacket and picked him up. "You greedy fool. You put us all at risk so you could line your pockets."

Jasper went red in the face and spluttered an incomprehensible protest. The tall man dropped him like a stone. Jasper hit the ground with a groan and whimpered. "I don't know what you're talking about, Del."

The guy called Del kicked Jasper in the stomach, and the smaller man gasped in pain. "We said no names, you eejit. This is just another example of why you should never have been hired in the first place. You're not cut out for this line of work."

Still moaning, Jasper rolled into the fetal position and drew his knees up to his chest. "Please don't hurt me. I didn't mean any harm. It was all Cara's idea. I'll give you the cash I took if that's what you want."

"Unless you want to end up like Cara, you'd better start talking."

Lenny and I looked at one another. Was Cara the woman in our bathroom?

"How much does this P.I. woman know?" Del continued. "Have you spoken to her?"

"She's gone around asking questions," Jasper said between gasps, "but I didn't tell her anything."

Del loomed over his prey. "Are you sure?"

"I swear. I haven't said a word to anyone." Jasper rolled onto his side and struggled for breath. "What did you mean about Cara? Is she all right?"

"Let's just say she's no longer part of this operation." I could hear the smirk in Del's smug voice.

"I'm sorry about the cash," Jasper whined. "Cara put the screws on me. She said she'd go to the guards and tell them everything if I didn't give her money."

"Why didn't you come to us?" Del demanded. "We could've taken care of her and avoided this mess. The boss is fuming that we have to bring the date forward."

"I didn't tell you because I didn't want anyone to get hurt." The man sounded almost sincere. "Tell me what I need to do to make it right. I can give you all the money I took."

Del's laugh sent chills down my spine. "If this job works out, we'll get a lot more cash than anything you've stolen from this dump. You're getting to be a liability. Do you know what the boss does with liabilities? Do you want to know what happened to Cara?"

Jasper whimpered. "Please. Don't hurt me."

The tall man leaned in close. "We're going to do a lot more than hurt you."

I sucked in a breath when he drew a knife from his pocket and held it to Jasper's throat.

The smaller man's tears rolled down his ruddy cheeks. "Please don't," he said. "I'll do anything…"

Whatever response Del might've made to this extravagant promise was lost by Lenny's sonic boom of a sneeze.

"Sorry, Maggie," he whispered. "I couldn't hold it in."

I sucked in a breath, my feet rooted to the spot.

Del and his burly pals whirled around. "Who's there?" he growled.

Yeah. I'm totally going to tell the dude my location.

"Search the place," Del snarled at his companions.

But before his lackeys could carry out his order, the fire alarm clanged into life with earsplitting efficiency.

Swearing, Del and his friends raced for the elevator. Meanwhile, Jasper staggered to his feet and took off in the direction of the fire exit, dragging his case behind him.

"Let's get him." I kept my eyes on my quarry and sprinted across the store.

In front of the fire exit, Jasper turned abruptly and reared back at the sight of me. Without uttering a word, he jammed his suitcase into my path, and I stumbled over it, turning my ankle when I landed. A sharp pain shot through my ankle, making me gasp. I made a grab for him, but I'd lost precious seconds. Jasper disappeared through the door. Gritting my teeth through the pain, I shoved the suitcase out of my way and pushed the door. It wouldn't budge.

"He's locked it," I shouted to Lenny. "I can't get the door to open."

"Maggie? Are they gone?"

My heart lurched, and a familiar figure emerged from behind a rack of winter coats. "Tom? What are you doing here?"

The man looked sheepish. "I've never been on a stakeout before. I wanted to see how the professionals do it."

"Did you set off the fire alarm?"

He nodded. "Even if Jasper has been stealing from me, I couldn't let them slit his throat."

"I don't imagine that your customers would appreciate a bloodstain in the middle of the floor. Bad for business." I hobbled over to Tom, wincing with every step.

"Did I mess up?" Tom slicked back his comb-over with an unsteady hand. "I was only trying to help."

"I know you were. Thank you for distracting the masked guys. Unfortunately, we still have no proof that Jasper has been stealing from the cash registers."

"But he had money in his pockets," Tom insisted, "and he stole that suit."

"We don't know that for sure," I said. "We're

assuming the bulge in his suit pockets contained cash, but we didn't see it. We also didn't see him take a suit. It'll be our word against his. And until those dudes showed up, he was careful not to appear on camera."

"But what about the stuff we overheard?" Tom demanded. "It sounds like those guys are in some kind of gang."

"That's the impression I got, but apart from knowing one guy is called Del, we have no idea who they are. All the surveillance footage will show is three guys dressed in black wearing balaclavas."

Tom looked crestfallen. "So we have nothing to give to the police?"

"We have this." I patted the suitcase that had facilitated my sore ankle. "And we have anything you can tell us about Jasper's background."

"I can't tell you anything that isn't in the personnel file I gave you." Tom wrinkled his nose. "Jasper seems too much of a fool to be a master criminal."

"He can't be all that stupid," I said. "From the sound of it, he's responsible for stealing cash from your store, and he's been getting away with it for weeks."

Lenny lumbered into view. "Yo, dudes. Any sign of the guards yet?"

"Not yet, but they'll be here soon."

At the sight of my assistant, Tom Dennehy jumped backward, his face leached of color. "Where did he come from? What is he wearing?"

"Tom, meet my assistant, Lenny Logan. Lenny, this is Tom Dennehy."

The men shook hands, Lenny pumping with enthusiasm as he always did, and Tom grimacing at the pressure.

"If it's all right with you," Lenny said, "I'd like to take a look at the men's changing cubicles. I'm betting Jasper has a hiding place for the money."

"Go for it. In the meantime, Tom and I can take a look in this case." I grinned at the older man. "Want to do the honors? It's your first time on a stakeout, after all."

Tom flushed with pleasure. "I don't mind if I do." He unzipped the case gingerly. Inside, it was filled with expensive men's shirts and designer watches. "There's got to be around fifty shirts in here, and they're all in the over-one-hundred-euros price range. As for the watches—" Tom shook his head, dazed, "—they cost several hundred each."

"Have you noticed missing stock?" I asked.

"No. We might miss the odd item until we did a full inventory, but not on this scale."

"Dudes, you gotta come see this." Lenny emerged from the changing area with a triumphant smile on his face. "I found his hiding place for the cash, and there's a pile of shirts and watches in there, too."

Tom and I followed Lenny into the men's changing area. He opened the door to the fourth cubicle and gestured for us to look inside. The cubicle consisted of a full floor-to-ceiling length mirror, a rack for hanging clothes, and a plush leather seat with a velvet cushion.

"Check this out." Lenny inserted a finger into the hollow underneath the cushion and tugged out a black fabric bag. "This hooks onto the inside of the seat. My bet is this is where he's been hiding the cash. No one would ever think to look here. Even if you shake the seat, nothing falls out."

"Well done," I said, genuinely impressed.

Tom Dennehy wiped the sweat from his brow. "Where are the shirts and watches you mentioned?"

"They're in the next cubicle."

The store manager opened the door and peered inside. A neat pile of packaged shirts lay on the floor, next to a box of packaged watches. Tom bent down and picked up a box. He removed the watch and examined it closely. And swore under his breath. "Counterfeit. I can't be one hundred percent certain, but my gut tells me it's not genuine."

"What about the shirts? Do you think Jasper exchanged them for the real deal?"

Tom opened a package and examined a shirt. A thunderous expression descended over his mild features. "They've been stealing my stock and replacing it with counterfeit goods."

"Do you want us to continue searching the store?"

Tom shook his head. "We're done here for the night. Let's wait for the police."

As if on cue, my phone rang. The name flashing on the display was Gavin's. "Hey, Maggie," he said when I answered. "The staff entrance door was wide open. Everything okay?"

"We're all right. Take the elevator to the men's department."

"I'm on it."

I barely had time to put my phone back into my pocket when the elevator pinged, and the doors began to slide open. "That'll be the cops." I turned to Tom. "By the way, you don't happen to know anyone named Del?"

Tom frowned. "No, I don't think so. I can ask around, though."

"It might be safer not to," I said. "Leave that part to Lenny and me. We can assume the Cara the men referred to was the dead chick in our bathtub."

"Maggie?"

The familiar gravelly voice jolted me. I gasped and whipped around to see not Gavin but Liam Reynolds step into view, his handsome features rigid with tension. When our eyes met, his narrowed.

"What dead chick?"

9

"What are you doing here?" My gaze moved from my boyfriend to the girl beside him, registering her presence for the first time. Was she Liam's reason for ditching our date? "Hey, Hannah. I didn't expect to see you until after the new year."

My boyfriend's face tensed, emphasizing the shadows under his eyes. "It's a long story. We can discuss it later. For now, tell me what craziness you've gotten yourself involved in this time. What's all this about a body in the bathtub?"

"And why is Lenny dressed like a zombie?" Hannah stared at my assistant in fascination. "Cool outfit, by the way."

Lenny beamed. "Thanks, but I'm a mannequin. I guess I could use it as a zombie costume, too, though."

Before I could voice a response, Gavin, dressed in plain clothes, stepped out of the elevator.

Liam rounded on his brother. "Why didn't you tell me Maggie found a dead body in her bathtub?"

Gavin shot me a warning look. "We haven't released the details of that case to the newspapers yet. I'd rather Maggie and Lenny not discuss this in public."

"I'm not public," Liam muttered. "I'm her boyfriend. Surely I have a right to know if Maggie is involved in another murder inquiry."

"Sure you do," I said tartly. "Just as I have a right to know what the heck is going on with you. What happened to 'I won't be available for the next couple of days?'"

"Never mind about that." Gavin bristled with impatience. "I need to know what's been going on here tonight."

Tom Dennehy emerged from the shadows and ran a trembling hand over his greasy comb-over. "Masked intruders," he wheezed, sounding as though he were on the verge of a heart attack, "with knives."

"One knife," I interjected, "that we know about."

"How can you be so blasé?" Tom shuddered. "Do you encounter armed robbers regularly in your line of work?"

"Only dead people," Hannah said, deadpan, "but that's usually during her free time."

"You're a great kid, but why aren't you waiting in

the car?" I shot her father a death glance. "And why aren't you down there with her?"

"Your text to my brother said an employee with a suitcase was acting suspicious," Liam said, on the defensive. "You never mentioned armed intruders."

"There were no armed intruders at the time I sent the text."

"They were with me when your text came through," Gavin explained. "When Liam heard you were in danger, he insisted on coming, and he didn't want to leave Hannah alone in the car."

I raised an eyebrow. Hannah was almost nine years old. Couldn't she stay on her own for a few minutes, especially if Liam thought I might be in danger? He verged on being overprotective with his daughter. It wasn't like him to bring Hannah into a situation that could end in an arrest.

"Why don't you talk to Maggie later?" Lenny suggested. "Mr. Dennehy and I can tell you all you need to know about what happened here tonight."

Gavin exchanged a long look with his brother. "Fair enough. Maggie and Liam can accompany Hannah down to the car, and I'll take Maggie's state-ment after." He tossed his brother the car key. "If you finish chatting before I come down, I'd appreciate Maggie hanging around to talk to me. And if you see the backup car I ordered, send them up here."

Respecting my preference for the stairs, Liam and Hannah followed me down the staff staircase and out onto the street. Gavin's black VW sedan was parked outside the building. Liam pressed the automatic key. "Hop into the back, Hannah. I won't be long."

The girl gave him the side-eye. "Sure, Dad. I'll leave you two to fight and get kissy-kissy."

Given her father's thunderous expression and my irritation with him, I doubted the kissy-kissy part was going to happen.

When Hannah was seated in the back of the car and distracted with her iPad, I said, "Liam, we——"

To my astonishment, he silenced me with a kiss. My initial impulse to shove him away and demand to know what was going on lasted less than a second. The sensation of his warm lips on mine melted the tension in my neck and shoulders and erased all thoughts of the craziness of the last two days. In spite of my vow to confront my boyfriend about his cryptic message, I wrapped my arms around him and snuggled closer, inhaling his comfortingly familiar scent and allowing him to tease my face and neck with his stubble.

"I've missed you, Maggie," he murmured, stroking my hair. "I'm sorry I had to cancel on you yesterday."

I pushed back and looked up at him. The angle of the streetlight bathed one side of his face in a soft yellow glow and left the other in shadow. "What's going on, Liam? You've been distracted for days. I was starting to think you were having doubts about us, but that kiss said otherwise."

His eyes widened in surprise. "You thought I wanted out of our relationship? Absolutely not."

I exhaled a breath I hadn't realized I'd been holding. "If we're not the problem, what's wrong?"

He wrapped his arms around me and hugged me tightly. "I'm sorry if I've been acting strange. It's been a stressful couple of weeks."

"If something is bothering you, you can always talk to me."

"I know." He broke the hug and rubbed his stubbled jaw. Under the streetlight, the dark shadows beneath his eyes contrasted with his winter-pale skin. "I got some bad news while I was on the training course. I didn't have permission to tell you—or anyone else. Even if I had, it wasn't the sort of topic I wanted to discuss over the phone."

An array of dire possibilities flashed through my mind. "You're not sick, are you? Is it Hannah? Or your ex? Is that why Hannah's in Ireland?"

"No, nothing like that. We're all healthy."

"Then what's wrong?"

His eyes met mine, and the fear in them chilled me to the bone. "Robyn received threats from a guy she successfully prosecuted a few years ago. He got parole two months ago, and on the day he got out, he showed up on her doorstep."

My eyes widened. "Oh my goodness. Did he hurt her?"

"Robyn wasn't home, thankfully, but her security camera recorded Weber, and she recognized him at once. Before he left, he put a threatening message through her postbox."

I shuddered and drew my coat tight around me. "Is he dangerous?"

"I'll say." Liam's mouth formed an uncompromising line. "Eight years ago, he beat a security guard into a coma during a petrol station robbery. I guess he was on his best behavior in prison, but it was all an act."

"Had he threatened Robyn before his release?" I asked, "Or did his threats come out of nowhere?"

"Right after his conviction, he yelled abuse at the judge and at Robyn, who was the prosecutor in the case. He said he'd kill them when he got out of prison. He later retracted this statement and wrote them letters of apology, claiming he'd lost his mind after being convicted and was sorry for any distress he'd caused them."

"An apology that dripped with insincerity."

"Looks like it." Liam's jaw tightened. "I don't always see eye to eye with my ex, but she's done nothing to deserve harassment and intimidation. She successfully prosecuted Gary Weber for a crime he committed, and he received a fair sentence."

"In others words, she did her job and saw that justice was served. How did the guy convince a parole board that he deserved early release?"

"To give a little background, Weber was convicted alongside his brother, Jim. Two years into his sentence, Jim died in prison. There was nothing suspicious about his death. He was known to suffer from heart disease.

However, in the letter Weber posted through Robyn's letter box, he accused her of being responsible for his brother's death. He claimed Jim would have received better medical treatment had he not been in prison."

"I'm sorry, Liam. That's awful. Does Hannah know?"

"Yes. That's why I had to cancel our dinner last night. Robyn's convinced the guy is following her around, and I believe her. Weber missed his scheduled meeting with his parole officer yesterday morning and is now on the run. As you know, I was supposed to have Hannah for the last week of her school holidays. Instead, I flew to England yesterday afternoon and brought her straight back here."

"Is Weber aware Robyn has a daughter?"

"I don't know, but the guy's obsessed." Liam's mouth pressed into a grim line. "It would be easy info to find out."

He was right. In this day and age, almost any information was a few mouse clicks away.

"How long will Hannah stay with you?" I asked. "Will she go back to her boarding school after Christmas?"

Liam ran a hand through his close-cropped dark blond hair. "I have no idea. It depends on how long it takes for the police to catch Weber. In the meantime, Robyn has a bodyguard, and Hannah will stay with me."

"What an awful situation. Robyn and I aren't

exactly besties, but I feel bad for her. She must be terrified."

"She is." Liam pulled me close. "I'm sorry if I made you feel insecure, Maggie. That was never my intention. I'd planned to tell you about Weber over dinner last night, but after he missed his parole check-in, Robyn called me in a panic and asked me to collect Hannah immediately."

"Please tell me she didn't use her cell phone to contact you."

"No." His lips twisted into a wry smile. "That's one pro to having a policeman as her ex-husband. She knew to put several layers of distance between the phone call and me. She bought a burner phone and asked a friend to contact Gavin at his station. He got word to me, and I booked a seat on the next available flight to London."

"Understandable. I'd have done the same in your position. Even if the threat to Hannah is minimal, I wouldn't want to take the risk." I bit my lip and dropped my eyes to my winter boots. "As for me being insecure, that's something I'm going to have to get over. Maybe I'm still feeling vulnerable after my breakup with Joe."

Liam regarded me with a serious expression and stroked a stray curl back from my face. "I'm not Joe, Maggie. I've never been unfaithful to any of my former partners. If I make a commitment, I take it seriously. And if I had doubts about our relationship —which I don't—I'd communicate them to you."

Hot tears stung my eyes at his words, and my heart swelled. "I believe you. At least the rational part of me does. I guess I need to work on the emotional side of me."

"I get that you're sensitive after your experience last year, but you can't live your life worrying and overanalyzing every word I say, or everything I do. It's not healthy—not for you and not for us."

"I know." I swallowed past the lump in my throat. "I'm sorry. I don't want to be paranoid. That's not who I am in any other aspect of my life."

He pulled me close and dropped a kiss onto my forehead. "Don't be sorry. If anyone should be apologizing, it's me. I should've found a way to communicate with you and let you know what was going on. If Robyn, the least tech-savvy person I know, can figure out how to use a burner phone and a go-between to cover her tracks, then surely I should have come up with a solution."

"How can I help?"

"At the moment, there's not a lot you can do. Gavin's wife works from home, and she's agreed to look after Hannah while I'm at work this week. I swapped a few shifts with Sile, and that'll mean I can start my Christmas break two days earlier." He gave me a wry smile. "Besides, it sounds like you have your plate full here. Are you going to tell me who you found dead in your bathtub?"

"A woman who claimed I'd caused her injury by

selling her facial hair lightener instead of butt bleach, but I'm guessing it was all a ruse."

Liam's hearty laugh brought a smile to my face. "Only you, Maggie. How did she end up in your tub?"

"A dude called Del and his balaclava-clad cohorts killed her and tried to frame me." At his incredulous expression, I added, "They're connected to a case I'm working on. Somehow, they discovered I was a P.I. and working undercover as a sales assistant."

My boyfriend cracked up at this revelation. "Ah, Maggie. I can't think of anyone who makes me laugh more than you do, and I mean that in the best possible way. I can't see you as a sales assistant. You barely get away with serving customers at your aunt's café."

"Hey, I'm polite." I paused. "Most of the time."

Liam wiped tears of laughter from the corners of his eyes. "How did you end up working undercover at Dennehy's? You never gave me the specifics."

"I signed a confidentiality agreement, but I doubt it matters much now. Tonight's discoveries will hopefully help crack the case. I was hired to investigate missing money, but it turns out the stolen cash was just part of a larger operation."

"Ouch. No wonder the store manager was sweating."

"Yeah." I glanced at my watch. "I guess I should go back and give your brother my statement. Will you and Hannah wait for him?"

"Nah. I'll see if I can find a taxi to take us back to the house. I'm staying overnight at Gavin's place, and I'll catch the first ferry to Whisper Island in the morning."

"I'll send you a message to let you know when I'll be back," I said. "I can't imagine it'll take more than a day or two. Once I'm home, I can help watch Hannah."

"I'd appreciate that, Maggie, but I can't cut into your work time. If you and Lenny weren't working from Galway at the moment, I'd hire you for a few hours a week."

"Lenny's almost done with his case, too. He might be able to help. Am I allowed to mention Robyn's situation to him?"

"Yeah, go ahead, but it goes no further." The furrow between his brows returned. "The fewer people who know, the less chance of a leak."

"In spite of Lenny's laidback attitude, he's incredibly discreet when he needs to be. I wouldn't have hired him otherwise."

"I know. You're a good judge of character."

I stood on my tippy toes and drew him into a kiss. "Goodnight, Liam. I'll miss you."

"I'll miss you, too." He stroked back my hair and gazed into my eyes. "I wish I could stay with you tonight, but Hannah needs me."

"I understand. We'll have time together soon." I took a reluctant step toward the door. "I love you, Liam Reynolds."

"I love you, Maggie Doyle." He cast me a rueful smile. "I'd tell you not to go finding more trouble, but would there be any point?"

I grinned. "Probably not."

It took great effort to leave him and go back into the Dennehy's building. As I trudged back up the stairs to give Gavin my statement, I ran over my conversation with Liam. While I felt bad for Robyn, knowing the strain between Liam and me had a logical explanation was a weight off my shoulders. On a less positive note, the extent of my insecurity shocked me. It wasn't like me to be this paranoid. Maybe the split with Joe had wounded me more than I'd realized. Whatever the cause of my anxiety, I had to get it under control before it consumed me and wrecked the best relationship I'd ever had.

10

Once I'd provided Gavin with my statement, the police left the department store. Lenny, Tom, and I spent the next two hours looking for counterfeit goods. The ankle I'd hurt when Jasper tripped me up still ached a little, but it wasn't showing any signs of swelling. Hopefully, the ankle would be back to normal within a few hours. After a fruitless search of every floor, we called it quits at one o'clock in the morning.

Tom slicked back his comb-over and rubbed his tired eyes. "Thanks for staying late, guys."

"I'm not sure if I should be sorry or pleased that we didn't find anything else suspicious," I said. "I'm not enough of an expert in luxury goods to recognize a fake."

Tom inclined his head. "I know watches and jewelry, but that's all. I'll ask the department supervisors to conduct a discreet search tomorrow."

"Don't you mean today?" I pointed to the clock on the wall.

The store manager followed the direction of my finger and groaned. "I need to get up in a few hours."

"Did your first stakeout live up to your expectations?" I asked dryly.

The man's boyish smile shaved ten years off his age. "It was rather fun, even if I nearly peed my pants."

"Next time you want to join us on a stakeout, give me a head's up," I said, enjoying the look of horror on Tom's face.

"I think I've had enough excitement tonight to last me a lifetime," he said. "In the future, I'll stick to watching stakeouts on the telly."

"Do you need me to come into the store tomorrow?" I asked. "Or do you consider Movie Reel Investigation's case to be closed?"

Tom's brow creased. "Until the police catch up with Jasper and that Del fellow, I'd feel more comfortable if you stayed."

"I can do that, but I'd like to get back to Whisper Island before the weekend." I suspected Tom's enthusiasm to keep me at the store had more than a little to do with the fact that he'd soon be down two members of staff, but I could roll with staying a day or two longer. I hated loose ends.

Lenny and I parted from Tom at the staff exit and headed back to our hotel on Eyre Square. This late, the streets were almost empty, and the flashing festive lights seemed incongruous without the familiar crowds of shoppers.

"Where do we go from here?" Lenny turned up the collar of his coat and dug his hands into his pockets to ward off the cold.

"I'd like you to research people named Del who live in Galway. Did you think his accent was local?" Although I'd lived in Ireland for nearly a year, I still struggled to differentiate between regional accents. They all sounded the same to me.

"Yeah," Lenny said without hesitation. "He has a Galway accent for sure. I'll see what I can find. I doubt this was his first time breaking the law."

"That's what I suspect," I said. "I'm sorry for getting us into this mess. I assumed the job was just about stolen money. Organized crime is way out of our league."

"It's been more exciting than sitting in front of the computer staring at surveillance footage."

I shivered and stuck my hands into my jacket pockets. "Personally, I'd rather do the job I was hired to do and get out."

"Want me to continue my search for info about Jasper?" Lenny asked. "And maybe the dead chick, too?"

"Yes, please. Gavin's going to see if he can find a Cara to match Ms. Butt Bleach's description, but I doubt he'll pass the info on to me." A thought occurred to me, and not for the first time that evening. "Didn't you find it weird that Gavin didn't tell Liam about us finding the dead woman in our bathtub? I was certain he would."

"Perhaps he's not allowed to talk about the case, even to a fellow police officer," Lenny suggested. "After all, the guards are being pretty cagey with the info they're providing the media."

"I've noticed. It doesn't make sense." I replayed the events of the last couple of days in my mind. "I found it strange that an inspector showed up to our place so quickly. It's usually beat cops who are first on the scene, and then it gets passed up the chain. I was distracted by the body when you called emergency services. Did you mention she'd been strangled?"

He frowned and thought for a moment before answering. "I think so. I'm pretty sure you mentioned the cause of death to me before I made the call."

"That's interesting," I mused. "Craddock acted like I'd electrocuted him when I asked if there'd been other strangulations recently. I bet the police are working on a big case that's somehow connected to Cara's murder."

"And her murder is linked to whatever's happening at Dennehy's," Lenny added. "We need to find out more about Jasper, Cara, and the Del dude."

"That sort of research lies in your area of expertise. While you're busy looking up criminals and wrapping up the case at The Costume Emporium, I'll use my last days at Dennehy's to question the staff. The time for subtlety is over."

"Good plan." Lenny looked at me, a small smile

on his lips. "You're in a better mood than earlier. How'd your talk with Reynolds go?"

"Good regarding our relationship. Not great in other ways."

We reached our hotel and Lenny held the door open for me. While we walked across the hotel lobby and up the stairs to our rooms, I filled him in on the basics of Robyn's situation with the guy she'd helped to convict for assault and armed robbery.

When I'd finished my tale, my friend whistled. "Poor old Liam. Robyn's a witch, but she's the mother of his child."

"Exactly. And she doesn't deserve to be threatened. I hate to admit it, but it was a relief to know Liam's strange behavior had nothing to do with me. I was starting to wonder if he'd gotten bored."

Lenny roared with laughter. "There is no way anyone could get bored with you around, Maggie. Exasperated? Maybe. Bored? Never."

"Still, it was weird for him not to confide in me, so you can see why I was worried. I'm the one who's reluctant to talk about family and personal stuff. He's more open than I am."

"He canceled *one* date. That's hardly a reason to panic. Don't you think that your paranoia might be because you care a lot about Liam? Maybe you're nervous because you've reached the six-month point of dating, and you're wondering what's going to come next."

My gut twisted. "If you're talking about an

engagement ring, no way. My divorce only came through in August. I don't want to remarry that quickly."

Lenny grinned. "But you're not ruling out another marriage."

"No," I said cautiously, "but it's not something I'd like to rush into."

"I get that, and you're right to take things slow." He cast me a sly smile. "Even if you're crazy about him and he's crazy about you. I might need to trot out my dad's old suit sooner than you think."

A sudden image of Liam waiting for me at the altar flashed through my mind. *Whoa.* I needed to rein in my emotions. It wasn't like me to get sappy, but then, it wasn't like me to get angsty over a guy I was dating. "I'll see you in the morning, Lenny. And no more talk of weddings."

THE NEXT MORNING, I trudged into work, exhausted. The glittering holiday ornaments and the constant stream of festive songs on the store's music system were sensory overloads. I needed a caffeine hit, and I needed one fast.

When I reached the cosmetics section, Nuala Kearns glared at me. "You need to redo your concealer, Maggie. We can't have you looking like you haven't slept. The customers expect cosmetics sales assistants to look the part."

I opened my mouth to argue, but I closed it again. She was right. I looked like I'd been dragged through a bush, and I was supposed to be selling makeup. I took my makeup kit into the restroom and redid my face, paying particular attention to the telltale bags under my eyes. When I returned to the cosmetics section, Tracey was busy with a customer, and Nuala was preoccupied checking stock. I grinned. Tom Dennehy had wasted no time in issuing the department heads with instructions to conduct a discreet search for counterfeit products.

Casting a last glance at the back of Nuala's head, I snuck into the break room. My purpose was twofold: grab a quick coffee, and score a lunch date with coworkers I hadn't had a chance to speak to yet. To my astonishment, the only person in the room was none other than Evan Manning. The man lounged by the machine, drinking an espresso as if he didn't have a care in the world. Looking at his innocent expression, you'd never guess he'd knowingly facilitated one theft, and probably several more. Perhaps he was a cooler customer than I'd given him credit for.

I ran my finger down the work roster pinned behind the door. No, I hadn't misremembered. The man wasn't scheduled to work today.

I sauntered over to the coffee machine and flashed him a warm smile. "Hey, Evan. Why are you in today? Did someone trade places with you?" I emphasized the words "trade places."

"Jasper asked me to cover for him. He's out with

the flu." Evan's tone was smooth, but his pink cheeks told another story.

"Poor guy." My tone dripped with insincerity.

Evan flinched, but he recovered his composure quickly.

While I made my espresso, I chattered about inconsequential topics, all the while gauging Evan's reaction. Nope, he wasn't as composed as he'd like me to believe. A sheen of sweat gathered on his forehead, and his voice was a notch higher than usual. Either Jasper was on the run, or the police had taken him in for questioning. And they'd catch up with Evan soon —I'd contact Gavin the instant I got the chance.

Nuala stuck her head around the break room door and glowered at me. "We need you out here, Maggie. Now."

I drained my disposable coffee cup and threw it into the trash. "Later, Evan."

I felt his eyes bore into my back as I exited the break room. My first act when the door closed behind me was to text Gavin. Once I'd hit Send, there was nothing left for me to do but return to my station in the cosmetics section.

The rest of the morning flew by. We had a steady stream of shoppers. With only one week to Christmas, everyone was stocking up on last-minute holiday gifts and supplies. Shortly after my lunch break, a familiar voice exclaimed, "What on earth are *you* doing here?"

I glanced up and gasped when I recognized my friend, Jennifer Pearce, from Whisper Island. I pressed a finger to my lips. "How may I help you? Would you like me to show you our new Beautalicious lipstick display?"

My friend looked startled, but she was smart enough to get the hint. She allowed me to drone on about various brands of lipstick, even though I was quite sure she was far more knowledgeable on the subject of luxury makeup than I was. When Tracey was far enough away, I whispered, "I'm working undercover."

Jennifer's eyes creased in amusement. "I guessed as much. I'm here to do some last-minute Christmas shopping." She glanced over her shoulder. "But I should warn you, Melanie Greer and her ladies-who-lunch pals are in Galway for a boozy shopping trip. When I last saw them, they were having a liquid lunch, and they said they were coming to Dennehy's later."

"Seriously? Melanie and her cackling coven are coming here?" I groaned. "Ugh. That's all I need. They'll blow my cover."

Melanie Greer had been my teenage nemesis, and the girl my first boyfriend had cheated on me with. To be fair, he'd married her, and they'd been together for over ten years. However, Melanie and I still sparked off one another. An inveterate gossip, there was no way Melanie would keep quiet about seeing me.

A cackle of laughter drew my attention to the front of the store. As if on cue, Melanie and three of her golf club friends sailed over the threshold, already laden down with shopping bags.

Sweat gathered under my tight collar. How was I going to prevent Melanie and her cronies from telling the entire store that I was a private investigator?

11

From the manner in which Rita Ahearn tottered on her high heels, Jennifer's description of the women's liquid lunch hadn't been an exaggeration. Melanie's other companions included Linda Reilly, whose husband had recently bought the island's yacht club, and Samantha Vincent, co-owner of the property developers who owned and managed my cottage.

I swore under my breath. "Time for me to do a disappearing act."

"I'll try to create a distraction," Jennifer said, "but keep your back to them."

Before Jennifer could fulfill her promise, Rita lurched forward and descended upon the makeup section, making a beeline for my supervisor. "Nuala," she trilled. "It's lovely to see you."

With mounting horror, Jennifer and I watched as

Nuala Kearns blocked my escape route and air-kissed Melanie and her friends.

I exchanged a panicked look with my friend. "What the—"

She regarded me with sympathy. "Doesn't one of Melanie's aunts work in a department store? I'm sure she mentioned it at some point."

"She does?" I scrutinized my supervisor and groaned. Now that she was standing beside Melanie, the family resemblance was plain to see. Melanie wasn't as emaciated as her aunt, but they both had the same almond-shaped dark eyes and silky hair, which in Nuala's case probably had help from an expensive colorist.

Glancing over Nuala's thin shoulders, Melanie's eyes widened when she caught sight of Jennifer and me. Her gaze shifted from Jennifer to me and she drew back. "Maggie? Fancy seeing you here." She looked pointedly at my black uniform. "And in such an uncharacteristically flattering outfit."

"Do you two know each other?" Nuala demanded, skewering me with her accusatory stare.

"Oh, yes," her niece said with relish. "Maggie's the one who found Mummy's body."

From her intonation, it'd be easy for a stranger to assume I'd killed the woman. "I'm also the one who found *Mummy's* murderer," I pointed out with more heat than was strictly necessary. "A murderer who's now behind bars."

"Very true," Melanie conceded, "but that doesn't

explain why you're working here." She raised her eyebrow in an ironic arch. "Are you on another case?"

"Please keep your voice down," I pleaded. "People aren't supposed to know."

"We've had nothing but drama since she came to work here," Nuala interjected, eager to share her grievances. "She caused a customer to injure her private parts earlier this week."

Melanie didn't appear in the least surprised by this news. "Oh, that's nothing new. Maggie's a magnet for disaster. She's always tripping over dead people."

It was on the tip of my tongue to add that Ms. Butt Bleach had been deliberately placed in my bathtub for me to find, rather than me stumbling over her, but I kept my mouth shut. Cara's name still hadn't been released to the media, so photographs of the dead woman hadn't yet been circulated, and Nuala and my other coworkers still didn't know of the murder victim's connection to me and the store.

"Maggie is a walking catastrophe," Linda Reilly added with relish, even though I was certain she and I had never exchanged a single word.

"Total," Rita Ahearn added. "I don't know how many times my poor husband has been called out to extinguish fires she started."

Nuala Kearns regarded me with alarm. "Don't tell me she's a pyromaniac."

"No," I snapped. "Merely a lousy cook. Are you guys here to laugh at me, or do you want to buy something?"

"Whoa," Linda said. "Prickly much?"

Nuala stuck her nose in the air. "I'll serve these ladies, Maggie. You run along and have your break."

"I already had my break," I said sulkily.

"Then take another one." The flinty edge to Nuala's tone made it clear that this was an order. Normally, I'd have been delighted to escape, but I knew only too well that Nuala would use the opportunity to pump Melanie and her friends for information about me. And in my brief acquaintance with Nuala, I knew she'd use whatever she learned to annoy me. Seriously, the sooner I got out of this store, the better.

Jennifer gave me an uncharacteristic hug. "I'll call you later, Maggie." The lawyer enveloped me in an uncharacteristic hug, and whispered into my air, "Don't let them get to you. Those women give female dogs a bad name."

Snorting with laughter, I parted from Jennifer and sailed past Melanie and her friends without sparing them a backward glance.

Siobhan was in the break room, playing with her phone. She frowned when I came in. "What's up with you?" she demanded. "You've got a face like a wet weekend."

Coming from her, this observation reeked of irony. "Isn't every weekend in Ireland wet?" I quipped and threw myself onto a sofa.

Siobhan revealed a surprisingly pretty smile. Since I'd known her, I'd never seen her smile before. "You might be right, but I'm hoping the weather stays nice for the next couple of weekends. I have plans."

"Oh, yeah? Are these holiday plans?"

"Sort of. My boyfriend is planning a big dinner for my birthday next week. It falls two days after Christmas, so it tends to be overshadowed by the holidays."

"That sounds like fun. Have you guys been together long?"

The woman's typically granite gaze softened. "We'll have been together two years this Friday. We met at a music festival in the freezing cold."

I grinned. "That sounds romantic. Do you have plans to mark the occasion?"

"I think Derek has something up his sleeve. A group of us are going on a trip to Whisper Island for the Our Lady's Tears festival."

I jerked to attention. At the last second, I stopped myself from revealing that I lived on Whisper Island. "Is that the cave festival?"

Siobhan nodded. "Yeah, I haven't been since I was a kid. I remember it being a laugh."

"Doesn't it have something to do with a weeping statue?"

"That's right," Siobhan said. "A statue of the Virgin Mary allegedly cries a few days before Christmas. It's all nonsense, of course. The statue is in a damp cave. I'd say it's got water dripping off it the whole year round. At any rate, the locals have turned it into a festival. It extends way beyond the cave.

There're stands and music and games. Kind of like a Christmas market."

"It sounds like fun." My aunts had mentioned the festival to me before I'd left for Galway, but I hadn't paid attention to the details.

Siobhan glanced at her watch and pulled a face. "Duty calls. Later, Maggie."

"Bye, Siobhan." I flashed her a friendly smile. "Hey, maybe we can grab lunch together."

The woman gave a noncommittal shrug. "I guess. I'll be in the canteen as usual."

Okay, then. Not an enthusiastic acceptance, but I wanted the opportunity to chat with a few of Siobhan's coworkers from the household appliances section.

After she left, I drank a coffee and let the minutes tick by. Hopefully, Melanie and her pals would have moved on from splurging on makeup by now. Stretching my stiff neck from side to side, I opened the door and stepped back into the busy store.

On my way back to the cosmetics section, I passed a large display featuring a family of mannequins laden down with shopping bags. I gasped when the male mannequin winked at me. I put my hands on my hips and glared at him. "Lenny? What are you—?"

Before I could finish, a guy wearing a Santa Claus costume came barreling right at me. I leaped to the side, barely managing to save myself from being mowed down. The man inside the costume was sweating profusely. The two spots of rouge that had been painted on his cheeks as part of his costume blended in with his red face. With the white wig and fluffy white beard, the guy could have been any age from thirty to sixty. The man reached up to straighten his wig, and I caught sight of the expensive watch on his wrist—a watch similar to the one I'd seen Jasper wearing last night.

Breathing hard, the man in the costume took off running. Santa Claus was an ideal costume for a guy who wanted to roam the store incognito and retrieve cash from his various hiding places. Santa, when he wasn't in his grotto, went around the store greeting customers and having his picture taken with children. That would allow Jasper to go all over the department store without arousing suspicion.

"That's him," I said to Lenny. "That's our man."

A small child stared at me. "Mummy? Is that lady talking to a mannequin?"

The mother regarded me with alarm and clutched the hand of her offspring as though I were a wild animal about to pounce.

Santa's progress had been hampered by a group of caroling children. I seized the moment and sprang after him. Lenny the mannequin followed suit, leaping from his stand to a chorus of shrieks from the surrounding customers. Ignoring the commotion behind me, I raced after Santa.

"Slow down, Jasper," I yelled. "The game's up."

Startled, Santa looked at me over his shoulder, lost his balance, and stumbled.

I dove through the air and tackled him to the ground. Lenny hurled himself on top of us, and we rolled in one ridiculous heap across the store floor.

A crowd gathered to watch the action. I straddled Santa and pinned his arms to the ground. "Let's see how clever you are now." I pulled off his Santa hat, and Lenny yanked at the beard. The man screamed in agony.

"Uh, Maggie? I don't think this is fake."

"Of course it's fake," I snapped. "Jasper can't have grown a beard in less than twenty-four hours. Maybe it's just stubborn glue."

"Get off me, you lunatics," Santa cried. "The beard is real. That's why I'm in such demand as Santa."

"If you are the store's official Santa, why were you running in such a suspicious manner?"

A loud fart erupted beneath me, followed by fumes so noxious that I gagged.

"Ew. Seriously? Did you just fart on me?"

Santa's only response was a series of gas explosions strong enough to power a rocket. Lenny and I scrambled for safety.

"Dude," Lenny said, examining the back of Santa's red costume. "Did you just mess your pants?"

"That's what I was trying to tell you." Santa moaned from his fetal position. "The toilets in the grotto are out of order. I must have eaten something dodgy for lunch."

"Look," said a child in the crowd, delighted with this turn of events. "Santa pooped himself."

I glanced at Lenny, and we both groaned.

In the middle of the chaos, a red-faced Tom Dennehy appeared. He looked from me to Lenny, and back again. "I want you two off the premises immediately. I'm sorry, Maggie, but this won't do. You've caused nothing but trouble since you arrived."

"I did warn you." Nuala Kearns appeared out of the crowd, a smug expression on her thin face. "Maggie's not cut out to work at a respectable establishment like ours."

"Respectable? There's nothing respectable about the reason Mr. Dennehy employed me in the first place." I turned to Tom. "I apologize for my mistake, but you have to admit that Santa was acting pretty suspicious."

"The man has a stomach complaint," Tom snapped. "If you and your ridiculous friend hadn't accosted him, he probably would have made it to the toilet in time and avoided disaster."

"Stress on the word *probably*," I said stubbornly. "You don't know that for sure. As I said, I regret that we contributed to the scene Santa was already making, but we were only doing the job you hired us to do."

"I didn't hire you to tackle Santa Claus. Traumatizing small children wasn't part of your job description." Tom turned his attention to Lenny. "Are you wearing one of our designer suits over that obscene costume?"

"Hey, there's nothing obscene about my outfit," Lenny protested. "As for the suit, I nicked it off the real mannequin. I needed to look the part, you know?"

The store manager's face turned purple. "Take it off immediately. If I find so much as a loose thread on that suit, I'll deduct the price from your invoice."

I sighed. I'd have to attempt damage limitation another time, preferably when Tom had had a chance to calm down. "Come on, Lenny. Let's go get changed."

Aware of the stares of the curious crowd, and the smirks coming from Nuala and Melanie's direction, Lenny and I trudged through the store on our walk of shame.

Down in the staff changing area, my friend broke the silence. "I'm sorry, Maggie. I was worried about you. That's why I told The Costume Emporium that I couldn't come in today. I had a feeling something would happen. I'm not usually a guy who gets gut instincts, but I had one about you coming here today. I'm sorry if I've wrecked our business's reputation."

I massaged my aching temples. "Don't worry about it. I'll talk to Tom when he's had a chance to calm down. Regardless of what happened today, he owes us money. After all, we provided him with the identity of the thief and uncovered a larger problem in his store."

By the time I emerged from one of the staff changing cubicles in my street clothes, Lenny had removed the suit. I eyed his costume, now revealed in all its glory. "Please don't tell me I have to walk home with you in that outfit."

My friend grinned. "I chucked my coat under a bench down here, but that doesn't cover the entire costume."

"Why does that not surprise me?" I glanced down at the folded uniform in my arms. "I guess I'll give this to Nuala. I need to collect the bag I keep under the counter in the cosmetics section anyway."

Lenny grabbed his coat and the suit. "I'll come with you. I need to return this to whoever deals with dressing mannequins."

I put on my backpack and Lenny and I took the staff staircase to the first floor. When we reached our floor, we went out into the shopping area. To our left, Christmas music floated down the winding passage that had been transformed into Santa's grotto. A vision of our tussle on the ground with the store Santa brought a bubble of laughter up my throat. Lenny turned a gurgle into a cough. I tried not to look at him, but a giggle escaped me. "I wish the Dennehy investigation hadn't ended in such a dramatic fashion," I said, "but man, that Santa…"

An earsplitting screech pierced the air, followed by distressed wails. We looked at each other. "I'm pretty sure an adult is creating that cacophony," I said.

Lenny nodded. "And I'm pretty sure it's coming from Santa's grotto."

"Maybe one of the elves also had a bad kebab," I added dryly.

We started toward the cosmetics section, but a series of screams from various people stopped us in our tracks, all coming from the area of the grotto.

"Either there's been an outbreak of dysentery in the joint," Lenny said, "or something else is very wrong."

In unison, we turned and ran toward the noise. When we reached our destination, a group of mothers and children stood weeping in front of the garishly decorated grotto. Every year, Dennehy's holiday grotto was sponsored by a different brand, each of whom added their own touch to the atmosphere. This year's sponsor was a popular beer company, and they'd gone all out with barrel-themed items, including a flashing neon barrel, and a huge wooden barrel filled with gifts.

One woman pointed at the source of their distress. "Look at Santa," she sobbed. "It's awful."

We followed the direction of her gaze. Headfirst in his barrel, only Santa's bottom half was visible, pristine in an unsoiled pair of red velvet pants.

"Does the store have two Santas?" Lenny asked. "Because there's no way the guy we tackled could get cleaned up and back here in the time since we last saw him."

"As far as I know, there's only one. Whoever this guy is, we need to get him out of that barrel."

We raced over to the barrel and hauled out the body. It landed on the ground with a thud. I rolled the man over and recoiled. Staring up at me, dead eyes bulging, was Jasper Ramsbottom.

12

L enny came up behind me and leaned down to take a look at Jasper. "Whoa. Santa looks ready for a body bag."

Behind us, a small boy let out a howl. "Santa's dead? Does that mean there'll be no Christmas?"

"Have some consideration," one of the mothers snapped at my assistant. "These poor children have had an awful shock."

I spun on my heels and glowered at her. "If you're so concerned about your kids being scarred for life, how about moving them along? Hanging around staring at the corpse will make the experience more traumatic."

Glaring at me as though I were responsible for the dead guy in the barrel, the woman herded a gaggle of wailing kids out of the grotto.

At this juncture, Tom Dennehy pushed his way through the gathering crowd, accompanied by a broad-shouldered man with a tool belt. The red-faced anger Tom had exuded earlier had been replaced by a chalky white pallor. "Customers are saying someone's injured." The store manager caught sight of the body and reeled back, colliding with his burly companion. "What's happened? Is he dead?"

"I should think that was obvious." I put my hands on my hips, still smarting over the unfairness of his accusations earlier.

"Santa got strangled," Lenny supplied helpfully. "Dude won't be coming down any chimneys this Christmas."

Tom loosened his tie and patted his brow with a handkerchief. "Maybe he had some sort of fit. He was sick earlier."

"Nope," I said. "Take another look at the body. Recognize him now?"

The store manager took a reluctant step closer to the corpse. After a couple of seconds, he recoiled. "That's Jasper Ramsbottom. Why's he wearing a Santa costume?"

"My guess is that the pooper was the real store Santa, and Jasper took his place." I indicated the dead man's neck. "See those marks? His assailant throttled him."

Tom Dennehy swayed and grabbed a pillar to steady himself. "No way."

The guy with the tool belt sidestepped the body. "I'll, uh, go check on those out-of-order bathrooms."

The store manager continued to stare into space. "This can't be happening. Not in my store."

"It can and it is." I pulled my phone out of my purse and hit the number for emergency services. When someone answered, I rattled off the address and explained what had happened. Hopefully, someone had already called it in, but I couldn't count on it. After I'd disconnected, I slipped my phone back into my bag and scanned the grotto. "Any idea where the original Santa is? Is he still in the restroom?"

A woman dressed in an elf costume emerged from the crowd. "Donal's throwing up. He's in a bad way."

"Have you seen this guy before?" I pointed out the dead body.

The woman took an instinctive step back before squaring her shoulders and forcing herself to look at the dead face of Jasper Ramsbottom. "I don't recognize him, but I only started working here last week. Apart from my lunch break, I mostly stay in the grotto, helping to move the crowd along."

"Are you just back from your break?" Lenny asked.

"Yeah. I get thirty minutes."

"Who helps Santa while you're gone?" I asked.

"No one. This time of day is usually quieter. That's why I take a late lunch."

"So when you're away, Santa is alone in the grotto?"

"That's correct. Donal takes his lunch break just

before me. While he's gone, the grotto's closed, but I stay here to make sure no one steals the presents."

"In other words," I mused, "the grotto should always have at least one member of staff present."

"That's right. Dennehy's has a system whereby parents can order specific presents for their children. That's a little fancier than what most stores do. Parents reserve tickets for certain times, and they bring their kids to meet Santa and get their presents."

"What about spontaneous visits to Santa?" I asked. "Are those possible?"

"Yes." The woman pulled a tablet from the depths of her felt elf bag. A few swipes brought today's schedule up on the screen. "We have specific slots during the day where the people who reserved presents can come and collect them. The rest of the time is open. Parents buy tickets, and the tickets entitle each child to a gift of a certain value."

"That's odd." The maintenance guy approached from my left, the frown lines on his forehead deeper than before. "I checked the toilets, and there's nothing wrong with them. Who stuck the out-of-order sign on the door?"

Tom blinked, an expression of confusion settling over his pale face. "I have no idea. I only heard about it when Donal said he'd been forced to find another bathroom because the ones in the grotto weren't working."

I sucked in a breath and looked at Lenny. "Are you thinking what I'm thinking?"

"Probably. I don't think the real Santa ate a bad kebab. I think he was poisoned, probably with a large dose of farting powder."

A pained groan escaped Tom. "Why do you think he was given farting powder?"

"Because your store sells it in the toy department," Lenny supplied in a cheerful tone. "I noticed it last night during our stakeout. There's an entire section devoted to jokes. If you give someone three or four sachets of the stuff, he'll get the trots."

The maintenance guy grunted in agreement. "He's right. I gave my brother an overdose when we were kids."

Tom's mouth opened and shut several times before he uttered a word. "I had no idea we sold that stuff," he spluttered. "How can that be legal?"

"It's your store," I pointed out. "You ought to know what you're allowed to sell and what you're not."

The store manager regarded the corpse. His Adam's apple bobbed. "You don't think Jasper died from farting powder?"

I shook my head. "No way. I've seen strangled bodies before. This man was murdered."

Tom shook himself, reminding me of a dog who'd just been in the water. "People don't get murdered in my store."

I rolled my eyes. The guy needed to pull himself together. "People can get murdered anywhere."

The cosmetics section supervisor tottered down

the ramp to the grotto, accompanied by Melanie and her tipsy cohorts. Nuala pursed her lips when she saw me. "I should've known *you'd* be involved."

"Not another body, Maggie." A spasm of distaste crossed Melanie's pretty features. "I'm beginning to think you give off an aura of death."

Rita Ahearn's plump hands flew to her face. "Is she the killer?"

"No," I snapped. "I'm here in my capacity as a private investigator."

"Police. Let us through." Gavin Reynolds shoved his way through the throng, Inspector Craddock hot on his heels.

"You again." Craddock's hard eyes moved from me to the murder victim. "With another dead body."

Gavin regarded me with a resigned expression. "You realize I'm going to have to take you both in for questioning. This is the second corpse you've found in two days. I can't ignore this coincidence."

"To be precise, I only found the *first* body," I pointed out. "This guy was discovered by a group of parents and kids who were due to see Santa at two o'clock. Lenny and I showed up on the scene after they started caterwauling."

"Those are the crazy people who attacked Santa," a small boy said, pointing to Lenny and me, "and they made him poo all over the place."

"That's right," his mother said, clutching her offspring's hand tighter. "I remember the weirdo in the mannequin costume. If they scared Santa into soiling his pants, maybe they scared him to death."

I snorted in exasperation. "Don't be absurd. The Santa you saw us tackle to the floor is still in the restroom being sick." I met Gavin's bemused gaze. "I thought the real store Santa was Jasper in disguise. When he was running through the store, I assumed he was making a getaway and gave chase."

"Then who's the dead man?" Craddock demanded.

"This really *is* Jasper Ramsbottom," I said. "And no, we have no clue why he's wearing a Santa costume."

Gavin took Lenny's unusual outfit in his stride, but Craddock was less forgiving. "Are you in the habit of walking around dressed like a freak?"

"Only when I'm working undercover," Lenny said, either oblivious to Craddock's sarcasm or choosing to ignore it. "Hey, I've been meaning to ask you. Did the dead chick in our apartment use facial lightener on her rear end, or was that just an excuse to get Maggie fired?"

"*What?*" Nuala Kearns's scarlet lips formed a perfect O. "That customer *died?*"

"She was murdered," Lenny supplied with relish. "Maggie found her dead in our bathtub."

"Your customers are dying?" wailed a woman in the crowd. "I'm getting out of here."

Craddock skewered Lenny with a glare. "We asked you to keep quiet about the bathtub incident."

My friend shrugged. "Sorry, dude, but what can you expect from a freak in a costume?"

"Why are the police being so cagey?" I cut in before Craddock exploded and arrested Lenny on the spot. "I expected to see more details of the case in today's newspapers."

Gavin flushed, suddenly finding his police boots fascinating. "It's not our decision to make. The order comes from higher up."

"We need the pair of you to accompany us to the station while forensics get to work." Craddock turned his reptilian gaze to Lenny. "And I want no more cheek out of you."

"Aren't you going to question the people who first discovered the corpse?" I crossed my arms over my chest.

Gavin gestured to two uniformed police officers who'd positioned themselves on either side of the grotto's entrance. "They'll take care of that."

I jutted my jaw. "If you want to speak to me at the station, I want my lawyer present. There's no reason for you to insist on questioning Lenny and me before getting statements from the first people on the scene."

The crowd parted, and Jennifer Pearce swept into view, looking every inch the successful lawyer that she was. "I'm happy to represent Ms. Doyle until a criminal law solicitor can be found."

"We also need to speak to Mr. Logan," Craddock said sarcastically. "Will you be representing his interests as well?"

Jennifer treated him to her most officious legal stare. "Yes, I'm happy to represent both Ms. Doyle and Mr. Logan." She shifted her focus to us. "Neither of you say another word until we've had a chance to talk in private."

THE POLICE STATION where Craddock and Gavin worked was housed in a blocky building close to Eyre Square. Unlike the small station on Whisper Island, this station appeared to have a permanent staff at the front desk. The two police officers ushered Lenny, Jennifer, and I through a waiting room filled with a varied collection of drunks, including a guy in a reindeer costume.

The instant my assistant showed signs of stopping to chat, I tugged him away from the inebriated reindeer. "No more costumes."

"It's an awesome outfit," he protested. "I just wanted to ask where he bought it."

"Trust me, Lenny. Movie Reel Investigations doesn't need to add a reindeer outfit to its growing range of disguises."

While Lenny waited outside for his turn to be questioned, Gavin Reynolds showed Jennifer and me into the same interrogation room we'd used yesterday. My boyfriend's brother went through the motions of explaining how the interview would work, and that he would record it. Having spent several years in the police force, I knew all of this already, but I understood he was legally obliged to talk me through the process, especially now that this was a formal interview with my solicitor present.

Craddock began by repeating questions I'd already answered about the body in the bath, and eventually steered the interview toward today's incident. "Can you describe to me your first meeting with Jasper Ramsbottom?"

"I'm not sure we ever officially met. I knew his name because the guy who gave me a tour of the department store mentioned it. Jasper Ramsbottom's not the kind of name I'm likely to forget."

"You mentioned that you and Mr. Logan spotted suspicious behavior on the surveillance footage and decided to stake out the store."

"We'd already planned a stakeout for last night," I said, "but the surveillance footage gave us an idea of who might be stealing cash from the store."

"And that person was Jasper Ramsbottom?"

"Yeah. With Ms. Butt Bleach as an accomplice."

Gavin coughed into his fist. Craddock's bushy eyebrows formed a demonic V. "Ms. Butt Bleach?"

"The woman in the bathtub. You haven't seen fit to supply me with her name, in spite of questioning me about her murder. Jasper and the masked dude named Del mentioned she was called Cara. Is that correct?"

Craddock ignored my question. "Are you certain

your confrontation last night with Mr. Ramsbottom
didn't get violent?"

"My client asked you a question," Jennifer cut in
smoothly. "Why are you reluctant to confirm the first
murder victim's name?"

The inspector's weather-beaten features grew red.
"We've been instructed to keep the name quiet."

"But surely not from a person you're questioning
over her murder," Jennifer said. "My client has a right
to know who she's being accused of murdering."

"We're not accusing Ms. Doyle of any crime."
Inspector Craddock flinty gaze moved to me. "Yet."

"Cara Mackey," Gavin said, avoiding Craddock's
warning growl. "Does the name sound familiar?"

"No. As I said in my statement after last night's
stakeout, Del and Jasper mentioned Cara, and I
assumed she was the woman in my bathroom." I fixed
the two policemen in place with an intense stare.
"What did the pathologist say about her butt?"

Craddock's harsh features twisted into an expression of distaste. "That's none of your business."

"I believe it is," I replied in a buttery tone. "After
all, if Cara's rear end showed no signs of injury, it
implies she deliberately set out to get me fired from
Dennehy's."

"Ms. Doyle has a point." Jennifer's expensive
fountain pen swept across her notepad. "If you press
charges against her or Mr. Logan, I'll need to know
that information."

"Plus the estimated time of death," I added.

"Lenny and I have a right to defend ourselves against false allegations, and the easiest way to do that is to prove we weren't anywhere near the victim at the time she died."

"The pathologist puts the time of death between six-fifteen and six forty-five." Gavin avoided looking at his superior officer. "And the victim's rear end showed no signs of injury, neither from a chemical substance or anything else."

"Let's get back to Jasper Ramsbottom," Inspector Craddock snapped, visibly fuming at Gavin's insubordination. "Did your confrontation with him last night turn physical, Ms. Doyle?"

The man's oily tone made me want to hurl. "When I was chasing Jasper, he shoved his suitcase at me to slow my pace. I stumbled and hurt my ankle, giving him the opportunity to get away. Lenny and Tom Dennehy can back me up."

"Have you checked the surveillance footage from the cameras?" Jennifer demanded. "Maggie wasn't making any attempt to avoid them. At least part of the confrontation with Mr. Ramsbottom must be visible on the recordings."

Craddock shifted uncomfortably in his seat. "We're working on it."

"While you work on it, my client is going home," Jennifer said firmly.

"Wait," Craddock shouted. "We haven't started questioning her about the second murder."

"For heaven's sake," I snapped, ignoring Jennifer's

murmured warning. "You can't possibly think that Lenny and I killed Jasper. Check the store's surveillance cameras. We have to appear on them almost constantly, and witnesses saw us in the store the whole time during the time frame that Jasper must've been murdered. Why aren't you talking to Evan Manning about Jasper's death?"

"Mr. Manning is currently speaking to two of our colleagues," the inspector said. "We haven't forgotten about him."

"Unless you have concrete evidence to tie me to either murder, I want to go home. And by home, I mean Whisper Island. Feel free to look me up if you have any more questions, but you'd better make them relevant." I pushed my chair back and got to my feet.

In one fluid movement, Jennifer picked her bag off the floor and stood to join me. "We can see ourselves out, gentlemen. I'll join Mr. Logan in the waiting room, but I hope you won't waste our time with pointless questions."

Without a backward glance, I marched out the door and strode through the packed waiting area, avoiding eye contact with the drunks.

"Gosh, Maggie," Jennifer said in a low voice. "Life is never dull around you."

I stopped by the exit and reeled around. "I'm sorry Jasper was killed, but this is the first time finding a body has been a relief. It lets Lenny and me off the hook for both murders, even though I wish it had happened in another way."

"Don't get cocky," Jennifer warned. "Craddock might not be able to pin Jasper's murder on you, but you and Lenny are still his prime suspects for the first murder."

I looked at my friend in exasperation. "But that's crazy. We had no reason to kill her."

"You were a cop. You know that motive plays less of a role in real-life murder investigations than on TV. You and Lenny had both means and opportunity. You'll need to make sure your alibis are watertight." Jennifer squeezed my arm. "Why don't you say goodbye to Lenny and go back to your hotel? I assume you won't be returning to the department store."

"I don't see any point in going back. With Jasper and Cara dead, the missing cash business will fall under the double murder investigation."

"In that case, pack your bags and go home. I'll stop by your place this evening and give you an update."

"Okay. I appreciate you taking the time to look out for Lenny and me."

"No worries. It beats holiday shopping. I'm not in the mood for Christmas this year." She grimaced. "Before I split up with Nick, my parents booked a trip to Barbados over the festive season. They invited me to join them, but I don't want to be in the way. It's their fortieth wedding anniversary cele-bration."

"Come to my place," I said on impulse. "Liam

and I are hosting Christmas dinner for Hannah, my aunts, uncle, and cousin. You're welcome to join us."

The lawyer's serious expression brightened. "Are you sure I wouldn't be intruding?"

"Not at all. We'd love to have you."

Jennifer's happy smile broke through my grumpy mood. "Thanks so much, Maggie. I'll look forward to it."

Behind us, Gavin emerged from the interrogation room and beckoned to my friend.

"I'll say goodbye to Lenny and let you two deal with the cops." I glanced at my watch. "If I hurry, I should make the two o'clock ferry."

13

On my first day back on Whisper Island, I typed up my notes on the department store case and sent my final invoice to Tom Dennehy. I sighed as I hit Send. After the discovery of Jasper's body, I could kiss goodbye to any hope of a glowing reference from Tom, even if I had discovered the store thief's identity.

Our parting had been frosty. Tom was sore that a murder victim had been found in his store, even though that hadn't been my fault. He was under pressure to recoup the cash lost due to the thefts, and the discovery of Jasper's corpse had triggered an exodus of customers on what would have been one of the store's best sales days of the year. While I sympathized with Tom's predicament, I'd done the job I'd been hired to do, and I'd completed the task in less time than I'd estimated. Being blamed for a situation I hadn't caused rankled, but all I could do was cross my fingers that Lenny's job for The Costume Emporium would score us a recommendation we could emblazon across Movie Reel Investigation's website.

After I'd finished the paperwork for Dennehy's, I ran through my short list of current clients and checked on our progress for their cases. We had three open investigations at the moment, excluding the Dennehy's job. Two of the cases were Lenny's: the costume manufacturer and the Whisper Island Hotel, who'd commissioned us to improve their security system. My only ongoing open case was for my aunt Noreen's business rival, Dolly O'Brien, owner of The Cupcake Café. Dolly had hired me to investigate her soon-to-be ex-husband, whom she suspected of hiding bank accounts from her lawyer. Dolly's case was non-urgent—the divorce process in Ireland took several years—and there was nothing I could do on it for the moment.

Once I'd finished my notes and paid a few outstanding bills, I went downstairs to the Movie Theater Café. After a week away, I wanted to reconnect with my aunt and her customers and find out what I could do to help at tomorrow's festival.

A couple of years ago, my aunt had fulfilled her dream of renovating an old movie theater into a movie-themed café. The café was located on the main thoroughfare of Smuggler's Cove, the island's only town. When I'd opened Movie Reel Investigations, Noreen had offered me the use of the old projector room for my office. Instead of paying rent, Lenny and I helped out in the café a few times a week.

When I entered the café, several customers were seated at the themed tables. Among them were my friends The Spinsters—Miss Flynn and Miss Murphy —as well as the Two Gerries. Gerry One, a.k.a. Gerry Logan, was Lenny's grandfather. His friend, Geroid O'Sullivan, was equally old and equally grumpy.

Gerry One squinted at me through his one good eye. "Hello, Maggie. How's the private investigation business? Are you keeping my grandson out of trouble?"

A vision of the two dead bodies Lenny and I had found in the last week flashed across my mind. "More or less."

The old man chuckled. "That's not what I hear. Well, at least the lad's having fun. You'll need to steer clear of my daughter-in-law, mind. She's none too pleased about this private investigator lark. Hasn't spoken a word to Lenny since the day he joined your agency."

"I didn't realize she wasn't happy about his new career." Although now that I thought of it, Linda Logan had been frosty at the last Movie Club meeting. I'd put it down to her having a head cold.

"It'll blow over in a few months," Gerry One said as if reading my thoughts. "Linda had the daft idea that Lenny would take over the electronics shop after she and Jim retire." The old man snorted. "If they had any sense, they'd take my advice and sell up now while they still have the chance to make a few quid on the sale. That shop is doomed."

Gerry One's opinion echoed mine. A small electronics store like the Logans' faced stiff competition from online stores and large chains on the mainland. "I don't like being the cause of tension between Lenny and his parents. I figured they'd be sorry to lose him from the store, but I had no idea his mom wasn't talking to him."

"Don't worry about it, Maggie. My grandson loves working for you. I haven't seen him this excited in years."

A smile stretched across my face. "We're having fun." *Dead bodies notwithstanding.*

"Would you like a cup of coffee, love?" Noreen called from behind the counter. She'd dyed the tips of her jet-black hair navy blue, a look more usual in younger women, but Noreen could pull it off.

"Coffee would be great, thanks." I nodded to the two Gerries. "Later, guys. Enjoy your tea."

I chose a seat at the Bette Davis table. Once Noreen had fixed my coffee and a cup of tea for herself, she came over to join me. "I like the hair," I said, taking my espresso cup. "What made you decide to change it?"

My aunt waved a hand in a vague gesture. "Ah, you know. I wanted something different. The new color makes me feel a few years younger, even if I don't look it."

I cast a glance across the road at The Cupcake

Café. Dolly was outside, adjusting the front window's lavish holiday ornaments. Her fluffy blond hair was piled high on top of her head, and her tight jeans and low-cut top made her look younger than fifty-plus.

"You've looked worried since you came back to the island," Noreen said, drawing my attention away from her main business rival. "Is this because of the murder at the department store? It's all over the newspapers."

I screwed up my nose. "Lenny and I saw the corpse."

My aunt patted my hand. "Well, of course you did. You're always finding bodies."

I didn't add that Dead Santa had been the second body we'd found in less than a week. The details about the woman in the bathtub were still vague in the newspapers. The only reason to keep the particulars under wraps was if the police suspected Cara's murder was connected to a larger investigation.

Noreen took a sip of tea. "I saw your sister on the telly last night. She's done well for herself with that blog thingy."

In Ireland, "doing well for oneself" meant making money, but when delivered with the sarcasm Noreen had used, it wasn't a compliment.

I wasn't in the mood to discuss my sister, but I could see that my aunt wasn't going to leave the topic alone. And in spite of all my issues with Beth, she was as much Noreen's niece as I was. "Her channel has taken off over the last few months," I said. "I believe she's now worth several million dollars."

"I don't quite understand what it is that she does. Something about makeup?"

"Beth is a beauty blogger and vlogger." At my aunt's blank expression, I elaborated. "She posts reviews of makeup and skincare products on her website and her YouTube channel. The channel also includes makeup tutorials and interviews with makeup artists."

"How does that make her all that money? Can't any old person upload a video to YouTube?"

"I don't know exactly how it works," I admitted. "Mom mentioned something about affiliate links and sponsorship deals with a few brands. Last summer, Beth collaborated with a makeup brand to create an eye shadow palette. Apparently, it was a bestseller."

Beth's palette was so popular that Dennehy's had sold out of their latest order before I'd started working there and were anxiously awaiting more stock.

My aunt leaned forward, curiosity warring with her dislike of my sister. "Is it true that she'll be in a film next year?"

"You know as much about that as I do. Beth and I don't exactly keep in touch."

"Do you think she'll visit Whisper Island while she's in Ireland?" she asked. "I haven't seen Beth since your wedding." And on that occasion, my sister had barely spoken to Noreen.

"I doubt she'll stay long enough." And even if she

did, Beth would never deign to set foot on a remote island. She'd disdained the island when we'd visited as kids. Why would she bother visiting as an adult?

Noreen patted my hand. "It can't be easy having a sister like Beth. She was always a prima donna. Your parents gave her far too much attention. Do they still spoil her?"

"She's the youngest." My diplomatic words were belied by my bitter tone.

"It wasn't fair," my aunt said, unwittingly opening sores I'd convinced myself had healed years ago. "I told your parents it wasn't right to label you girls. They didn't do it to your brothers."

I shrugged, trying to downplay how much our parents' treatment had hurt me. "Beth was prettier than me when we were kids. Still is."

"You've grown into a lovely-looking woman," Noreen said. "And you've a good head on your shoulders, as well as a good heart."

"Given the success of Beth's channel, I'd say her head's pretty firmly screwed on, too."

Noreen nodded. "Labeling her as the beauty and you as the brains wasn't healthy for either of you. I don't believe in slotting children into categories based on one feature."

Growing up as the homely sister hadn't been fun, and I'd been determined to make my parents proud. So it had come as a nasty shock to me when our parents had decided Beth's career in cosmetology was the perfect choice for her, whereas my efforts had barely warranted comment, let alone praise.

In an effort to impress our parents, I'd followed the path they'd laid out for me and joined the police force, made a "good" marriage, and tried to live the life that was expected of me. But it was never enough. Now that I was divorced and had left the San Francisco PD, my parents were barely speaking to me. I'd received a curt email on my birthday, but any effort to keep in touch was on my side. Their rejection stung more than I cared to admit.

I took a hasty sip of coffee to banish such maudlin thoughts and burned my tongue in the process. "How's business at the café? Are the new teen nights proving popular?"

"So far, so good. Last month's film was a success, and the kids couldn't get enough of your non-alcoholic punch recipes. You came up with some fantastic ideas to help me expand my business during the low season." My aunt's gaze strayed from me to the front window, through which her rival's café was visible.

"How's The Cupcake Café doing?" I asked over the rim of my coffee cup. "Is it still as popular as it was when it first opened?"

My aunt wrinkled her nose. "I'm not sure. This close to Christmas, we're both seeing an increase in trade. Dolly has the advantage of offering goods that attract both passing trade and café customers. While I get some takeaway orders, my baked goods are mostly purchased by people in the café."

"But you have the advantage of a larger space that you can offer to clubs."

A fact my aunt exploited to the full. Every weekday evening, at least one of the island's many interest clubs used the café for their meetings. In return, they bought food and drinks.

"True," Noreen admitted. "I guess I'm feeling irritated with Dolly over the Paddy Driscoll business. Did you hear they're stepping out together?"

My eyebrows shot up. I couldn't picture the grumpy farmer with the glamorous woman who ran The Cupcake Café, but this was Whisper Island, a place with a limited dating pool. "Are you sure?"

"I've seen them together."

The hurt in my aunt's voice had me reaching for her hand. "I'm sorry, Noreen."

"Don't be, love. Paddy and I have always been on and off. It's my fault for assuming he'd always be available."

She had a point. If my aunt had genuinely wanted to commit to her friend-with-occasional-benefits, she'd had decades to make up her mind. "No offense, but Paddy's not exactly a catch. He's moody and temperamental. I've never understood what you see in him."

My aunt's smile was wan. "Habit, probably, and a lack of choice. The island isn't overflowing with single men in their fifties. The part that upsets me most is that the woman he's seeing is Dolly."

I'd suspected this. My aunt hadn't been pleased

when her teenage rival had returned to Whisper Island after splitting up with her husband. To add insult to injury, Dolly had opened a café directly across the road from Noreen's. "You'll just have to make sure that your café is the one everyone wants to go to tomorrow."

My aunt perked up at the mention of the Our Lady's Tears festival. "I have a fantastic menu planned for the day. We'll have a stand on the street to catch passing trade, as well as great deals inside."

"Now that I'm back on the island, I can help. What do you need me to do?"

My aunt drew her brows together and considered my question. "An extra person would be useful. I've roped Philomena and Julie into running the café while I take care of the stand outside. How do you feel about hanging around in the cold, serving donuts and mulled wine to tourists? The stand opens at ten and closes at three."

I laughed. "As long as I get to sample the wares, I'm good. And if you need more than one extra pair of hands, I know Lenny will also help if he's around."

"How's his job at the costume place going? Isn't this his first job on his own?"

"Yes, and it's going very well. I'm impressed."

"I'm delighted for you both. I don't wish you any more dead bodies, but I hope your business thrives."

I laughed. "I've seen more dead bodies since I moved to Ireland than I did working for the San Francisco PD." This was an exaggeration, but only slightly.

Even I had to admit that my reputation as a dead-body magnet wasn't entirely misplaced.

"Let's hope that Santa in the department store was the last murder victim you find." My aunt grinned. "For this year at least."

14

That evening, I helped Noreen set up for the Movie Club meeting. Due to tomorrow's festival, we'd shuffled the schedule and used the Unplugged Gamers' Thursday evening slot for the Movie Club. It would be our last meeting of the year, and we intended to do it in style.

My aunt peered at the drinks menu over the rim of her glasses. "You've done a wonderful job with tonight's cocktails."

"Thanks," I said, beaming with pride. "I hope they taste as good as they look on paper."

Tonight's movie was James Dean's *Rebel Without a Cause*. I'd spent the afternoon creating a fun cocktail menu that paired the holiday season with the youthful Fifties vibe of the movie. For the festive half of the menu, I'd added a Winter Sidecar, Hot Toddy, and Cinnamon Twist Irish Coffee. The Fifties-inspired recipes included a Mudslide, Pink Squirrel, and Rum Runner, as well as a couple of non-alcoholic cocktails.

"Yo, Maggie. Hey, Noreen." Lenny ambled into the café, pulling a suitcase behind him. "I just got off the ferry. Okay if I dump my stuff in the kitchen?"

"Go for it," I said. "Your cocktail apron is hanging on a hook on the back of the kitchen door."

After Lenny had deposited his suitcase and backpack in the kitchen, he shrugged off his winter jacket to reveal his suit, the Seventies-style creation that had once been his father's. The suit looked as though it had survived a nuclear war, but Lenny wore it with an enviable nonchalance. He tied his apron around his waist and joined me behind the counter.

"How does it feel to be back on the island?" Noreen asked him.

My friend grinned. "Awesome. Being in Galway for a few days was fun, but I'm glad to be home."

I glanced at my watch pointedly. "Want to go over the drinks menu together and get the ingredients lined up?"

"Sure thing." Lenny looked me up and down. "Cute outfit, by the way."

I patted down my shirt. "Thanks. I found a bunch of great vintage clothes in a charity store in Galway."

Formal dress wasn't mandatory for the Movie Club members, but many members chose clothes that reflected some aspect of the night's movie. My outfit consisted of a pair of vintage Fifties women's pants and a shirt, and I'd finished my look with a high pony-tail tied with a red ribbon.

Lenny rubbed his hands together. "Two cases wrapped up. Not a bad week for Movie Reel Investi-gations."

"Apart from the two corpses," I added dryly.

My friend grinned. "Apart from those. Have you heard anything from our good pal, Inspector Craddock?"

"Nope. I'm hoping no news is good news, but I wish the cops would hurry up and give us back our phones and laptops."

"Word." Lenny scratched his scraggly beard. "I have a bunch of computer equipment, but that partic-ular laptop is my favorite."

I lined up several cocktail shakers, and we arranged the various ingredients on the counter. "Your grandfather mentioned Linda isn't thrilled with your new career."

My friend's face fell at the mention of his mother. "No. Neither is Dad. They'll come around to the idea eventually. I just need to give them time."

His confidence rang false. "I'm sorry, Lenny. I had no idea my job offer had caused a rift between you and your parents."

"Not your problem, Maggie. They'll have to deal with the situation, and I'll have to give them space to come to terms with my decision." He scratched his beard and rearranged the bottles on the countertop for the fourth time. "Even if you hadn't offered me the opportunity to work for you full-time, I never planned to stay at my parents' shop forever."

"Okay," I said. "Just know if you want to talk about it, I'm here."

"Thanks, Maggie." A smile appeared on his lips. "Want to taste test one of your new cocktails?"

I laughed. "Definitely. Bring it on."

Over the next thirty minutes, the café filled with Movie Club members, and my friend and I were kept busy preparing drinks.

"No sign of Reynolds yet," Lenny said after he'd loaded a tray with the latest order of cocktails. "Is Hannah already on the island?"

"She arrived today. Liam sent me a message to say he was picking her up this afternoon. They're due to stop by later."

My cousin approached the counter and grabbed the tray Lenny had loaded with drinks. "Nice menu, Maggie. The club members are saying it's the best one yet."

"Thanks, Julie. How did you get roped into acting as a waitress?"

"How do you think? Noreen bribed me with the promise of a box of donuts. I'm not a huge donut fan, but those cherry-filled ones she makes for the festival are divine."

"You're making my mouth water in anticipation."

"Honestly, they're the only redeeming feature of the festival," my cousin said. "The idea of celebrating a crying statue is bizarre even by Irish standards."

"I hear it brings in a lot of money," I said, a touch of irony in my voice. "So much so that Noreen was willing to change the night of the Movie Club meeting from Friday to Thursday."

"The money is *why* the Islanders make such a big deal out of it," Lenny added. "Whisper Island is dead this time of year. The festival attracts tourists, and the islanders make bank."

"I don't think I've seen this famous statue, but if it's in a cave, it's not exactly a surprise that it has water dripping down it."

My cousin rolled her eyes. "It's ridiculous. The cave is out of bounds all year except on the day of the festival. Of course the statue's wet more than one day a year. Everyone knows that, but no one cares."

From across the café, a florid-faced man whistled. "Hey, Julie. Any sign of those drinks?"

"Keep what's left of your hair on, Tom. I'm on my way." Julie carried the tray across the room to a table surrounded by Tom Ahearn and his wife, Rita, as well as Paul and Melanie Greer.

At that moment, Julie's mother, Philomena, passed the counter with her friend, Sister Pauline McLaughlin. Her eyes widened when she saw Lenny. "You're the very man I was looking for."

My assistant shot me a questioning look. "Dude, don't look at me. I don't have a clue what she wants from you."

"Your grandfather told me you bought a bunch of costumes in Galway." My aunt gave Lenny a beatific smile. "One of those costumes wouldn't happen to be a Santa costume, would it?"

Lenny blinked in confusion. "Why? Do you want to borrow it?"

"Not exactly." My aunt beamed at him. "I'd like to borrow you in it. I'm organizing the annual Christmas Eve pageant. When Gerry mentioned your costume collection, I thought adding a visit from Santa for the younger members of the audience would make a lovely addition to the program."

"Uh…" Lenny cast me a rescue-me look.

"Don't look at me for help," I said, making a valiant attempt not to laugh. "You're the one who went crazy buying costumes."

"Wonderful." Philomena clapped her hands together in a gesture of delight. "The kids will have so much fun. I'll call you tomorrow to discuss times."

Before Lenny could form a coherent protest, my aunt skipped off into the crowd with an agility I hadn't known she possessed.

"Did I just get roped into playing Santa?"

"Yep." My smile was gleeful. "You should have cut her off the moment she mentioned the pageant."

"I'm going to have words with Granddad," Lenny said grimly. "If he's so keen on me dressing up as Santa, he can borrow my costume and play the role himself."

"What's the big deal? You loved wearing your clown and mannequin costumes," I pointed out. "The

Santa outfit will be the ideal excuse to try out your padded suit."

Lenny groaned and put his face in his hands. "The last two Santas I've encountered came to bad ends. One messed his pants, and the other got murdered."

"Yeah, I hear you. I'm pretty much over Santas."

"I gotta figure out a way to get out of it," he muttered.

"Good luck with that," I said with a laugh. "Philomena is one scary lady when thwarted, and she's determined to make you Santa."

"And I always thought Philomena was more placid than Noreen."

"She's quieter than her sister," I conceded, "but she's got a will of iron."

Our conversation was interrupted by a fresh onslaught of thirsty club members. Lenny and I returned to our mixing and shaking until Noreen rang the gong to signal the final round of drinks orders before the movie started.

Liam and Hannah arrived just as Movie Club members were filing into the theater. They made a beeline for me. I noted the shadows under Liam's eyes and his concerned expression every time he glanced in his daughter's direction.

"Hey, you." I gave him a quick kiss across the counter. "Hi, Hannah. Have you unpacked?"

"Yeah." She tugged at one of her plaits. "I didn't bring much stuff, though."

"Do you want to help me set up the projector?" Lenny asked her, emerging from the kitchen with a tray filled with clean cocktail glasses.

The girl's expression brightened. "I'd love to."

After Lenny had propelled Hannah in the direction of the stairs, I turned to Liam. "How's she coping?"

His mouth tightened. "Hard to tell. She's clammed up. I guess she's missing her mum. And she's worried about her. I keep wondering if telling Hannah the truth was the right move."

"You made the right decision. Hannah needs to know what's going on. Apart from anything else, it's for her own safety."

"I don't think she's in danger." Liam rubbed a hand across his jaw. "But I'm not prepared to take the risk. She'll stay here with me until they catch Weber."

"Have the police made any progress?"

A muscle in his jaw flexed. "Not so far."

"Keep the faith," I said gently. "They'll catch him soon."

"I hope so. The man's not stable." His mouth twisted. "It makes me sick knowing he's at large."

"You're certain he hasn't made a direct threat against Hannah?"

"Weber hasn't mentioned Hannah in any of his communications with Robyn. Like I said before, we're not even sure he knows she has a child, but we can't take the risk. The police consider the threats made against her credible, and neither of us wants Hannah put at risk."

"Has she reconnected with Caoimhe yet?" On Hannah's previous visit to Whisper Island, she'd become friends with Caoimhe Greer, Melanie's daughter, and they'd kept in touch via email after Hannah had returned to school in England.

Liam grinned. "Oh, yes. First thing after unpacking, she went over to their house to hang out. She wants to go for a sleepover tomorrow, but I'm not sure it's a good idea. I don't want to put the Greers in danger."

"I'm sure it'll be fine. As you said, Weber doesn't know she's here."

"I know you're right," he said, "but I'm not sure I could sleep with Hannah away."

I touched his arm, feeling the familiar tingle of awareness flicker through my body. "I could come and keep you company."

My offer brought a grin to his face. "I'd love your company, Maggie, but I'm not sure you want to be around me when I'm worried and moody."

"Don't be ridiculous. I'm your girlfriend. I want to be there for you when you're stressed."

"I note you didn't mention the 'moody' part." His grin grew wider.

"I can cope with moody. Heck, after the week I've had, I can rival you."

He laughed. "We need to get over the grumps with a comedy."

"If you'd feel more comfortable keeping Hannah with you, why don't I pick up Chinese food for us tomorrow night? You two can find a comedy for us to watch."

"Sounds good. Are you attending tomorrow's festival? I'm a little freaked out by the crying statue."

"I'll be at the festival, but I'm avoiding the damp cave," I said with a wry smile. "I've offered to help Noreen run her mulled wine stand."

"Mulled wine sounds a lot better than freezing your behind off in the cave. I was supposed to be off duty, but one of the reserves is down with the flu. I need to replace him for a few hours. Would it be okay if you kept an eye on Hannah for a couple of hours? I'm sure she'd enjoy helping you and Noreen."

"No problem. We can go Christmas shopping together when I'm finished helping my aunt." I laughed. "That's assuming we can find anything to buy on the island."

Liam's crinkly smile brought a warm feeling to my chest. "I trust your excellent shopping instincts to find something worth buying."

The second gong sounded, indicating the start of the movie. I removed my apron and joined Liam on the other side of the counter.

He slipped his arm around my waist. "It feels good to have you back."

Before I could respond, the bell above the café door jangled. A distinguished man entered. He wore his silver-gray hair slicked back in a ponytail, and his royal-blue suit was custom-made. He looked vaguely familiar, but I couldn't place him. He was followed by a burly guy stuffed into a suit whose every movement screamed "bodyguard."

At the sight of the third new arrival, my stomach went into free fall. Sweeping into the café, wafting perfume and sex appeal, came the glamorous form of my sister.

15

B eth posed at the entrance, waiting for all eyes to take in her spectacular figure and long, honey-blond hair. She'd chosen a Fifties-style evening gown for the event and paired it with a mink stole that looked genuine. My sister focused on the small crowd of Movie Club members who hadn't yet taken their seats in the movie theater. "I hope we're not late." Her husky voice and come-hither smile exuded a sex appeal I'd never managed to master.

Years of resentment surged through me and formed a malevolent lump in my chest. I took an instinctive step closer to Liam, and his grip on my waist tightened.

"Beth?" Our aunt Philomena pushed her way to the front of the crowd, paused, and then barreled toward my sister. "It *is* you. What a lovely surprise."

With admirable dexterity, Beth managed to deflect

the impending hug and turn the greeting into an air-kiss. "Nice to see you again, Philomena."

"What are you doing on Whisper Island? Maggie didn't mention you were coming to visit." Our aunt looked at me, her expression a mix of hurt and accusation, neither of which were warranted. In spite of being just as surprised as Philomena at my sister's sudden appearance, an irrational sensation of guilt settled in my stomach.

"I'm here on business." Beth gestured to the gray-haired man. "Do you know Con Ryder?"

No wonder the guy looked familiar. Con Ryder was an Oscar-winning film director who specialized in romcoms that packed an emotional punch. I wasn't a fan of his work, but he managed to attract a star-studded cast to all his projects.

Noreen staggered forward, her hand on her chest. While my sister's dramatic entrance had failed to impress her, my movie-buff aunt was rendered incoherent at the sight of her favorite living director. "Mr. Ryder?" she spluttered. "Welcome to the Movie Theater Café. We're honored to have you here."

Con Ryder's oily smirk made me want to hurl. "The pleasure is all mine. When Eliza mentioned her aunt had renovated an old cinema, I was intrigued."

"We're about to watch *Rebel Without a Cause*. Have you seen it?" Noreen flushed. "Well, of course you have. I'm sure you've seen all the classics."

"Yes, but it's been a while. I hope you don't mind us showing up unannounced."

"Oh, of course not. You're most welcome." Recovering her composure, Noreen turned her attention to my sister, her lips tightening. "Hello, Beth. I didn't expect to see you here."

"Hi, Noreen," my sister gushed, either oblivious to my aunt's frosty tone or choosing to ignore it. "I couldn't visit Ireland and not see my aunts."

I rolled my eyes. Whatever Beth was doing here, it wasn't playing catch-up with our father's family. She had an agenda, and that agenda had to be connected with Con Ryder.

"Where are you staying?" Philomena looked from my sister to me. "With Maggie?"

"Oh, no. We're staying at the Whisper Island Hotel. I didn't want to inconvenience Maggie." My sister looked over Philomena's shoulder, and our eyes met for the first time in a year.

"Hi, Beth," I said evenly. "Last time you were here, you swore you'd never come back."

My sister's tinkling laugh grated on my already frayed nerves. "Last time I saw you, you were still married."

Touché. I'd never been able to outbitch Beth.

"Her ex-husband's loss is my gain," Liam said smoothly, still holding me close.

Beth pretended this was the first time she'd noticed the man at my side. "Are you two an item?"

"No," I drawled. "I just let random men drape their arms around me."

Con Ryder's pompous sneer gave way to a laugh of genuine amusement. "Who's this, Eliza?"

Beth's rigid stance indicated her reluctance to introduce me to the director. "Con, this is my sister, Maggie. Maggie, Con."

"Is that so?" Ryder's eyes twinkled with merriment, stripping him of the arrogant attitude he'd displayed earlier, and pumped my hand in a firm handshake. "Delighted to meet you, Maggie. We must have dinner with you while we're on the island."

"Uh, sure." Why did this man want to hang out with me? Or was his mention of dinner just a meaningless Hollywood promise?

Liam stepped forward and shook hands with Ryder and Beth. "Liam Reynolds, Maggie's boyfriend."

Philomena beamed, apparently blind to the tension between my sister and me. "Well, isn't this lovely. Are you staying for Christmas, Beth?"

My sister batted her expertly applied false eyelashes. "I'd love to, but it all depends on Con." She laid a scarlet-taloned hand on the arm of the man accompanying her.

"I'm going to be filming on the island next spring," Ryder said in his smooth baritone. "We're here to get a feel for the place."

"I'm hoping to be part of the project," Beth added, cooing adoringly at the director.

My heart sank. The news that my sister might stay on the island for Christmas was bad enough, but the idea that Beth would be back in the spring gave me heart palpitations. Whenever I was with my sister, the years dissolved into a toxic puddle and I was a kid again— always at a disadvantage, and never quite good enough. My vulnerability around Beth annoyed me almost as much as she did.

A gasp made me whirl around. Hannah stood at the foot of the stairs, Lenny at her side. "Is that *Eliza Donati*?"

"Yeah." Lenny, bless him, didn't sound impressed. "She's Maggie's sister."

Hannah's eyes widened. "Seriously? They look nothing alike."

Beth smirked. "Isn't it hilarious? No one ever believes we're related. I guess it's our different hair colors. And I'm younger, of course."

"Yeah," I drawled, "by ten months."

Hannah took a tentative step toward my sister. "I watch you on YouTube all the time."

"Oh, you're just adorable, honey," Beth gushed. "How old are you?"

Hannah flushed in delight. "I'm eight, nearly nine. Will you give me your autograph, please?" She pulled a hot-pink notebook out of her backpack.

"Of course, darling. I adore meeting fans."

Lenny shot me a look of sympathy, and Liam dropped a kiss on my temple. I leaned into my boyfriend, the comforting warmth of his closeness easing some of the tension in my body.

Beth made a great fuss of signing Hannah's notebook, eliciting the first smile I'd seen on the girl's face since she'd arrived on the island.

Staring at her notebook reverently, Hannah returned to us. "Isn't Eliza awesome?"

"Fabulous," I said dryly. "Enjoy the movie, Beth. I'm sure we'll catch up soon." *Preferably in another lifetime.*

Liam took the hint and ushered Hannah and me through the crowd and into the movie theater.

Despite being a fan of the movie, I barely registered tonight's screening of *Rebel Without a Cause.* Beth's abrupt appearance had rattled me. I loved Whisper Island, and I considered it to be my territory —fair or not. Looking back to our childhood, I'd felt the same way then. While Beth had found the island and its inhabitants boring, I'd reveled in the summers we'd spent here. Now that I'd made this place my home, seeing Beth here was jarring.

As if sensing my distraction, Liam took my hand in his. "It'll be fine," he whispered. "She won't stay long."

"I know." I rubbed my thumb against his warm skin. "I just hate the way I revert to teenage behavior when she's around."

"It's the same with me and my brother Jamie. We've never gotten on."

I rested my head on Liam's shoulder and relaxed for the remainder of the movie. The instant the credits began to roll, I was aware of my sister's presence. She and Ryder had secured a place in the middle row and now made a great show of sidling past people to get out. If I found Beth unbearable now, she'd be ten times worse if she got a role in a movie.

Following the throng out of the theater, I joined Noreen at the café's exit to say goodbye to the club members.

A whiff of Beth's heavy perfume signaled her approach. "Lovely to see you again, Maggie," she purred, giving me the limpest handshake I'd ever experienced.

"Before this evening, I didn't realize Eliza had a sister living on the island," Ryder said when it was his turn to shake my hand. "Wouldn't you rather stay with Maggie than shack up with us in a hotel, Eliza?"

From the look of horror that flitted across my sister's face before she got her emotions under control, that would be a no. "I've already unpacked," my sister said in an unnaturally high voice, "and I'd hate to inconvenience Maggie."

Our eyes met in a rare moment of understanding. "I'm sure Beth would find my cottage cramped," I added. "It's pretty small."

"Nonsense." Ryder's expression grew serious. "Families should be together, especially at Christmas. Why doesn't Eliza move in with you for the next few days? It'll give her a chance to get a feel for the island and its inhabitants, and immerse herself in the environment her character lives in."

"Well, I—" The words stuck in my throat.

"That's settled then," Ryder said with the air of a man used to getting his way. "Eliza can move into your place tomorrow. I'll collect her each morning in time to scout locations and discuss the script."

My sister and I stared at one another in horror, both apparently robbed of our powers of speech. Beth's raised shoulders and tight lips mirrored mine.

Sensing the mounting tension, Noreen cut in. "Will you be at the Our Lady's Tears festival tomorrow, Mr. Ryder?"

"What on earth is that?" the director asked with a laugh. "A festival for weeping women?"

"A festival to celebrate one particular weeping woman," I said dryly. "A statue of the Virgin Mary in a cave is alleged to cry once a year."

Ryder arched his eyebrows. "How quaint."

"The island will be packed with visitors," Noreen said, beaming with pride. "The Movie Theater Café participates every year with fresh donuts and mulled wine."

"The mulled wine sounds interesting," Ryder said with a half smile, "but I think I'll skip the cave."

As I had similar plans, I couldn't help smiling in return.

After more gushing and air-kissing, my sister and her companion departed, the burly bodyguard detaching himself from the shadows and trailing after them. Liam, Hannah, and I stayed to help Noreen tidy the café.

"I wonder why your sister didn't tell us she was coming," my aunt mused.

"Beth likes to make a grand entrance," I said with a hint of acid. "Giving us advance warning would dilute the effect."

This comment brought a smile to Noreen's lips. "She's rather dramatic. A film role would be just the thing for her."

"Do you think that'll pan out?" Liam asked. "Aren't film people notorious for making promises they don't keep?"

"Con Ryder has a long-term male partner. We can assume he's not interested in Beth romantically, so why else would he waste time and money courting her if he wasn't serious about casting her?"

"Beth is a pain, but it would be fun to have a niece in a film. Your grandmother would have been delighted."

"I know," I said softly. "I still miss her."

Noreen squeezed my arm. "So do I, love. She'd have been very proud of you. She was always going on about how intelligent you were. Mammy would have loved the idea of you becoming a private detective."

I swallowed past the lump in my throat and nodded. "Granny always had a sense of adventure."

It took us an hour to restore the café to its former glory. Once we'd finished, Liam drove Hannah and me home to Shamrock Cottages, the complex of holiday houses where he and I were the only permanent residents.

"Night, Maggie." Hannah waved to me from her front door. "It was fun meeting your sister."

I bit back a tart comment about Beth. The kid had a right to enjoy my sister's channel. "Sleep well, Hannah."

After his daughter had disappeared inside their cottage, Liam rubbed a thumb over the frown line between my brows. "Don't worry about your sister. I bet she'll pitch a fit, and Ryder will back down on his determination to throw you two together."

"I'm not so sure about that. Con Ryder strikes me as the sort of man who's used to getting what he wants."

Liam laughed. "I'd say your sister is pretty good at asserting herself."

"Oh, yeah. Beth is used to people giving her what she wants." I bit my lip. "I hate feeling like this. Maybe it's end-of-year malaise. I don't know. First I was worrying about our relationship, and now I'm stressed about my sister being on the island."

"Don't be so hard on yourself, Maggie. You've had a lot happen over the last twelve months. A divorce, an international move, and starting a new business are all big events, and you've done them within the same year."

"Yeah, but they were for the best, and I'm in a good place now." I leaned into his chest and inhaled his familiar scent. "I have you."

"And I'm delighted you do, but has it occurred to you that you've been so busy, you haven't had time to process some of your feelings? You didn't just leave your ex when you moved here. You also left your family and friends behind."

"That's true, but my parents are barely speaking to me."

"Which has to be a source of stress, am I right? And then your sister shows up, and you're reminded that your parents have always given her unconditional affection."

"If you ever get bored being a cop, you should become a therapist."

He grinned. "No way. I like the variety of my job, even if it means tolerating Sergeant O'Shea."

I twitched at the thought of my nemesis, the work-averse older police officer who'd been head of police on Whisper Island until Liam had arrived. "Will that man ever retire?"

"Next summer." Liam's lips twitched. "Or so our district superintendent assures me."

I snorted. "I'll believe it when it happens."

"Me, too." He glanced back at his cottage. "I'd better tuck in Hannah. Do I get a goodnight kiss before I go?"

"Only if you give me one, too," I teased.

He laughed and wrapped his arms around me. "With pleasure."

16

The day of the festival dawned sunny but cold. I woke at five-thirty to find one of my running shoes on my chest, and Bran, my Border collie-Labrador mix, panting plaintively in my face.

I groaned and pushed myself into a sitting position. "You don't do subtle, do you, boy?"

The dog barked in agreement and wagged his tail, impatient to be on the move. He and the cats had stayed with Noreen while I'd been in Galway, and I'd missed them, especially my early morning runs with Bran.

I rubbed his head, and he rewarded me with a generous lick. "All right," I said with a laugh. "Give me ten minutes, and I'll be ready."

After I'd thrown on my running gear and prepared breakfast for the cats, Bran and I headed out into the chilly morning. No lights were on in any of the other seven houses that formed the Shamrock Cottages complex. Built on a slope with a spectacular view of the sea, each cottage consisted of two bedrooms, a kitchen, and a living room, as well as a small fenced-in backyard. In addition to the cottages, the complex sported a communal playground and a games room, neither of which I used.

Bran tugged on his leash and led me down the winding drive toward the road. When we reached the main gate, the dog veered to the left, heading in the direction of his favorite running route. We followed the road for five minutes and then took a path through the fields. In summer, these fields were a lush green that complemented the purple-gray stone that was a feature of the island. This morning, the light of my headband shone over a smattering of snow. The white landscape spread out before us, punctuated by bare trees and the odd farm building.

Once our feet hit the grass, I unhooked Bran's leash, and the dog took off at a rapid pace. I jogged after him, letting him lead the way. After a glorious half hour of chasing my dog through fields and woods, I slowed my pace to a light jog. Two joggers had crested the hill in front of us and were running in our direction, the lamps on their headbands casting a yellow glow across the white fields.

"Come back, Bran," I shouted. "We have company."

My dog was reasonably well behaved, but we rarely encountered other joggers on our runs, and these rare sightings sent him into paroxysms of joy. This occasion was no exception. Bran barked excitedly at the newcomers and showed every sign of greeting them with an enthusiastic crotch sniff.

"Oh, no you don't." I caught up with the dog and clipped on his leash. A moment later, the approaching joggers spotted us and slowed down. A burly figure in black running tights came into view, followed by a slim woman dressed in hot-pink running gear. A blond ponytail peeked out from beneath her hat.

"You've got to be kidding me," I muttered under my breath. An encounter with my sister was the last thing I needed before I'd had my first coffee of the day.

"Maggie?" Beth came to a halt in front of me and examined me from head to toe. "What are you doing here?"

"I should have thought that was obvious." I shifted my attention to the bodyguard and stuck out my hand. "I'm Maggie Doyle. We haven't been introduced yet."

"Luke Vaglietti." His handshake was of the crushing variety, and his accent was pure Brooklyn. "It's nice to finally meet you. Eliza is pretty quiet about her family."

"I'll bet," I said dryly, shooting my sister a sly grin. Had I misread the situation last night? Were they an item? Luke looked and acted the part of a bodyguard. He'd blended into the background at the Movie Club meeting like a guy who was used to disappearing when not needed, only to emerge from the shadows the instant he was required to open doors or scare off undesirables.

"Luke works for Con," my sister said. "That's how Con and I met."

Aha. So Luke was one of my sister's many conquests, to be used and discarded at her whim. Poor guy. Even in the poor light offered by our respective headbands, his adoration was plain to see. If he'd been Beth's ticket to Con Ryder, she'd dump him before the ink on her movie deal was dry.

I tugged on Bran's leash. "I'll let you two get back to your run."

"Wait a sec." Beth stepped forward, her headband light momentarily dazzling me. "I spoke to Con about this proposed visit."

"Did you manage to wriggle out of it?"

"He's adamant I should stay with you. He's even booked a table at the hotel restaurant for Christmas dinner, and he's expecting all of us to come, including Noreen and Philomena's family."

"Ouch," I said. "That's a no-can-do. I'm spending Christmas with my boyfriend, his daughter, and a friend. I'm not canceling on them."

"Oh, your boyfriend and his kid are already on Con's list, as well as whatever guy Julie is seeing. Adding your friend won't be a problem." Beth screwed up her nose. "I don't know how he managed it, but Con seems to know more about our family than I do."

I did a double-take. "Wow. Doesn't he realize people make plans for the holidays?"

My sister laughed. "Con's not used to people saying no. And I suspect Noreen and Philomena will jump at the chance to have dinner with him, even if it is on a holiday."

Unfortunately, she was correct. There was no way my aunts would turn down an invitation from Con Ryder, even if it meant canceling their annual turkey dinner.

I blew out a sigh. "There's no way you can change his mind before he starts inviting people?"

My sister shook her head. "He's determined."

"And because he hasn't yet signed a contract, you don't want to rock the boat."

"Exactly." She looked me straight in the eye. "Will it be so awful to have a house guest?"

My sister's beseeching tone didn't have the same effect on me as Bran's big doggy eyes had this morning. "I have a cramped guest room that I use as my office. When was the last time you slept in a single bed?"

"I'll cope. It'll only be for a few nights."

I sighed. "Define 'a few.'"

"Con's booked to stay at the hotel until the morning of the thirtieth. He wants to spend New Year's Eve in Dublin."

I performed a rapid calculation. "He wants you to stay with me for *eight* nights?"

"Please, Maggie. Con's totally into the whole big,

happy family thing, and part of the reason he's willing to consider me for a part in his next film is my Irish connection. He expects to see me with all of you over the holidays."

It was on the tip of my tongue to tell my sister to stick her movie deal where the sun didn't shine, but an emotion I couldn't pinpoint stopped me. "Okay. You can stay. But no complaining about the size of my house, the water pressure in the shower, or anything else that doesn't meet your high standards. Got it?"

"Absolutely." Beth beamed at me. "Thanks, Maggie."

Luke coughed discreetly. "It's pretty cold out here. We should probably get moving."

"Sure." Beth jogged on the spot as if she'd only just become aware of the temperature.

"I need to get home anyway." I slid my phone from my running belt and found a business card in its cover. I handed it to my sister, unsure if I was grateful or regretful that I'd remembered to pencil in my temporary number on my business cards while the police had my regular cell phone. "Send me a message later, and we'll arrange a time for you to move into my place."

Beth took the card and put it into her jacket pocket. "Have a nice day, Maggie."

"You, too." I nodded to Luke. "Nice to meet you."

They jogged off toward the woods that Bran and I had just left. Bran whined and pulled at his lead.

I smiled at the dog. "Are you ready for your breakfast?"

His whine grew louder and was accompanied by enthusiastic tail wagging.

I laughed. "I'll take that to be a 'Yes.'"

We headed home, where I showered and ate breakfast before getting into my Toyota Yaris and driving to Smuggler's Cove. The Yaris was the latest in the long line of vehicles I'd owned since I'd moved to Whisper Island. Its predecessors had all met bad ends, and I hoped the Yaris would last me a while longer. In spite of its lousy acceleration and aversion to hills, it was a nifty little vehicle.

Courtesy of the festival, the town center was closed to cars, so I parked at the elementary school and walked to the Movie Theater Café. When I reached the café, my aunt was arranging a donut fryer and various accoutrements on a stand positioned on the pavement, right in front of the main window.

"Hey, Noreen."

She shoved an errant blue-tipped strand of hair under her hat and smiled at me. "Morning, love. I hope you brought a pair of gloves with you. It's nippy out here."

I reached into my coat pockets and pulled out my gloves, a new pair I'd purchased yesterday. "I come prepared."

My aunt looked over my shoulder. "Where's Hannah? I thought you said she'd be joining us today."

"Liam's taking her to the police station for the first couple of hours of his shift. He'll walk her to the café on his way to the infamous Cave of Sorrows."

Noreen scrunched up her nose. "Poor dear. Does he have to attend the festival's opening ceremony?"

"Yeah. I'm happy to give it a miss. I'd rather be here with donuts and mulled wine than stuck in a damp cave." I joined my aunt behind the stand. "Want to show me what I need to do before people start mobbing us?"

My aunt nodded. "We'll have to make it a quick lesson. I see people heading in our direction."

In spite of the early hour, the town was already filling up with visitors. On the main street, every shop, restaurant, and café had erected a stand outside their premises in preparation for the passing trade.

While Julie and Philomena ran the café, Noreen and I spent the next several hours serving freshly fried donuts and mulled wine to a constant stream of islanders and tourists. As arranged, Liam brought Hannah to us at ten o'clock, and she flitted back and forth from the stand to the café, eating a large quantity of donuts and sampling the non-alcoholic hot punch.

By two that afternoon, I was chilled to the bone and the ankle I'd injured on the night of the stakeout throbbed. "I'm out of practice. I didn't realize how much sitting-down time we had at Dennehy's."

Noreen flexed her shoulders. "I'm looking forward

to having a warm bath this evening. The festival gets busier every year."

"Yeah. I thought you were exaggerating about the number of tourists who come over for the festival. I can't recall the last time I saw the island this busy."

"It's partly because the festivities are focused on a small area," Noreen said. "Everyone's either in the town or at the cave, and the cave's only a ten-minute walk outside Smuggler's Cove."

A group of tourists wearing Santa hats swooped across the street, chattering loudly, and descended upon our stand en masse. Above the uproar, rose a squeal of delight.

"Oh my goodness," cried a familiar voice, causing me to whirl around in surprise. "Is that you, Maggie?"

17

A woman in a bright red coat with a matching woolen hat swam into my line of vision.

"Hey, Tracey. It's good to see you." I nodded to her companions. "Hi, Siobhan. Hey, Barry."

Siobhan bristled at the sight of me, but Barry came over and hugged me.

"What are you doing here?" he demanded. "We didn't know where you'd gone when you disappeared from Dennehy's. We were told you weren't coming back."

"Nuala Kearns said you're a private detective." Siobhan glared at me in an accusatory fashion, the hostile wariness she'd displayed when we'd first met back in force. "Is Maggie even your real name?"

"Yes, it is. You mentioned you were coming to Whisper Island for the festival. I hadn't realized your plans included Tracey and Barry."

"They didn't." Barry grinned. "Tracey and I tagged along."

"It's good to see you. I'm sorry I didn't get to say goodbye before I left, but things moved fast after Jasper's murder."

Tracey shuddered and wrapped her arms around her slim frame. "The guards still don't know who killed him. All we've been told is what's in the papers. Jasper was responsible for stealing money from the store and had connections to some sort of gang."

"I can't see Jasper being anything but low-hanging fruit. He didn't have the brains to do anything but take orders." Siobhan's eyes narrowed. "Do you know who killed him, Maggie?"

"No." But I had my suspicions, Del being the obvious candidate.

"I wasn't particularly fond of Jasper," Barry said, his expression grave, "but him getting murdered? It's too gruesome to contemplate."

Keen to move the conversation away from Dead Santa, I gestured to the stand. "Can I offer you donuts and mulled wine to warm you up? They're on me."

Siobhan folded her arms across her chest and looked at the stand askance. "Is this another under-cover assignment?"

"No," I said evenly. "This is my aunt's café."

Noreen finished serving a customer and moved to my end of the stand to fetch more cups. "Did I hear you say you worked with Maggie in Galway?"

"That's right," Tracey replied. "We had no idea she was a P.I."

"Were you at the department store when Maggie found the body?" Noreen asked them, her eyes bright with excitement.

I sighed. My aunt basked in the reflected infamy from my tendency to find murder victims. "I didn't find the body, Noreen. A bunch of other people got there before me."

"I saw Jasper." Tracey's large eyes were damp with tears. "It was horrible."

Barry put a comforting arm around her. "Even if Jasper took that money, he didn't deserve to be killed."

"If you want those donuts, you'd better hurry up." Siobhan jabbed a gloved finger at her watch. "I promised my boyfriend we'd meet him down by the harbor."

I supplied my former coworkers with food and drink. Siobhan grabbed her donut and muttered her goodbye. She was already striding down the street while I wished Tracey and Barry happy holidays.

"We must get together in the new year," Tracey gushed. "I want to hear all about your work as a private investigator. That way, I'll be prepared if I'm ever cast as a P.I."

Barry pulled a face behind Tracey's head, and I coughed away a laugh. I'd never seen Tracey act, but Barry had been subjected to several of her performances and claimed still to bear the scars.

"Hi, everyone," trilled an upbeat voice. To my

horror, Beth glided over to the stand and sniffed the donuts. "These smell divine."

My shoulders slumped. Seriously, why did my sister have to show up twice in one day?

"Oh my gosh. Are you *Eliza Donati*?" Tracey's hand flew to her mouth in an exaggerated gesture. "I watch your channel."

Beth preened at this enthusiastic greeting. "Yes, I'm Eliza. Are you a friend of Maggie?"

The cosmetics sales assistant looked at me in surprise, and then back at my sister. "You two know each other?"

I sighed. My sister had been on Whisper Island for less than twenty-four hours, and I was already tired of the inevitable incredulity when people discovered we were related. "We're sisters."

Tracey's eyes widened. "Seriously? That's amazing. Is it true you'll be in a Con Ryder film?"

"Possibly." Beth tone was coy. "I'm certainly considering it."

Tracey pulled a card out of her enormous purse and shoved it at my sister. "I act and direct, and I'm in the process of making my first film. Could you please give my card to Con Ryder? I'd love to discuss the project with him."

Beth's smile froze. From her rigid expression, I couldn't tell if she was put out that Tracey was using her to get to Con, or irritated that my former coworker hadn't asked for her autograph. "Con doesn't take unsolicited business cards," she said after an awkward pause. "And he prefers to make his own movies."

Unperturbed by this snub, Tracey shoved her business card into Beth's jacket pocket. The move was so sudden and outrageous that I almost bit my tongue. "Trust me," Tracey said, "he'll be interested in this project."

"Are you two coming, or what?" Siobhan yelled from further down the street. "We're late."

With an air kiss and a smile, Tracey waved goodbye and hurried to join the other woman. Giving Beth and me a knowing wink, Barry followed his friends.

"My, that's one pushy lady," Beth said when they were out of earshot. "I can't believe she shoved her card into my pocket. Seriously, who does that?"

For once, I found myself in wholehearted agreement with my sister. "A very determined individual who doesn't have a snowball's chance of getting her movie financed."

Beth jerked her shoulder in a dismissive half-shrug and banished Tracey from her mind. "My last-ditch attempt to persuade Con to let me stay at the hotel failed. It looks like I'm moving in with you."

"When? I won't be home until late this evening." And preferably never if Beth was going to be there.

"Would eight work for you? I have your number. I'll send you a message if it's later than eight."

"Eight should be okay," I said reluctantly. "As I

said, don't expect luxury. My cottage is comfortable for one adult. Two will be a squeeze."

"Oh, it'll be fine." Beth gazed through the windows and into the Movie Theater Café. "I'm going to ask Philomena and Julie about Christmas," she said in a lowered voice. "I figure if they agree, Noreen won't refuse."

My sister was many things, but stupid wasn't one of them.

"You're probably right. Just make sure Con knows that Liam, Hannah, and my friend, Jennifer, are also coming. If he insists on having the whole family present, they're part of the deal."

"That won't be a problem." Beth rolled her eyes. "Con loves entertaining a large audience."

After my sister went into the café, I returned to my position beside Noreen, and we served the seemingly endless line of customers for another thirty minutes.

"It's almost time for you to finish your shift," Noreen said between customers. "Do you want to fetch Hannah and get going?"

The line of waiting customers snaked down the street. "I can't leave you to deal on your own."

Philomena emerged from the café, carrying another steaming saucepan filled with mulled wine. Hannah followed with a tray piled high with extra cups.

"Did I hear you say Maggie needs to go?" Philomena looked from Noreen to me. "Go ahead, love. With Beth helping out, Julie has the café under control. I can take over for you out here."

I raised an eyebrow. My sister was serving customers? "If that's okay with you, I'd like to take Hannah shopping."

I rubbed my numb hands together and blew on them. In spite of my gloves, my hands were frozen after hours outside.

While Philomena transferred the mulled wine into its warmer, Noreen unrolled more one-euro coins. "I don't feel comfortable having this amount of cash hanging around," she murmured under her breath, "especially out on the street. Would you mind popping by the bank and depositing what we've brought in so far today, Maggie?"

"No problem. I can go whenever works for you."

"You'd better make it now," Philomena interjected. "The bank closes early today because of the festival."

"I'd forgotten all about that." Noreen's forehead creased. "They're only open until three today."

I glanced at my watch. "If Hannah and I hurry, we'll make it before they close."

"I'm sorry to make you rush," Noreen said. "I should have thought of it earlier."

"Don't worry about it." I glanced at Hannah, who was jumping up and down to keep warm. "Want to speed-walk to the bank?"

The girl raised her eyebrows and jerked a thumb at the throng of people meandering along the main street. "I don't think we can move fast with that crowd."

I laughed. "We'll do our best. Want to race me?"

A broad smile spread across her freckled face. "You're on."

AFTER HANNAH and I had said goodbye to my aunts, we headed down the main street toward the bank. I'd placed the metal box Noreen used to transport money to and from the bank in a discreet shopping bag so as not to advertise that I was carrying cash.

"No speed-walking for us today after all," I said, dodging a woman pushing a stroller.

Hannah swerved to avoid a group of drunk guys in their twenties. "I still intend to beat you to the bank, but I don't want to push anyone."

"Unfortunately, push-or-be-pushed seems to be the standard operating procedure today," I said. "Hang onto my arm and let's go."

We maneuvered our way through the crowd and headed in the direction of the harbor. The bank was located a few doors down from the library where Philomena worked. Under normal circumstances, it was a five-minute walk from the Movie Theater Café, but the masses of people hampered our progress.

"Hey, Maggie. Hey, Miss Hannah." Lenny shoved through the crowd and fell into step with us. "How's it going?"

I pulled a face. "Slowly. We need to get to the bank before it closes."

My friend grinned and held up a moneybox. "Snap. I told my dad I'd deposit today's takings from the electronics shop. He and Mum knocked off early for the festival."

"Want to hang with me, Maggie, and Dad?" Hannah asked. "We're going to eat lots of food."

Lenny smiled down at the little girl. "I'd be honored to hang with you, Hannah."

When Hannah skipped ahead of us, I asked, "Is your mother speaking to you again?"

"Not really." The hurt showed on Lenny's face. "She's monosyllabic."

"I'm sorry. I have family woes, too," I said gloomily. "Beth is moving into my cottage tonight. Why didn't I tell that director dude to take a flying leap? Did I take a blow to the head or something?"

"No. He bamboozled you. I don't know if it's because he wants Beth to bond with her family, or if he just wants to save on hotel costs."

I snorted. "I'll bet it's the latter. Beth won't like that. If he cheaps out on hotel accommodation, he's hardly going to pay her the fee she'd like to become accustomed to."

"No offense, but your sister is a dose of misery. I wouldn't want her to stay at my place."

"No offense taken. I agree with you. I'm surprised Beth didn't get her way. She usually does, and I've never known her to give up easily."

Hannah, who'd skipped back to join us, stared at me, open-mouthed. "You don't like Eliza? But she's awesome."

"Maybe her makeup tutorials are awesome," I conceded. "I've never watched them."

"But she's your sister. How can you not like her?" She scrunched up her forehead. "I've always wanted a sister."

My assistant and I exchanged a look over Hannah's head. "Siblings can be complicated," Lenny said after a pause. "Trust me on this."

We reached the end of the street and crossed over the square to the library. Hannah stopped to admire the huge Christmas tree at the center of the square.

"Maybe on some level, Beth does want to recon-nect with you but can't come out and say it," Lenny said when the girl was out of earshot. "And let's face it: if you were as disinterested in her as you claim, why did you buy that magazine when we were in Galway?"

My cheeks grew warm. "I'd forgotten all about that. Did I leave it in your hotel room?"

He nodded. "It was still in the bag with the toiletries you bought me."

"It was an impulse buy," I muttered, slowing my pace as we neared the bank to allow Hannah to catch up with us.

Lenny held the door open and bowed to Hannah. "Ladies first."

She giggled, and we stepped inside.

A long line of people waited for a free cashier. At five minutes before closing time, Lenny and I weren't the only people on the island who'd decided to do a little last-minute banking.

Jennifer Pearce waved to us from the end of the line. We went over to join her.

"Hey, you," I said. "How's it going?"

"Fine. Just crazy busy." She held up a metal box similar to the one in my carrier bag. "I told Aaron I'd deposit cash we had in the practice before the weekend. Then I'm going to catch the ferry over to the mainland and finish my Christmas shopping."

"Don't you want to go to the festival?" Hannah asked. "Maggie and I are going shopping after the bank and then meeting Dad later. I want to buy Christmas presents from the stands."

Jennifer, whose tastes ran to finer products than handmade wooden reindeer, schooled her features into a neutral expression. "I don't think the festival stands have what I'm looking for."

"I'm not a big fan of this festival," Lenny said as we shuffled up one place in the line. "It attracts way too many outsiders and turns into a drunken party before evening."

The blast of cold air on my back indicated the arrival of another bank customer. "Noreen forgot to give you this." A breathless Beth came to join me in the line, clutching a second money box in her gloved hands. "With the rush of customers on the stand, she forgot to add the cash from the café to the box she gave you."

"Thanks. Sorry you had to run all the way."

My sister's flushed appearance wasn't as expertly polished as it had been when she'd first swooped down on the stand. "It's okay." She wrinkled her nose. "I was relieved to get out of that café for a few minutes."

Lenny and I exchanged amused glances. "I wondered how long you'd last behind the counter," I said. "Did Philomena guilt-trip you into helping out in the café?"

Beth's coral pout transformed into a smile. "How did you guess?"

"Because that's how she operates. She smothers you in kindness, and then you feel you can't refuse. The trick is to anticipate the danger and run before she can pounce."

"Philomena even got me to agree to play Santa at the Christmas pageant," Lenny supplied in a morose tone. "I can't believe I let myself get sucked into agreeing."

"I'm sure you'll make an excellent Santa," I said, deadpan. "You can put Movie Reel Investigation's new disguise wardrobe to good use."

Beth handed me the money box and glanced at her watch. "I guess I'd better get back."

"Thanks for delivering the box. I'll see you later at my place."

"See you then."

My sister reached out to open the door. Before she could turn the handle, the door burst open, ushering in an arctic breeze. Five individuals wearing Santa Claus costumes marched into the bank, forcing Beth to leap to the side to avoid a collision. The Santas each held a large sack of presents in front of their padded stomachs. Their movements and attitudes indicated that these guys weren't a bunch of friends having fun at the festival.

A memory stirred. As if in slow motion, the newspaper headlines from the night I'd found Ms. Butt Bleach in the bath ran through my head. Wasn't there something about a gang of Santas terrorizing Galway? An icy fear snaked down my spine. They couldn't be on Whisper Island. That would be absurd. Wouldn't it?

My unspoken question was answered in the next second. With a flourish, the Santas dropped their sacks and revealed Colt AR-15s concealed underneath.

18

The Santa at the front of the pack grabbed my sister by the hair and shoved her onto the floor. He pushed the muzzle of his weapon against the back of her head and growled at the terrified bank occupants. "Do as we say, or the beauty queen gets a bullet."

By unspoken agreement, two of the Santas surged into forward motion, descending upon the counters. "Hands on your heads," one of the robbers yelled at the terrified bank employees, before turning to address the rest of us. "Same goes for you."

A chorus of gasps and whimpers rippled through the crowd as we watched the robbers haul the bank's staff out from behind the counters. The staff shuffled out into the foyer, arms held high and limbs shaking. Beth appeared to be too stunned to register what was happening. Her mouth froze in an O of surprise, the sort of fugue state a person goes into when their gut knows something bad is happening, but their brain hasn't caught up.

Rage tore through me in a searing torrent. I wasn't fond of my sister, but she didn't deserve to have her life threatened. None of us did. On instinct, I reached for the place my holster used to be when I was a cop. Old habits die hard.

"Everyone on the floor," roared the Santa who appeared to be the spokesman of the group. "Careful, now. No sudden movements."

Lenny, Jennifer, and I kneeled on the cold tiles, our hands on our heads, but Hannah stood rigid, too shocked to move.

I pulled the girl down beside me and held her tight. "It's going to be okay," I whispered. "Just stay calm and do what they tell you."

"Hands on your heads," the head Santa roared at us.

I shot him a look that could bore holes in granite before I complied. Beside me, Hannah trembled so violently that her teeth chattered. My fingers curled into fists. When this was over, I'd make those guys pay. One way or another, I'd make sure they saw the inside of a jail cell for putting a child through this experience.

"Now, here's how this is going to play out." The spokesman gestured for the last two of his cohorts to move closer to us. "I want all of you to place your phones and smartwatches on the floor in front of you. My pal with the red sack is going to collect them.

While he does that, you're going to put whatever cash you have on you into the green sack. Anyone who doesn't cooperate gets one in the head. Got it?"

A murmur of strained assent rose up from the crowd. I took my sweet time in putting my phone on the floor for collection. When it was my turn to hand over the goods, I hit Liam's number on speed dial while placing my phone face down on the tiles. It was a long shot, but worth a try. The Santa with the green sack picked up my phone and tossed it in with the other phones without checking the screen. I exhaled the breath I hadn't realized I'd been holding, and registered the stench coming from the bag. Had someone thrown a stink bomb in there? If so, good for them.

The guy with the green sack yanked Noreen's cashboxes out of my grasp. Seeing her hard-earned money disappear brought bile to my throat. My aunt had worked hard to ensure that today was a success, and she was counting on the extra cash to get her through a lean January. I itched to show the Santas my karate moves, but they were all heavily armed, and I couldn't risk endangering my sister or any of the other hostages.

"Hands back on your heads," snarled the head Santa, "and stop sniveling. If you cooperate, you'll be fine. Any attempts at heroics won't end well." The man turned to the Santas who were in charge of the bank employees and inclined his head. "Your turn, lads."

The Santa nearest to the bank manager, Joseph McCarthy, hauled him to his feet. "I need you, and her."

At this cue, the Santa next to him grabbed a red-haired teller named Angela and forced her to stand.

The first Santa hissed into the bank manager's ear. I wasn't familiar with how bank security worked on Whisper Island, but it was unlikely to be as sophisticated as at a larger branch on the mainland. However, the staff would be able to access at least some money, and cash appeared to be the gang's goal.

After the robber had finished issuing instructions, the manager took a hasty step to his right. His captor let out a string of expletives and slammed a fist into the man's face. At the crack of a breaking bone, I winced. That had to hurt. Joseph McCarthy staggered back, blood streaming from his nose.

Ignoring the command to keep her hands on her head, Jennifer put her arms around Hannah and shielded the girl's eyes. It was hard to tell which of them needed comforting more—the child or the adult.

"I said no funny business," the head Santa snarled. "Try a trick like that again, and the redhead gets a bullet to the brain as well as the beauty queen."

Angela's eyes widened in terror and her mouth formed a silent scream. My fingers curled into fists. These idiots had no right to terrorize innocent people. I didn't know Joseph and Angela well, but they'd always been friendly and helpful whenever I saw them at the bank or the café.

The Santa who'd hit Joseph put his masked face against the bank manager's bloody nose. "Unless you want more broken bones, do as I told you."

Joseph, obviously still dazed after receiving a punch to the head, struggled to focus his eyes. The Santa dragged him through the staff gate and out of my range of vision.

A taut silence spanned the room, the tension palpable. The acrid scent of fear-induced perspiration pervaded the atmosphere. I prided myself on keeping calm in almost any situation, but an icy trickle of sweat slid down my back. The seconds stretched, each one seeming longer than the last. My sister's initial expression of stunned disbelief had transformed into a pure rage that mirrored my own.

While I fantasized about enacting an action film-style takedown of the bank robbers, I memorized every detail of the three Santas who remained in the foyer. The Santa I judged to be the leader of the pack was male and well over six feet. It was impossible to tell if his black boots contained shoe lifts to make him taller. I had to hope not. The man's voice and height were the only potential identifying factors. The masks and padded suits made it impossible to say much else about their appearance, and the piercing blue of their eyes through the eye slots of the masks was the classic mark of cheap colored contact lenses.

The two other Santas left in the foyer were a few

inches shorter than their leader. They could have been male or female, but from his movements, I was pretty sure the one closest to the door was a guy.

After several long minutes, the Santa holding Angela hostage emerged from the staff section of the bank. He'd thrown his yellow sack over his left shoulder, and it looked full. Finally free, Angela stumbled toward her coworkers, and half fell to the floor.

The Santa who'd attacked the bank manager followed a moment later, shoving his hostage in front of him and raising his sack in triumph. "Our job here is done, lads," he said to his partners in crime.

By now, the guy collecting cash had reached the last bank customer. Once the woman had placed the contents of her wallet into the sack, the robber stepped back and whistled a festive song off-key.

"Thanks for your cooperation." The leader's voice dripped with sarcasm. "We wish you all a very merry Christmas. We'll sure have one."

Laughing, the Santas sprang through the staff gate and out the fire exit, disappearing with their loot.

The instant the door slammed after the Santas, I leaped to my feet and surveyed the scene. Customers cowered on the floor, shaking with fear. The bank's employees hunched in front of the counters, wearing dazed expressions on their pale faces. Beth hadn't moved a muscle since her captor had left. Even Jennifer had lost her usual poise—in her stunned stupor, she didn't appear to notice that she'd spilled the contents of her purse all over the floor during her haste to hand over her cash.

I helped my sister to her feet and led her over to my friends. "Can you stay with Hannah for a sec?"

The kid would be okay with Jennifer and Lenny, but Beth needed a sense of purpose to snap her out of her state of shock.

My sister blinked at me unseeingly. "Sure."

"Can I come with you?" Hannah demanded, eyes wide with curiosity. Unlike Beth and my lawyer friend, she appeared to be recovering from her ordeal at a rapid pace.

"I'd feel more comfortable knowing you were with Beth and Jennifer. I won't be long." I raised my voice and addressed the crowd. "Excluding Joseph, is anyone hurt? I saw some of you fall to the floor pretty hard."

A plump woman I recognized from the library let out a sob. "I think I sprained my wrist when I landed."

Brid Kelly, a trained nurse and a member of the Movie Club, pushed herself off her knees and stood. "Let me have a look at that wrist, Patsy."

Slowly, the other people in the bank unfurled from their positions on the floor. Joseph McCarthy held his bleeding nose and looked as though he'd seen a ghost. In the distance, the wail of a police siren floated through the windows. Maybe my trick with the phone had worked. I had no idea how much Liam would have been able to hear, but I'd figured dialing his number was worth a shot.

I addressed the bank manager. "Did you press the emergency button?"

The man regarded me blankly, still in shock. "No, but I threatened to. That's why the guy punched me."

Of all the idiotic things to say to a guy with a lethal weapon… Perhaps I was being harsh. With Ireland's strict gun laws, the bank manager had probably never seen a firearm up close before today.

"Do you have whiskey in your office?"

The bank manager stared at me, perplexed by my question. "Uh, yeah. Do you want a glass?"

"No, but you should have one. And call the cops while you're in your office, just in case those sirens aren't for us. When you've done all that, let Brid Kelly have a look at your nose." My attention shifted to the fire exit door. "I'm going to see where they dumped our phones."

"Nearby is my bet." Lenny uncoiled his lanky form from his position on the floor and joined me midstride. "If the robbers were clued in enough to demand our phones and smartwatches, they're unlikely to hang onto them. They'll know they can be used to follow their tracks."

I reached for the door handle, but Lenny stopped me. "Are you sure this is safe, Maggie? What if the Santas are still out there? Shouldn't we wait for the police?"

"The castrated cops of Ireland don't have guns.

What good will they be if the Santas are still there? Besides, they won't be. They'll put as much distance between them and the bank as possible, and they'll dump their costumes."

"You're very confident."

My words sounded braver than I felt. "It's unlikely the Santas had a getaway vehicle near the bank. The entire town center is a pedestrian-only zone today. Their best bet is to blend in with the crowds of tourists, and that means getting rid of their costumes, guns, and sacks."

"You have a point, and I want to find my phone."

My friend's words galvanized me into action. Taking a deep breath, I squared my shoulders and opened the door. "Let's do this thing."

19

A chill wind hit me the instant I stepped outside. I scanned the narrow cobbled lane for any sign of the Santas, but it was deserted. The lane ran between the back of bank and the high wall of a seafood packing warehouse. The only windows were placed up high and designed to let in light, not afford the warehouse employees a view of the lane.

"The security camera's bust." Lenny pointed at the lone camera placed above the bank's fire exit.

I grunted. "Figures. Let's look for whatever they dumped. At the very least, I expect we'll find the phones and smartwatches. They won't want to be traced."

"About that…" My friend sounded mighty cheerful for a guy who'd experienced a bank robbery. "Once the coast is clear, I need to get my laptop from my parents' shop."

"Dude, we've been robbed at gunpoint. Why the sudden concern for your laptop?"

Lenny's smile turned smug. "My parents are lax about security at their shop. Whenever they ask me to deposit money at the bank, I always insert an electronic tracker until I've handed over the cash."

I spun around to face him. "Whoa. Are you saying the robbers are carrying a tracking device in the sack with the money?"

"Bingo." He grinned. "I've done it for years. First time it's come in handy."

I broke into a fit of laughter. "Lenny, you're a genius."

"I aim to please." With a newfound swagger, my friend sauntered down the lane, dodging puddles of slush that had formed on the uneven surface. "I don't see any brightly colored sacks hanging around. Where do you think the Santas chucked our phones?"

I pointed to a Dumpster at the end of the lane. "That seems the obvious choice."

He groaned. "Aw, man. I'm supposed to meet my family after this, and Mum will expect me to look—and smell—respectable."

"I want to find the phones, not remove them from wherever they were left. The Santas wore gloves, but the police will still want to check for hairs and fibers."

Lenny grimaced. "Yeah…I kinda need them not to see my phone."

I raised an eyebrow. "Do I want to know why?"

"I, uh, stuck something in the case and I don't want the cops to question me about it."

I crossed my arms over my chest. "Is this the not-so-secret ingredient you add to your brownies?"

"No way. I wouldn't ask you to help me retrieve an illegal substance. It's just…" Lenny's cheeks turned pink, "something I'd rather the police not see."

I'd rarely seen my friend flustered. Whatever was in his phone case must mean a lot to him. Swallowing a sigh, I found my ever-present emergency detection kit in my jacket pocket and pulled on a pair of disposable gloves. "Glove up, and help me get this open."

The Dumpster was huge, and it took all our strength to open the heavy lid. Noxious fumes emanated from within, making us gag.

"Gross." I wrapped my scarf around my mouth and pulled a flashlight from my pocket. "Help me up, and I'll see if the sack is in there."

Lenny hoisted me up, and I shone my flashlight into the dark interior, illuminating the red felt sack.

"It's here." I coughed at the stench from the Dumpster. "I'd suggest tossing a coin to see which of us goes in, but our festive friends fleeced me."

"No worries. This is my problem, not yours." Lenny helped me down before removing his jacket and scarf. "Will you give me a leg up?"

"Sure."

After much huffing, puffing, and swearing, I succeeded in helping Lenny climb onto the edge of the Dumpster. My friend had barely had time to lower himself into the smelly interior when the fire exit door burst open, and Liam tumbled into the lane. He'd lost his uniform cap, and his hair stood up in wild tufts. "Maggie?"

"Stall him," Lenny pleaded from within the Dumpster. "I need time to find my phone."

Seriously, this week… "Hey." I plastered a smile on my face and waved to my boyfriend.

Liam staggered to a halt when he spotted me, color returning to his ashen face. He broke into a run and enveloped me in a crushing hug. "Thank goodness."

"Hey, go easy on my ribs, buddy." I leaned against him and inhaled his familiar scent.

He laughed and eased the pressure. "I was so worried when I got your call, and when I didn't see you in the bank…"

"My trick worked?" I asked, my voice muffled from me being held tight against his chest. "I wasn't sure how much you'd be able to hear."

"I heard enough to know you were in trouble. I called Sile and arranged backup."

I hooted with laughter. "Backup from the reserves or Sergeant O'Shea?"

"Thankfully, neither. With the number of visitors on the island for today's festival, the district superintendent sent over extra officers."

When Liam released me, I took a reluctant step back. I wanted to snuggle against his chest and let him soothe away the stresses of the day, but we had five armed robbers to deal with first. "You need to stop everyone from leaving the island. I doubt the bank robbers will haul their loot onto the ferry in the bright green sack they used to collect it, but they'll try to smuggle the cash off the island somehow."

Sile Conlan, the young police officer who'd joined the Whisper Island Garda Station last summer, appeared in the fire exit doorway. Whenever I saw her in her uniform, I had to fight the urge to laugh. Even without her nose and eyebrow rings, Sile couldn't shake the Goth look. She'd pulled her jet-black hair into a severe updo, but her heavy white makeup, burgundy lipstick, and don't-mess-with-me expression screamed attitude. Sile scoured the lane. "Did you find them, Sarge? Oh, hi, Maggie."

"Them?" Liam looked at me, and his eyes narrowed in suspicion. "Where's Lenny?"

"He's…" I sought for a suitable reason for my friend's absence and came up blank, "preoccupied."

Sile curled her lip. "Chasing bank robbers? At the speed he runs, they have nothing to worry about."

At the outraged squawk from within the Dumpster, Liam's eyebrows shot up, but Sile was too far away to hear.

"I want everyone boarding the ferry searched for the stolen cash," Liam said briskly, walking toward her and ensuring that she didn't approach the Dumpster. "Is anyone scheduled to fly off the island today?"

The young police officer furrowed her brow. "The

only helicopter registered is at the hotel. I'll ask them to make sure no one uses it."

"Place a guard at the helipad," Liam said. "We can't risk them escaping. If you make the calls, I'll finish searching the lane with Maggie."

Sile eyed me with suspicion before turning back to Liam. "Yes, boss."

After the young police officer had returned to the bank, Liam regarded the Dumpster. His eyes twinkled with merriment, and his shoulders heaved. "You can come out now, Lenny. The coast's clear."

"Thank goodness," came the muffled voice from within. "I'm dying in here."

Liam peered into the Dumpster, and Lenny handed him the sack with all the phones and smart-watches. Once Liam had deposited the sack on the ground, he helped Lenny climb out of the Dumpster.

"Ew." I took a step back from my friend and held my nose. "Dude, you stink."

"Sorry about that. Trust me. Dumpster-diving was *not* how I pictured spending my day." Lenny turned to Liam, an expression of innocence on his face. "At least I found the phones. The bank customers will be pleased."

Liam crossed his arms over his chest and toed the sack. "Want to tell me what you were looking for, Logan? I know Maggie wouldn't let you tamper with potential evidence for no reason."

Lenny scratched his scraggly beard, his eyes darting in my direction.

"I want nothing to do with this craziness," I said. "All I did was give him a leg up."

Liam sighed. "Did you remove a phone from the sack, Lenny?"

"Only my own," Lenny said, on the defensive. "I'm sick of cops taking my stuff. Maggie and I still haven't gotten our gear back after your brother and his odious fellow officer confiscated them on Monday."

My boyfriend opened his palm. "Hand it over, and we'll pretend this never happened."

Muttering, Lenny retrieved the phone from his pocket and slipped the device out of its case. "Here. Thieves, the lot of you."

Liam's lips twitched. "I need the case, too."

My friend drew back, clutching the phone case tight. "Why?"

"Why don't you want me to see it?" Liam countered.

"This isn't a police state." Lenny bristled with outrage. "A man's entitled to a bit of privacy."

Liam's eyes narrowed. "Are you hiding drugs in the phone case?"

"No, I—"

"Give it up, my friend," I interjected. "We've wasted enough time over that stupid case. Liam and Sile have five Santas to catch."

Liam whirled around to face me. "Only five? I understood the gang robbing places around Galway had six members, including the getaway driver."

"Maybe they originally had six, but if one of their members was Jasper Ramsbottom, he's currently in a body bag at the morgue. And if they have a getaway driver, he's unlikely to be in the town today."

"True. We had a devil of a time getting the squad car through the crowds." Liam's gaze fixed on me. "Why do you think Jasper was connected to the bank robbers?"

"We know he was involved in something more serious than stealing cash from the department store, and he died wearing a Santa suit. It's not proof, but it's a coincidence worth investigating."

"And your brother and that obnoxious inspector dude were cagey about the corpse in our bathtub," Lenny added. "She was linked to Jasper, and I suspect they were both involved in a bigger operation than stealing cash and goods from the department store."

Liam grinned and held out his hand. "I still want your phone case."

Muttering under his breath about police brutality and violation of personal privacy, Lenny handed over the goods. As Liam looked inside, my friend turned an interesting shade of beetroot.

"Come on," I said. "You've gotta tell me what's in there."

Liam snapped the case closed, his lips quivering. "That'll be between Lenny and me."

"Come on, guys," I protested. "I tell you every-thing. Well," I amended, "more or less."

My boyfriend hoisted the sack of phones over his

shoulder and walked back toward the bank. "I'll get everyone to identify their belongings before we bag them for prints."

"You won't find any," I said. "The Santas are pros. In addition to wearing gloves, they had padding under their suits, neatly disguising their respective builds. They all wore colored contact lenses, Santa boots, and masks under their beards. I don't know if the boots contained shoe lifts to make them appear taller."

Liam swore fluently in Gaelic and English. "Our Lady's Tears is supposed to be a fun festival in the run-up to the holidays. These buffoons have turned a family day out into a nightmare."

"I do have some good news for you." Lenny's expression turned smug. "If you let me get my laptop from my parents' shop, I should be able to tell you where the Santas are."

My boyfriend's eyebrows shot up. "How?"

Lenny repeated his story about placing a GPS tracker in one of the rolls of cash from the electronics store.

Liam whistled. "I'm impressed. Okay, you've officially bought my silence over what I saw in your phone case."

"No fair," I objected. "Now I'm dying to know what it is."

"Tough luck," Lenny said. "If you promise to make us one of your awesome holiday cocktails this evening, I'll fill you in on the fate of my GPS tracker."

"All right," I grumbled, hating not being a part of

the action, "but only if we all agree to brainstorm the connection between Jasper and the Santas. I've got some theories I want to run by you both."

"Deal," Liam said, "and apologies in advance if I'm late. I have no idea how long I'll have to work tonight. Is it okay if I leave Hannah with you?"

"No problem. She can hang with me and stop me from killing Beth." I was only half joking. The prospect of my sister moving in filled me with dread.

Hoisting the sack of phones over his shoulder, Liam held the fire exit door open for Lenny and me. "I'll be in touch, Maggie. In the meantime, you'll need to give your statement to Sile or Garda Walsh."

Was it my imagination, or did Liam's voice quaver when he uttered Sile's name? I looked from my boyfriend to Lenny. My friend's cheeks had turned bright red. *Interesting.* I'd wondered more than once if he had a crush on the young police officer, but now wasn't the moment to contemplate Lenny's love life. With my mind working overtime and a spring to my step, I walked into the bank. I had to figure out a way to convince Liam to let me help with the investigation, and I had an idea how to make that happen.

20

Back in the bank's foyer, the staff and customers who'd endured the robbery were calmer than they'd been before Lenny and I had gone out into the lane. I noticed the half-empty whiskey bottle beside Joseph McCarthy and smiled. The good old Irish cure-all had worked its magic.

Sile Conlan and a male police officer I presumed was Garda Walsh were taking statements from the bank hostages. Some were still in shock. Others were embarrassed to have lost their cool. I was just plain mad. My aunt had worked hard to earn the cash those guys had stolen. She didn't deserve to be ripped off. And no one should be made to fear for their life.

After Liam and Lenny took off for the Logans' electronics store and Lenny's laptop, I made a beeline for Beth, Jennifer, and Hannah. "How are you guys doing?"

"I'm bored," Hannah said, wrinkling her nose. "I wish we could go back to Dad's cottage."

"Your dad has to work, but I said you could come home with me. We'll leave as soon as the police let us go. I even have one of Noreen's lasagnas in my freezer. Would you like that?"

Hannah's tummy rumbled, making us all laugh. "Defo. I'm starving."

I shook my head in bemusement. If I'd consumed half the number of donuts the girl had devoured this morning, I'd never want to eat again. Oh, to be eight years old. I turned to my sister. "I'm sorry you had to go through that."

"I'll live. If Con wants me to play a hostage in a bank robbery, I can draw from real life experience." Beth gave me a trembly smile, and her eyes filled with just enough tears that they didn't spill down her face in a mascara-streaked mess.

Whoa. Where were these uncharitable thoughts coming from? My cheeks grew warm, and I shifted my weight from one foot to the other. Maybe Lenny was right. Perhaps the events of the last year had hit me harder than I'd thought. The old me hadn't let my resentment of my sister fester. Or had I? And I didn't recall displaying the insecurity I'd shown when Liam had canceled our date during previous relationships. Then again, I probably should have been warier in the case of my ex-husband.

"Are you okay, Maggie? You look like you're miles away."

Jennifer's voice jerked me back to the present. I noted her wan face and the worry lines etched around her eyes. "I'm fine, thanks. What about you?"

"I'm okay." The lawyer shivered, making her words a lie. "I don't know why, but those Santas freaked me out. Maybe it's after the dead Santa at Dennehy's."

"Masks are freaky. There's something about not being able to see a person's face that gives me the creeps." My words triggered a memory, an aspect of the robbery that didn't quite fit into place. "Hey, Beth? Why did the guy who held the gun to your head keep referring to you as the beauty queen?"

My sister batted her impossibly long eyelashes. "I have no idea. Maybe he knows me from my YouTube channel."

"While trawling the internet for makeup tips on disguising himself as Santa Claus? Yeah, I don't think so."

Beth shrugged. "He could be a drag queen on the side. Who knows?"

"Maybe he saw Beth's photo on the news," Jennifer suggested. "Her collaboration with Con Ryder was all over the media, both print and online."

"It's possible," I mused, running the scene through my mind in the hope of unearthing a clue. "The robbers burst through the door, and Beth leaped to the side to avoid a collision. She was wearing her full outdoor clothes: hat, scarf, gloves, and the collar of her winter coat was turned up."

"It was freezing outside," my sister said, on the defensive. "It gets chilly at home, but I've never experienced anything like the wind on this island."

"The leader of the group grabbed her," I continued, "and shoved her onto her knees, facing away from him. Why did he call her the beauty queen? Just a random phrase, or did he know who Beth was?"

"I am rather good looking," my sister said huffily. "He might have been referring to my beauty."

"That's one option. The other is that the guy knew who you were before he walked through that door."

"Is that significant?" Jennifer frowned. "We've already considered the possibility that the man had seen your sister on social media or in the newspaper. If I recall correctly, there was a recent article about the Santa gang that was featured on the day the news of your sister's visit to Ireland."

"That's right. On Monday evening. I saw the headlines. No, what I meant is that the Santas—or at least the one who grabbed Beth—knew she was in the bank."

"Admittedly, I'm still not myself after the robbery," Jennifer said, rumpling her forehead, "but I'm afraid I don't follow."

"If the gang saw Beth enter the bank, it limits the number of places they could have been hiding before they barged in here. Five people dressed in Santa costumes are kind of hard to miss. Lenny, Hannah, and I arrived just a couple of minutes before Beth did, and we didn't see them. There must be witnesses who can say from what direction they came."

"Isn't it down to the cops to find that out?" my sister asked. "I don't think a bank robbery, even one you witnessed, is material for a private investigator."

I didn't inform her that I'd been involved in several murder inquiries since moving to Whisper Island, both before and after I'd founded my private detection agency. "I guess you're relieved the Santas didn't decide to add kidnapping to their resumé. You'd fetch a decent ransom."

"Maggie, you're ghoulish." Beth gave an exaggerated shudder. "Apart from having a gun held to my head, I got off rather lightly. They didn't bother robbing me. I suppose they noticed I'd given the second moneybox to you."

"They didn't make you empty your purse?" I drew my brows together. "That doesn't make sense."

"I'm sorry if that disappoints you," my sister drawled, "but I have to admit I'm relieved."

"It doesn't make sense," I murmured, thoughts rampaging through my head in a mad jumble. "Why didn't the Santas rob Beth? And why did they target Whisper Island? The bank doesn't contain the amount of cash they'd get at a bank in Galway."

On the other hand, security measures weren't as tight here as in a city, and the island was packed with visitors today. In a crowd of strangers, it would be easy for the gang to blend in once they ditched their costumes. The guns could be disassembled and put into backpacks along with the cash they'd stolen. Plenty of visitors were planning to stay the night due to the notoriously rough sea. I didn't blame them. A choppy crossing in daylight wasn't fun. In the dark, it could be terrifying.

As I watched Sile and the other police officer move around the bank, I felt a sudden pang of envy. I didn't miss being on the police force, but I recalled the exhilaration of being on the scent of a big case all too well. Although Movie Reel Investigation's involvement had ended the day I'd left the department store, my interest in the investigation hadn't. I had to figure out a way to get involved, and Jennifer was my best bet. I waited until Hannah and Beth were giving their statements to the police and seized the moment. "Can I ask you a favor?"

My question surprised the lawyer out of her vague state. "Sure. What's up?"

"Can I tell Liam that you've hired me to investigate Nesbitt & Son's stolen money? You don't have to pay me. I just need an excuse to pump him for info about the case."

"Actually, I was considering asking Aaron if we could hire Movie Reel Investigations to speed up our insurance claim." Aaron, Jennifer's boss and the only living Nesbitt of Nesbitt & Son Solicitors, loathed negative publicity. An intensely private man, he valued his reputation and wouldn't want his firm tainted by association with a bank robbery.

"Only if you're sure," I said. "I'm not fishing for

work. All I need is an excuse to persuade Liam to share details of the investigation."

"I'll have to square it with Aaron, but I don't foresee it being a problem. And if it is, feel free to tell Liam we've hired you anyway." Jennifer glanced at her watch, and a pained expression flitted across her attractive features. "The ferry I'd hoped to catch to the mainland left fifteen minutes ago. I don't suppose there's any point in traveling to the mainland today. By the time I get there, it'll be too late for a relaxed shopping spree."

"'Relaxed' and 'shopping' aren't words that go together in my opinion," I said dryly. "Particularly not this time of year."

Jennifer smiled. "Oh, I get a buzz from the crowds. Some people are stressed, sure, but a lot of them are in a festive mood."

"Speaking of the holidays, my sister's director pal is insisting we all eat Christmas dinner with him at the hotel. You're included in the invitation."

The lawyer's face lit up. "Seriously? I'd love to meet Con Ryder. I only saw him from a distance at the Movie Club. He's my favorite film director."

"Noreen's, too." I sighed. "I guess I'll have to accept that I'm spending Christmas with my sister."

"I get it," Jennifer said quietly. "My sister hasn't spoken to me in five years."

I regarded her with renewed interest. It had taken months to move our relationship status from acquaintances to friends, but I still knew very little about Jennifer's past. "Your family lives in Dublin, right?"

She hesitated for a fraction of a second too long before responding. "Most of them. My sister is based in London."

The lawyer's tight expression indicated that this was a painful topic. Before I could press her for more details, Sile returned with Hannah. The police officer's mouth formed a grim line, but the girl bounced with excitement.

"It's so much fun visiting the island," she exclaimed. "I don't find dead bodies or get held at gunpoint in London."

I met Sile's bemused gaze over Hannah's blond head. "I'm pretty sure your parents wish your visits here involved less drama."

Sile consulted her notebook. "Can I speak to you next, Maggie? I need to know exactly what you observed."

"Sure." I turned to Hannah. "Once I've finished speaking to Sile, we'll take off."

The girl's face fell. "Do we have to? I love watching the police at work."

"I'm delighted you're having fun," I said dryly, "but I'm looking forward to getting out of here."

"You and me both," Sile said. "I want to finish questioning the witnesses and then catch up with the sarge."

Jennifer looked at her watch. "I'm sorry, Maggie, but I should get going. If I'm not going to make it to the mainland today, I need to do some last-minute holiday shopping here on the island." She wrinkled her nose. "Goodness knows what I'll find."

"Nothing that isn't handmade soap, pottery, or genuine woolen products," Beth said dryly. "I looked around the stores this morning."

"If you want to go wild, I saw a lovely diamanté statue of the Virgin Mary in the window of McElligott's jewelry store."

Jennifer's eyebrows arched. "Diamanté?"

"Yep. For the bargain price of three hundred euro, it could be yours."

"I'll pass, thanks," the lawyer said dryly. "I'll give you a call later, though, and let you know what I did find."

"Sounds good." I looked at my sister and drew a breath. "Could I leave Hannah with you while I talk to Garda Conlan? After everything that's happened, I don't want her to be on her own."

Hannah rolled her eyes. "I'm fine, Maggie. Seriously."

"I'll tell you all the behind-the-scenes beauty blogger gossip," my sister said, putting her arm around the girl's shoulders.

Hannah's face lit up. "You will? Awesome."

Having passed on my babysitting duty, I followed Sile into a small office at the back of the bank. It was decorated with trophies and medals from various Irish sports. Gaelic football and hurling, if I had the names right. Joseph McCarthy was an enthusiastic member of the island's Gaelic Athletic Association, more commonly known as the GAA.

Sile sat behind what I presumed was Joseph's desk, and I took a seat across from her. "Any news from Liam?" I asked. "He and Lenny must have traced the cash by now."

The young police officer shook her head. "I've heard nothing so far. For all we know, the robbers checked the cash for trackers and dumped the device in the middle of a field."

"Even if they got rid of it, they'll have a hard time getting the money off the island." I grimaced. "Unfortunately, they struck me as pros. I bet they have a plan in place."

"That's my guess," Sile said morosely. "I did what Sergeant Reynolds ordered. Everyone getting on the ferry is being searched for the stolen cash, and the helipad is out of bounds. We've placed guards at both harbors in case the robbers use a private boat to get away. However, we can't patrol every cove. We've notified the coast guard, but there's still a chance the robbers have already reached the mainland."

"Think positive. You're doing everything you can to catch them."

"Yeah." Sile tapped her notebook, and a grin spread across her face. "And that involves taking yet another statement from you. Given the number of times I've had to question you since I moved to Whisper Island, we should create a multiple-choice witness form just for Maggie Doyle."

"Jeez, thanks," I said. "Would you believe me if I told you I'm over the excitement of corpses and armed robbers?"

She laughed. "Nope."

"I thought not." I stretched my tired neck from side to side. "Okay, let's get this over with. After all the madness, I want a hot bath and an even hotter drink."

21

B y the time I'd finished giving my statement to Sile, it was after five and dark outside. Adjusting to the difference in latitude between Whisper Island and San Francisco had taken me a while. In the warmer months, Ireland had more hours of sunlight. In the winter, it was the other way around. At this time of year, it started to get dark at four and was pitch black by five every evening.

Beth had used the time I was with Sile to multi-task. As well as regaling Hannah with beauty blogger gossip that I suspected wasn't suitable for an eight-year-old, Beth had called Luke and asked him to drop off her bags at my place. "I told him to leave them outside your door. I assumed no one would steal my stuff. You live out in the middle of nowhere, right?"

"Judge for yourself," I said, slowing my car as we approached the turn into the Shamrock Cottages complex.

As I drove up the curving drive, I snuck a look at my sister. Her expression was priceless. "It's...quaint," she managed eventually. "And snug."

I pulled the Yaris into my parking slot and killed the engine. "I told you it was small."

We piled out of the car and walked over to the cottage. The mountain of luggage on my doorstep nixed all thoughts of a bath and a hot drink. I blinked. "Where are we supposed to put all this stuff?"

Hannah regarded the pile of cases curiously. "Is Beth moving in?"

"Only temporarily. In spite of the hundred-plus bags outside my house."

"Seriously?" Hannah bounced on the spot. "That's great. I didn't get a chance to ask her about her favorite makeup brands earlier. I'd love to be a YouTuber when I grow up."

"What happened to your plans to be a detective or a forensic scientist? I thought you and Caoimhe had plans to solve crimes together."

"Oh, you know," the girl said vaguely. "I want to keep my options open. And YouTubers are cool. I want to talk to Eliza about how she's made it work."

I trudged to my front door with zero enthusiasm.

My sister circumnavigated her mountain of baggage and treated me with a saccharine smile. "Would you mind helping me carry my bags inside?"

I gritted my teeth and put my key in the lock. "Sure."

I knew how that would pan out: Beth would direct

operations, and I'd play the role of a pack mule. My sister didn't disappoint. After I'd lugged the tenth bag into the cottage, I was ready to scream.

Beth sat on the sofa, listening to Hannah regale her with stories of her last adventure on Whisper Island.

"And then Maggie figured out who the real killer was and Caoimhe and I helped her catch him." Hannah delivered this announcement in dramatic tones.

"Wow." My sister flashed me a grin. "You guys live an exciting life. I thought nothing ever happened on Whisper Island. Between your adventure at the fort and the bank robbery, it sounds like it's all action."

"Caoimhe says nothing ever happened on the island until your sister moved here," Hannah supplied. "Maggie attracts all sorts of excitement."

Beth stared at me, her expression a mixture of horror and fascination. "I recall you being pretty boring," she said with her trademark lack of tact. "What changed?"

"I dumped Joe and got a life," I snapped, shoving open the guest room door with more force than I'd intended and hurling one of my sister's many bags inside. Mavis, my adopted cat, leaped off the bed with a hiss and shot out into the living room.

"Poor kitty cat. You scared her," Beth said reprovingly and leaned down to stroke the cat's soft fur. Mavis closed her eyes and purred. She snuggled up to my sister and rubbed her body against Beth's legs. Within seconds, the cat was on my sister's lap.

The traitor. It had taken months for Mavis to accept me, and even now, she made it clear that she merely tolerated me inhabiting her space. She'd reached a reluctant understanding with Bran and the other two cats but mostly kept her distance. Seeing her show affection to my sister made me crabby.

I dragged the last of Beth's bags into the bedroom. "I don't know how you'll have room to move in here."

Beth, Mavis purring on her shoulder, wandered into the room. She looked around and wrinkled her nose. "Don't you have a larger room for me? This is pretty cramped."

I crossed my arms over my chest. "I told you my cottage wasn't big. You'll just have to deal with the space available."

With these words, I left her to unpack. I stomped into the kitchen and switched on the oven to preheat for our lasagna. While the lasagna warmed up, I prepared a salad and homemade salad sauce, following one of Noreen's recipes.

Thirty minutes later, Beth emerged from the guest room. She'd changed into an extravagant outfit with red-and-black sequins and had completely redone her makeup. I bit my tongue while Hannah gushed over my sister's outfit and Beth gave the eight-year-old makeup tips her father wouldn't approve of.

At the same moment the timer on the oven pinged

to indicate that our lasagna was ready, the doorbell rang. I switched off the oven and went to answer the door. When I opened it, my eyes widened in surprise. "Lenny *and* Liam? I didn't expect both of you so early. Did you catch the robbers?"

"No such luck," Liam said grimly. "I guess they're long gone."

I stood back to let them in. "I've just made a lasagna. Do you want some?"

"Is it one of Noreen's?" Lenny asked.

I laughed. "Yes. I only reheated it. You're safe."

My friend grinned. "In that case, lasagna sounds great."

Lenny bounded into the kitchen, leaving Liam and me in the hallway. My boyfriend wrapped his arms around me and pulled me into a kiss. "I've missed you," he murmured.

I leaned into him and inhaled the familiar scent of his aftershave and washing detergent. "I've missed you, too. Which is ridiculous. It's only been a couple of hours."

"It feels longer. Time drags when I'm away from you." He kissed me again and we stood like that for a glorious few minutes, enjoying the comfort of one another's closeness.

Laughter from the kitchen reminded me of my duties as a hostess. I broke the kiss and stepped back. "We'd better get some lasagne before they eat it all."

Liam draped an arm around my shoulders, and we walked slowly toward the kitchen. "Lenny's tracking device didn't help us catch the robbers, but it has given us an idea of how they're hiding the cash. The GPS led us to an elderly man's garden shed. Inside, we discovered two thousand euro hidden beneath a loose floorboard."

I frowned. "The Santas took a lot more than that, Liam. Where's the rest of the money?"

"I have no idea. It's possible the guys split up after the robbery, and each hid cash in various locations. That method makes it more difficult for us to find all the money they stole, and a lot easier for them to retrieve the cash at a later date."

I absorbed this information. "It makes sense. With so much scrutiny on anyone leaving the island today, trying to remove the cash would have been crazy. This way, they can come back for it later, possibly even make several trips."

Liam nodded. "It's also possible they're still on the island. While the majority of the festival goers are day-trippers, some people opt to stay overnight."

"Will you continue to monitor the harbors?" I asked. "The robbers have to get off the island somehow."

"Yeah. For another day or two at least." My boyfriend rubbed his jaw and sighed. "The force is understaffed. The district superintendent can't leave too many extra police officers on the island for longer than a day or two. And for all we know, we've already searched the robbers and found nothing. The officers down by the ferries were thorough."

To my surprise, Beth had placed the salad bowl on the table and was dishing the lasagna onto plates. She glanced up when Liam and I entered the kitchen. "Hannah was hungry, so I thought I'd make a start on serving dinner."

"Uh, thanks," I muttered, ignoring Liam's bemused smile. "I'll take it from here."

"Homemade, I'm sure." My boyfriend flashed me a wicked grin. "I have fond memories of your aunt's lasagna."

I whacked him playfully on the arm. "My cooking is improving…slowly."

"Hannah says Jennifer has hired Movie Reel Investigations," Lenny said when we were all seated. "What does she need us to do?"

I shot a glance at Liam, who eyed me curiously. I hadn't gotten around to divulging this information to him yet. "Strictly speaking, we've been hired by Nesbitt & Son. Aaron and Jennifer would like us to make sure their insurance claim for the stolen money goes through smoothly."

My boyfriend burst out laughing. "Pull the other leg, Maggie. You persuaded Jennifer to let you use her as an excuse to get info out of Gavin and me."

I feigned indignance. "Nonsense. Would I do an underhand thing like that?"

He shook his head, but his smile was broad. "You're incorrigible, Maggie Doyle. Yeah, that's exactly what you'd do. You hate not being involved in the investigation, and you're convinced the bank robbery is linked to the case you worked on in Galway."

"It has to be. It's too much of a coincidence otherwise."

"What case is this?" Beth's eyebrows arched neatly over her perfectly made-up eyes.

Liam and I exchanged a look.

"I won't tell her anything she couldn't read in the newspaper," I said. "Pinky swear."

"Go on then. Most of the details are public knowledge by now. Did you see that the police released Cara Mackey's name at a press conference this morning?"

I paused mid-chew. "Seriously? Finally."

"Who's Cara Mackey?" Beth demanded. "Is she connected to the bank robbers?"

Frankly, I didn't feel like sharing the details of Ms. Butt Bleach and the Dennehy's case with Beth, but I wanted to discuss my theories with Lenny and Liam, and Beth was my guest. Given that I had no intention of saying anything inappropriate in front of Hannah, I had no excuse to get rid of my sister without being rude. I might not relish the prospect of having Beth stay at my place over the holidays, but couldn't be inhospitable.

While we ate our dinner, I gave Beth a sanitized summary of my adventures in Galway, including the discovery of Ms. Butt Bleach in Lenny's brother's bathtub and Jasper Ramsbottom's fatal encounter with a Christmas barrel.

"Wow," she said when I'd finished. "Hannah wasn't exaggerating when she said you were a disaster magnet."

"I believe Hannah phrased it more diplomatically than that," I said in a sardonic tone, "but whatever."

"Maggie thinks the dead dude in Galway is connected to the Santas who robbed the bank today," Lenny said between mouthfuls of lasagna, "and I agree with her."

"Did your brother ever find out where Jasper got his Santa suit?" I asked Liam. "Was it one owned by the store?"

"No. It was a different brand from the one they use." His glance flitted to Lenny. "As a matter of fact, it's a brand carried by that costume place you worked at. I checked their online catalog before I drove home."

I looked up from my plate. "So you think my hunch is right?"

Liam shrugged. "I'm keeping an open mind, but your theory is worth pursuing. We've collaborated on enough investigations by now that I know you have good instincts."

"What I'd like to know," Lenny said, "is what brand of costume Jasper was wearing. I should have checked when we found his corpse, but it only occurred to me after he'd been bagged and tagged."

My boyfriend slipped his phone from his pocket and checked the display. "The brand was Krazy Kostumes Inc."

Lenny perked up. "That's one of The Costume Emporium's own brands. As part of quality control, each costume has a serial number. If you check the serial number on the costume, The Costume Emporium should be able to tell you when it was purchased and by whom."

My boyfriend's jaw dropped. "Really? They put serial numbers on cheap costumes?"

"Not on all of them," Lenny replied. "The Costume Emporium is particular about its wares. Their costumes are competitively priced, but they pay attention to quality."

Liam chewed on his mouthful of lasagna, a thoughtful expression on his face. "I'm pretty sure Gavin and Inspector Craddock aren't aware that the costume can be traced."

"Get Gavin to check first thing tomorrow morning," I said. "We have the CEO's private number."

"Thanks, Maggie. I'll do that. Could you give me the number now? I'll send Gavin a text message right away."

"No problem."

I took out my phone and found the CEO of The Costume Emporium in my contact list. While Liam sent his brother a text, I cleared the plates from the table. "I don't have much for dessert, but I can offer the adults cocktails. Do you want a cookie, Hannah? I think I have some in a cabinet."

The girl grinned. "Is this the part when you try to

persuade me to watch TV with Bran and the cats so you can talk about interesting things?"

I laughed. "Smart kid. Seriously, though, Lenny and I do need to speak to your dad in private."

To my surprise, my sister spoke up. "Why don't I take Hannah into my room and give her a makeover?"

"Would you? I'd love that." The girl looked at her father pleadingly. "Can I, Dad? I promise I'll wash it all off before bed."

Liam didn't appear to be thrilled by the prospect of his eight-year-old daughter receiving a makeover from a woman wearing a black- and scarlet-sequined minidress. However, he correctly interpreted the warning look I sent him from across the table. "Okay, but behave yourself for Beth."

"It's so funny to hear people call you Beth," Hannah said as she and my sister left the kitchen, Mavis the cat trailing after them. "Eliza suits you much better."

"Clever kid," I said. "She knows just what to say to get into my sister's good books."

Liam pushed back his chair and crossed his arms. What's on your mind, Maggie?"

I lowered my voice so only Liam and Lenny could hear me. "I don't want Beth spreading my specula-tions around the island, but if I were part of the Santa gang, I'd make it look like I was in no hurry to collect the loot. And then I'd use the distraction of Christmas to get the money."

"So you think the gang is going to try to retrieve the loot over the next few days?" My boyfriend pondered this idea for a moment. "It makes sense. Today is the twenty-second. As of Sunday, stores will be closed, and everyone will be busy with family."

"Exactly. No one will be in their usual routine, and most people will be at home." I toyed with my water glass. "The police haven't connected the spree of robberies to the murders in Galway. How much manpower is the district superintendent going to leave on the island? He'll assume that the bank robbery today was a one-and-done, right?"

"That's his assumption. The bank is the only major source of cash on the island."

"Right. We can assume the robbers left all the cash on the island, and not just the money you and Lenny found with the tracker."

"It's possible they found the tracker and hid the money to put us off the scent," Lenny added. "It didn't look as if the tracker had been tampered with, but I can't be certain."

"True, but let's say the Santas didn't find the tracker and that hiding cash in small quantities is part of their plan."

"If they intend to collect the cash at some point over the holidays, how many of them will return to the island?" Liam mused. "I can't imagine all five will come back."

"I don't know. What I'd like to know is if Gavin and Inspector Craddock have had any success in tracking down that Del guy Lenny and I saw the night of our stakeout."

Liam hesitated for a moment before answering. "I'm not supposed to discuss the details of the case with you two. You know that."

"I'm sensing a 'but' here," Lenny said.

I leaned back in my chair and blew Liam a kiss. "Come on. Tell all. You know you want to."

My boyfriend grinned. "The last I heard, Gavin and his colleagues had had no luck in tracking down Del."

"Let's assume Del is one of the Santas," I said. "We know he's violent, and we know he killed Ms. Butt Bleach, and probably Jasper. And he's tall enough to fit the profile of the Santa's leader."

Liam squeezed his eyes shut and groaned. "I hate making assumptions about a case. I like facts."

"So do I, but what else do we have to go on?"

"I reckon your bro and his cranky colleague held back the details of Ms. Butt Bleach's murder because they believe it's connected to a larger case than the stolen cash at Dennehy's," Lenny said. "At the moment, the only case hitting the headlines is the Santa gang."

My boyfriend was silent for a long moment. "Okay," he said finally. "I'll talk to Gavin and Crad-dock and see what I can find out. I'll tell them Movie Reel Investigations has been hired by Aaron and Jennifer, and that might get them to agree to share a few details with you."

I beamed at him. "Awesome. Thanks, Liam"

"Not much about this case is awesome." My boyfriend's expression sobered. "If your hunch is right, the Santas will return to Whisper Island before long. I'm officially on my Christmas holidays as of tomorrow, but we all know we can't leave Sergeant O'Shea in charge of a case of this magnitude. My job is to convince the district superintendent to send in reinforcements until we find the money and the Santas, or whichever happens first."

I snorted. "Good luck with that."

I'd met the district supervisor, Garda Sile Conlan's father, and he'd struck me as a typical ambitious cop: arrogant and blind to anything that didn't serve to advance his career.

"Could Sile talk to him?" A frown creased Lenny's forehead. "Maybe persuade him to see sense."

Liam's smile was wry. "I doubt Sile can persuade her father to do much beyond losing his temper. They're not close. She joined the guards in spite of her father's position rather than because of it, and they have very different mindsets."

"Sile strikes me as a good police officer," I said. "She's capable of thinking outside the box."

"She's good at her job, but she lacks tact." He grinned. "Remind you of anyone?"

I stuck my tongue out at him. "You should be a comedian. Seriously, though, we need to come up with a plan of action. If Liam is going to dig for info from his brother, what are your plans, Lenny?"

"I'll keep looking for info on Del, Cara, and Jasper." He pulled a face. "Sorry, but I'm behind. Between wrapping up The Costume Emporium Case and helping my parents at their shop, I haven't had a lot of time to do a thorough search."

"No problem. If you take care of the internet searches, I'll deal with the bank robbery. I want to write down everything I saw and question people who were outside the bank just before and just after the robbery. Do you have names to share with me, Liam?"

"I have a few," he replied slowly, "but I'm not sure what you can get out of them that we didn't."

"I'm not sure either, but it's worth a try. People talk differently to a member of the public than they do to a cop."

"That's true." My boyfriend inclined his head and pulled a notebook and pen from his shirt pocket. "Okay. The list of witnesses is succinct. There was a large crowd outside the bank, but few people claim to have seen the robbers."

"How did they miss five dudes in Santa costumes?" Lenny demanded. "They weren't exactly inconspicuous."

"They changed into their costumes in the lane behind the bank." The scenario crystallized in my mind as I spoke, the details fitting together like missing jigsaw puzzle pieces. "The security camera at the back of the bank was broken, remember? They entered the lane as regular tourists and changed into their costumes. Once they were dressed, they used the main entrance to gain access to the bank. They risked being seen entering the bank, but using the main entrance was a lot easier than disabling the alarm on the fire exit door, plus it allowed them to overpower both the customers and staff."

"The sacks they used to collect the money and phones stank," Lenny said. "Did you notice that?"

I nodded. "Yeah. I wonder if they hid the guns and sacks in the Dumpster before the robbery?"

"I'll take another look at that rubbish bin," Liam said, making a note in his notebook.

"Why didn't their costumes smell?" I mused. "Were they not hidden in the Dumpster?"

"Having had the honor to hang out in said Dumpster, I can tell you it's at its widest at the top and tapers down to a narrower bottom." Lenny screwed up his nose at the memory of his time in the stinky interior. "There's enough space behind the Dumpster to hide cases. Rubbish collection was yesterday meaning the bin was nice and empty, and on the day of the festival, people were unlikely to go out into the lane."

"And then the robbers pulled off their costumes, shoved them into the cases with the loot, and took off. They must have moved fast. We weren't that far behind them." I sighed. "Okay, to sum up, Liam will talk to Gavin, Lenny will do his internet magic, and I'll talk to the witnesses outside the bank. Do you have that list of names for me?"

My boyfriend tore a sheet of paper from his note-book and handed it to me. "It's short, but you know most of the people on it."

I scanned the list, and my attention fixed on one name. A slow smile spread across my face. "Correction: I know them all. Barry White worked with me at the department store. He was on the island with a few coworkers for the festival."

Liam's eyes flew to meet mine. "That's another link to Dennehy's. I don't like this."

"Neither do I, but half of Galway was on the island today. It's not all that surprising." All the same, it was yet another coincidence. Like most cops, coincidences bothered me. "I'll contact Barry and see what he has to say. Want to meet tomorrow night to compare notes?"

Lenny nodded. "Sounds good."

"Yeah," Liam said and flashed me a cheeky smile. "Now are you ever going to make this famous winter cocktail for us?"

I laughed. "I'll get on it right away."

22

The following morning, I got up early to attend the beginners Irish class that my cousin Julie taught at the island elementary school. Unfortunately, I wasn't quick enough to sneak out of the house before Beth woke up, and she insisted on accompanying me.

"After all," she said loudly so everyone in the small classroom could hear, "Julie's my cousin too. And she did ask if I'd like to come along."

I gritted my teeth and exchanged an exasperated look with Günter, Julie's German boyfriend, who was taking the class with me. "The class started in October," I said to my sister. "You're not going to be able to follow."

"I have a natural affinity for languages," Beth replied primly. "After all, I communicate with people from all over the world on my YouTube channel."

"People who speak *English* with you," I pointed

out. "Have you ever been expected to speak French or Italian to any of your interviewees?"

My sister executed an elegant half-shrug. "I took language classes at community college. I could manage an interview in Spanish."

I doubted her Spanish extended beyond basic menu items. In the interests of harmony, I bit my tongue and kept my thoughts to myself.

"Good morning, everyone." Julie smiled at us from the front of the classroom. "We're going to start by looking at your homework, and then we'll jump into a vocabulary test on the various rooms in a house. Sound good?"

I'd just opened my homework notebook when the classroom door burst open and my old "friend," Sergeant O'Shea, bumbled in. Judging by the straining buttons on his police uniform shirt, the older police officer had already gotten into the festive spirit.

He scanned the room with glee. My stomach sank when he fixed his beady eyes on me. "Maggie Doyle, I'd like you to come and answer a few questions down at the station."

This statement was delivered with obvious relish, and I bristled at this intrusion into my private sphere. Nevertheless, I refused to give the man the satisfaction of knowing he'd gotten under my skin. I schooled my features into a neutral expression. "What's this about?"

His smug smile widened. "The shenanigans you were involved with yesterday."

"Are you referring to the bank robbery? If so, forty other people were involved in those *shenanigans*, including the five dudes who held up the bank with AR-15s. Any luck in tracking them down, by the way? Or is this dramatic entrance during my language class your way of tracing five armed and dangerous criminals?"

"Are you refusing to come to the station?" The guy sounded hopeful as if my unwillingness to cooperate would afford him pleasure.

"Don't get your skid-marked underpants in a bunch," I said, oh-so-subtly referring to an unfortunate encounter with Sergeant O'Shea's underpants during a previous case. "I'm always happy to assist with a police investigation."

"What's going on?" Beth's forehead formed a perfect frown as though she weren't aware of what had occurred yesterday. "You haven't found another body, have you, Maggie?"

"When would I have had the time? We've been together since the bank robbery. Do you recall me tripping over a corpse?"

"There's no need to get defensive. I'm not used to all this drama."

No, you're only used to creating drama. My sister's doe-eyed innocent act wasn't fooling me. Ignoring her, I shoved my books and pencil case into my backpack and grabbed my coat from the back of my chair. "I don't know how long I'll be. You'll have to find another ride back to the cottage."

"But what am I supposed to do all day on my own?" Beth opened her eyes wide and laid a predatory hand on Günter's arm. "Would you mind showing me around the island?"

My gaze slid to Julie, who was standing in front of the blackboard, chalk in hand. My cousin tensed, waiting to see how her boyfriend would react to being blatantly propositioned by a woman as stunning as my sister.

"Sure," Günter said blandly. "You're welcome to join Julie and me at the town hall. We promised her mother we'd help get the hall ready for the Christmas Eve pageant."

Beth pouted. "I'm not a pageant kind of person. I was hoping you'd give me a tour of the island."

Günter shrugged, unmoved by my sister's blatant attempt at manipulating him. "No can do. Pity you're not into pageants. We'll have fun."

Relief flooded Julie's face. We'd both seen how many men my sister had made fall at her feet when we were teenagers. Although I'd already slotted Günter into the good guy category, it was good to see him live up to my expectations. Even otherwise decent dudes tended to lose their heads in my sister's presence. Before I left to join Sergeant O'Shea, I winked at my cousin and mouthed, *He's a keeper.*

Outside the classroom, I rounded on the policeman. "Why do you want to talk to me? And why was it so important that you had to interrupt my class? I gave a full statement to Garda Conlan yesterday."

"You need to give a few more details about your involvement with the robbery and the murders in Galway."

"Seriously?" I jutted my jaw in defiance. "The police know I had nothing to do with the murders."

"We've established nothing yet." A self-satisfied smirk spread across the sergeant's fleshy face. "Except that your private investigation business keeps cropping up in our inquiries."

"Whatever about the Galway murders, how on earth can Movie Reel Investigations have anything to do with the robbery at the bank? I was there as a private citizen depositing the proceeds from my aunt's café. My business only got involved after the robbery when Aaron and Jennifer hired me to do some digging for their insurance claim."

"So you say." The older police officer's voice oozed complacence. "But you were on the scene when that woman was found dead. You were one of the first on the scene when the corpse in the Santa costume was discovered. And now you've been present at a bank robbery committed by a group of people dressed up in Santa Claus costumes. Plus your colleague is investigating embezzlement at a place called The Costume Emporium."

I opened my mouth to protest but shut it again. Sergeant O'Shea was waiting for me to incriminate myself. I couldn't risk saying anything he could twist to use against me. "I'm contacting my lawyer."

"Go right ahead, but you're not under arrest.

However, you might feel you need legal representation before long."

I glared at him but refrained from delivering the scathing retort that sprang to my lips. Unless he'd fabricated physical evidence against me, a tactic that not even the odious Sergeant O'Shea would stoop to, he was merely goading me. Holding my head high, I followed him out of the school building.

The police officer took great pleasure in escorting me to the squad car and gesturing for me to get into the back. "Ladies first."

"I prefer to take my own car," I said, daring him to force the issue.

The man's nostrils flared. "Suit yourself, but I'll follow you all the way to the station."

"Do whatever floats your boat." I turned my back on him and strode away.

His whistled off-key jig followed me to my car. Knowing he'd have to wait for me, I shot a quick text to Jennifer, asking her to meet me at the station. Even if I didn't think he'd invent evidence against me, I didn't trust the man. He was a master at twisting everything I said, and it was typical of him to pounce on me on a day when he knew my boyfriend wasn't on duty. Liam had been posted to Whisper Island earlier in the year to "ease O'Shea's transition to retirement," otherwise known as taking over as the de facto head of police on the island. O'Shea resented the younger officer's presence at what he considered to be *his* police station, and he took particular umbrage at Liam's insistence that he exerted himself and did some work instead of spending his days on the golf course.

When O'Shea and I entered the station, Sile Conlan was sitting behind a desk in the reception area. She raised an eyebrow in surprise when she saw me. "Hey, Maggie. I wasn't expecting to see you in here today."

I shot her superior officer a malevolent look. "That makes two of us. I wasn't expecting to be here, either."

Sile looked from me to O'Shea. Although she'd never said so directly, I knew Sile didn't think much of the elder police officer, and I'd heard from Liam that O'Shea delighted in making sexist remarks in her presence.

O'Shea led me toward one of the station's small interrogation rooms. When I entered the room, I sucked in a breath. Seated on one of the cheap plastic chairs was Inspector Craddock.

"Good morning, Ms. Doyle," he said with an edge to his tone. "Thank you for taking the time to join us."

I took a seat. "I'm always happy to help the police with their inquiries. I hope you're not in a rush because we'll be waiting for my solicitor to get here before I answer any questions."

Craddock's expression turned thunderous. "You've been brought here to voluntarily answer questions. You're not under arrest."

"Sergeant O'Shea forgot to mention the 'voluntarily' part when he marched me out of my language class." I crossed my arms over my chest and leaned back in my chair. "So yeah, we're waiting for my lawyer."

Ten interminable minutes later, a knock at the door indicated that our wait was at an end. Sile stuck her head around the door and addressed the older officers. "Jennifer Pearce is here to represent Maggie. Will I show her in?"

"Yes," O'Shea and Craddock said in unison before looking at one another in annoyance. Craddock was higher up the ranks than O'Shea, but Whisper Island Garda Station was O'Shea's territory. Sile obviously picked up on the tension, because she winked at me before ushering Jennifer into the room.

My lawyer friend was perfectly groomed in a maroon pantsuit and six-inch heels. "Good morning, Maggie." She nodded to the men. "*Gentlemen.*" The irony in her tone was plain for all to hear.

Jennifer took a seat beside me, smoothing invisible wrinkles from the front of her pants. "I'd like to know why my client has been brought in for questioning again. Has new evidence been brought to light connecting her with the murders in Galway?"

"Not exactly," Craddock began, "but her private investigation agency has been connected with three crimes over the last week."

"We've already established Maggie wasn't involved in either of the murders in Galway," Jennifer replied smoothly, "so I fail to see why you're here, Inspector Craddock."

The man's Adam's apple bobbed. I didn't like the guy, but unlike O'Shea, I didn't think he was incompetent at his job. He must have recognized the link between Jasper Ramsbottom and the Santa robberies.

"Did the information I passed on to Sergeant Reynolds help?" I asked sweetly. "Did Evan Manning have anything interesting to share about the missing cash at Dennehy's?"

Craddock's features stiffened. "I can't comment on an ongoing investigation, Ms. Doyle. I'm sure you understand."

Jennifer turned to me. "What information was this?"

"According to Lenny, the brand of Santa costume Jasper Ramsbottom was wearing when he died is one of The Costume Emporium's own brands. Lenny said each of their costumes has a unique serial code for quality control purposes. We passed this information on to the police. I also helped them locate Evan Manning, the guy we suspect helped Jasper Ramsbottom steal the cash."

"Did these helpful tips lead to your visit this morning?" Jennifer demanded. "If so, my client has a right to know if the information she shared with you bore fruit."

I doubted the legality of this statement, but it appeared to rattle Inspector Craddock.

"Evan Manning admitted he was a paid accessory

to the department store thefts," he muttered, "but he denies any further involvement with Jasper Ramsbottom and the counterfeit goods. He was serving customers at the time we suspect Mr. Ramsbottom was killed, so he's not a suspect in that case."

"What about the info about the costume serial numbers?" I demanded. "Did that result in a breakthrough?"

Inspector Craddock regarded me with an expression of loathing. I was unmoved by the man's dislike of me—the feeling was mutual.

"Jasper Ramsbottom purchased twenty identical Santa costumes from The Costume Emporium," the man said eventually. "Plus padding, masks, and festive sacks."

"In other words, my client passed on information that led to a breakthrough in your investigation." Jennifer's cool gaze pinned Craddock in place. "So why has she been brought in for questioning?"

The inspector shifted in his seat, a tense expression on his face. "I'd like to clear up a few inconsistencies in her statements."

"There are no inconsistencies in my statements," I snapped but shut my mouth when I felt Jennifer's arm press down on mine.

"My client is happy to cooperate with the police, but she isn't prepared to tolerate harassment. You've made it clear that you don't like my client, Inspector Craddock. If you have nothing concrete to connect

Ms. Doyle with either of the murders you're investigating, she and I bid you a good day."

Jennifer started to stand up, but Craddock held up a hand. "Wait. Look, I know Ms. Doyle and her assistant are asking questions about the murders. All I want to know is why."

I snorted. "Define 'questions.' We've discussed the murders, yes, and we have theories. However, I haven't questioned anyone since I left the department store on Wednesday evening."

"Then why did one of my officers see you talking to staff from Dennehy's yesterday?"

I raised an eyebrow. "I assume officers from your station were assigned to help out at yesterday's festival."

Craddock gave a slight inclination of his neck. "That's correct. One reported seeing you interrogate employees of Dennehy's department store."

"Your officer *saw* this?" Jennifer pounced on the description with enthusiasm. "Did he *hear* what was said, or did he simply assume that Maggie was using the opportunity to question her former colleagues?"

"Well…" An expression of discomfort flickered across Craddock's face.

"A few people I'd worked with at the store came over to the island for the festival," I said. "I didn't interrogate them, as you put it. Actually, they asked *me* questions because they'd discovered I'm a private detective and they were intrigued."

"Did they reveal anything useful about the murders?" Craddock asked, failing to feign disinterest.

"This is ridiculous. You didn't need to force me to miss a language lesson to ask me these questions. If you'd wanted to know what the Dennehy's crowd said to me yesterday, all you had to do was call me, Inspector. You have my phone number." I pushed my chair back and stood. "As far as I'm concerned, this interview is at an end. You're both using your positions as men in power to bully me, merely because you don't like me. What you want is a one-way exchange of information *and* an opportunity to goad me. That's not happening. If you want information my assistant and I gleaned as part of our investigations, get a court order."

On that merry note, I strode out of the room. I didn't stop walking until I reached the car park. When I arrived at my car, I slumped against the side, shaking. How dared those idiots try to incriminate me? I'd done nothing wrong. Okay, I'd snapped a few photos at the crime scenes, but about those, the police remained in blissful ignorance.

"Maggie, wait." Jennifer jogged to catch up with me.

I straightened my back, shoved my trembling hands into my coat pockets. "Those two are—"

"Any number of expletives in a variety of languages." Jennifer's smile was ironic. "I know you're angry, Maggie, but it's not wise to antagonize a man like Craddock. Unlike O'Shea, he's no fool, and he outranks Reynolds. Word has it he's very popular with the district superintendent."

"I don't care if Craddock is best friends with the chief commissioner," I said in an icy tone. "I know he sent O'Shea to haul me out of the classroom, fully intending to push the blame for the idea onto the man. O'Shea's a lousy actor. I saw how he reacted when the inspector tried to convince me that O'Shea had screwed up by not telling me I was being asked to voluntarily talk to the police. I don't trust Craddock. He's ruthless, and he wants a promotion. He sees cracking this case as his ticket to success."

"Perhaps the best thing for you to do under the circumstances is to share whatever you've discovered with him. Forcing him to get a court order will just annoy him and be a short delay."

"To be honest, Lenny and I don't know anything worth sharing that Craddock doesn't already know. The major piece of info was about the costume's serial number, and we passed that tidbit along to the police. I'd be more curious to see what Craddock has in his files."

Jennifer laughed. "I don't see that happening."

"No, but I can wish." I screwed up my forehead and replayed the scenario in the interrogation room. "It's time for me to start questioning the people who saw the Santa gang enter the bank. Liam, Lenny, and I came up with a plan of action last night, and we're due to pool our knowledge tonight. Want in on our brainstorming session?"

"I'd love to participate." The lawyer's controlled poise lapsed into a rare display of animation. "I must admit that working with you is more exciting than dealing with islanders' border disputes and drawing up wills."

This statement brought a smile to my lips. I'd often wondered how Jennifer tolerated the tedious work of a country solicitor's practice. "Okay. Swing by my place at seven this evening. I'll confirm the time with the guys. We can have dinner together, and I'll get you to taste test my new non-alcoholic Cherry Apple Punch recipe."

Jennifer laughed. "That sounds delicious. Why don't I collect takeout from the Chinese restaurant on my way? I have an insulated food box to keep it warm. Will Hannah and your sister be there?"

"No. Beth is dining with Con Ryder, and Hannah is staying overnight with Caoimhe Greer."

"Okay." The lawyer made a note on her phone. "I'll get enough food for the four of us."

"Perfect. Thanks, Jennifer." I opened the door to the Yaris and slid behind the wheel, fuelled by grim determination. "We're going to crack this case."

23

Before I started the engine, I sent Lenny and Liam text messages, confirming the time for our strategic brainstorming session and asking Liam to take Bran for his evening walk. After I pulled out of the police station parking lot, I headed down the main street of Smuggler's Cove and swung by the elementary school. I arrived just as the Irish class was getting out. My baser instincts wanted to dump Beth and leave her to her own devices, but she was my sister and my guest, however reluctant I was to acknowledge both facts.

Judging by her surprised expression when I beeped at her, my sister had also expected me to abandon her for the day. I rolled down the window, and she came over to the car.

She shivered in her fashionable taupe jacket that did little to ward off the chill sea wind. "Have you finished with the police already?"

I shrugged. "Looks like it. Want a ride? I can drop you somewhere."

"Sure." She opened the passenger door and slid onto the seat, placing her designer clutch on the floor between her feet. "I tried calling Con and Luke, but it went straight to voicemail. I guess they're busy touring the island."

I noted the wistful tone of her voice. "You truly want this role, don't you? What's the movie about, anyway?"

"It's about a woman who moves to Ireland to find her roots. Kind of like you."

"Is your character planning to open a private investigation agency?" I quipped. "If not, I doubt we have much in common."

"Touchy much?" Beth yanked her seatbelt into place. "Seriously, what is it you have against me? I'm making an effort here."

"You call being forced to spend Christmas with me 'making an effort?'" My grip on the steering wheel tightened, and I pulled out of the school parking lot. "Would you have bothered to contact me if you hadn't needed to come to Whisper Island for work?"

"Probably not," my sister said defiantly. "It's not like you *want* me here."

"Since when have you ever shown any inclination to hang out with me, Beth?"

"Why would I hang out with someone who doesn't like me? You've always made it clear that you find me dull and my interests ridiculous. Your expression when I told you I wanted to study cosmetology was priceless."

I swung the Yaris onto the coast road that would lead us to the first person on my witness list, switching on my windshield wipers to combat the light smattering of snowfall. "That is so not true. I didn't care what you studied. We don't have much in common, that's all."

"My whole life, you've looked down on me because I'm not as smart as you are." Beth's words lost some of their impact due to her lip-glossed pout. "How do you think it feels to be constantly defined by the way I look?"

"We're all defined by something. You just happened to have lucked out in the looks department."

"Looks don't last. Brains do. Why do you think I'm working so hard to make money while I can? If I can establish myself as an influencer in the makeup industry, hopefully I can start my own makeup brand one day."

"That's not a bad idea," I admitted, "but there's more to starting a makeup brand than knowing how to apply the products."

"I know that. I might not be as smart as you, but I'm not stupid. I'm taking a marketing class online. If I'm going to make this work, I only have a couple more years to establish myself. Once I hit thirty, it'll be harder to maintain my YouTube following."

I snorted. "Hey, I'm your sister, remember? You'll turn thirty next May, not in a couple of years."

"I mean my YouTube age. My viewers think I'm twenty-seven. Women in their teens and twenties are my demographic."

"Are viewers so fickle?" In spite of my natural aversion to my sister, I was curious. I knew nothing about the YouTube scene.

"Totally fickle." Beth's lips twisted into an ironic smile. "There's a reason I shaved two years off my age. I should have shaved more, but it's too late now."

We drove in silence for a few minutes, both lost in thought. My sister's anger had wrong-footed me. Did I judge her as harshly as she claimed? How would I have reacted if she'd reached out to me before I'd seen her visit to Ireland mentioned in the media and had the chance to feel slighted? The uncomfortable truth was that I didn't know. Depending on my mood, I might have said something snarky, and the conversation would have devolved into a fight.

"Oh, man." I slammed on the brakes and pulled over. "I forgot I was supposed to drop you somewhere. Where do you want to go? Back to my place?"

"Where are you going?"

I drummed my fingers lightly on the steering wheel. "I have to talk to a few people who witnessed the Santa gang go into the bank. Part of the investigation I've been hired to conduct for Jennifer and her boss."

"You're talking to witnesses?" Beth's sullen mood vanished. "Can I come with you?"

"No way. You're not an agency employee."

My sister gave me her wide-eyed, baby doll look. "Wouldn't bringing me make it more casual? I'm great at getting people to talk, particularly guys."

Yeah, I know you are. "I only have two men on this list, and I seriously doubt your charms will sway either of them into saying anything they wouldn't otherwise reveal." I was pretty certain Barry wasn't interested in women, and Paddy Driscoll was a grumpy old coot.

"Please, Maggie. What else do I have to do today?"

"You could take Günter up on his offer to help with the Christmas pageant preparations," I pointed out. "You seemed mighty keen to hang out with him earlier."

"He only has eyes for Julie." Beth delivered this statement with an air of surprise.

"I guess not every guy can fall at your feet." I restarted the engine and continued down the cliff-hugging road that led to the part of the island where I, Noreen, and Paddy Driscoll lived. The rough sea crashed against the rocks. If the Santa gang was crazy enough to take a boat out in this weather to collect their loot, they were in for a rough ride.

When we approached the entrance to Shamrock Cottages, Beth clutched my arm. "Please don't leave me here. I have no car, and I don't want to be stuck in the middle of nowhere all day."

"You can play with Mavis," I snapped. "You two seemed to get along last night."

"I like cats," my sister said simply, making me regret my sharp tone.

My foot lingered on the gas. Would having Beth with me be so bad? Her point about her presence making the interviews more natural wasn't entirely off base. I sighed. "All right. You can stick around."

My sister bounced in her seat, reminding me of Hannah. "Awesome. Thanks, Maggie. You won't regret it."

"Maybe I won't, but you might. Don't blame me if Paddy Driscoll sets his dogs on you. The guy's not exactly known for his hospitality."

My sister wrinkled her smooth forehead. "The name's familiar. Is he that farmer person that Noreen used to date?"

"Yeah, but don't mention him to her, okay?"

Beth's interest was piqued. "Why? Did it end badly?"

"Not exactly. They've been on and off for years, but Paddy recently started seeing Philomena's sister-in-law, Dolly O'Brien."

"Oh, my." Beth scrunched up her nose. "Is she the woman with the big hair who runs The Cupcake Café?"

"Yep. Right across the street from Noreen's place. So you can see why it's a sore subject."

Although the snow wasn't deep, Whisper Island's lone snow plow was responsible for the entire island.

Judging by the state of the road, this area hadn't received its attention for several hours. I drove at a slower pace than usual, passing fields bathed with white. By the time we reached the entrance to Paddy Driscoll's farm, it was past my usual lunchtime. I swung through the gates and drove up to the court-yard. Before I'd had the chance to kill the engine, Paddy's pack of dogs raced over to the car, barking and snapping their impressively sharp teeth.

Beth pressed her back into her seat. "They don't look friendly."

"Their owner isn't much better," I said in a dry tone. "He won't be rolling out the red carpet for us."

Alerted by the noise, Paddy's bulky figure loomed in his doorway. He glared at us before addressing his dogs. "Go on away with you, now," he roared. "Go back to your beds."

The animals stopped barking. Growling, they backed away from my car.

I opened my door. "We'd better hurry up in case they change their minds and decide we're their next meal."

Beth, whose side of the car was closest to the dogs, opted to scoot over to my side to get out. "This scene is straight out of a movie, and not one I want to star in."

"What do you two want?" Paddy snarled, stomping down the steps to meet us.

"My sister wanted to meet you," I improvised, rolling with the idea my sister had unwittingly given me. "She's researching for a movie role, and she needs to visit a genuine Irish farm to get the details right."

The man's eyes narrowed in suspicion. "Is that so? Of all the farms on the island, you happened to pick mine?"

"It's your charming personality, Paddy," I said, deadpan. "I described you to Beth, and she just had to meet you."

The grumpy farmer's lips twitched. "Is that so? In that case, we'll start with the cowshed."

The cowshed, while clean by farm standards, was not kind to our shoes. I gritted my teeth and resigned myself to an evening scrubbing mud and other substances from my winter boots.

Beth screeched when she stepped right into a pile of manure. "My new heels are ruined."

"Should have thought about that before you paid me a visit," Paddy grunted. "Add it to your list of details for that film of yours."

For the next thirty minutes, Paddy led us around the various farm buildings, not-so-secretly relishing Beth's facial expressions when she encountered more animal excrement and other delights. When we were visiting the horses, I broached the topic that had prompted my visit. "I hear you saw the bank robbers yesterday."

The farmer caught my eye and grunted. "So that's why you came sniffing around my farm. Are you investigating the case?"

"Aaron and Jennifer asked me to help speed up

their insurance claim." True, but not the whole story. "What did you see, exactly?"

Paddy shrugged. "A group of men dressed in Santa Claus costumes. Nothing you didn't already know."

"Are you sure they were all male?"

My question surprised the man. The grooves on his forehead deepened. "I assumed they were men."

"But you're not certain?" I pressed.

"They were wearing those silly outfits. Hard to tell a person's shape or size when they're decked out in that sort of rigmarole."

"Who was standing near you when you saw the Santas enter the bank?" I asked. "Anyone you knew?"

The farmer scratched his stubble and considered my question. "Tourists. No one I recognized."

"Can you describe them to me?" I pulled a pen and notebook from my purse.

"I wasn't interested in the tourists. All I wanted was to get to Murphy's Pub and have a pint with Stu Sheridan."

"So you can't think of anything that stood out about the people around you?"

The man's lip curled. "One of the girls had a tattoo on her neck. I don't like tattoos on women."

"In that case, remind me never to expose my butt to you," I said breezily, making Beth giggle.

"I've already seen your behind," the farmer said with a snort, "and I don't recall no tattoo."

Beth looked at Paddy and then me. "What on earth have you been doing, Maggie?"

"It's a long story. To summarize, the incident that saw me expose myself to half the population of Whisper Island involved a pair of split running pants and a mad chase after an escaping criminal."

"And I thought life in San Francisco was exciting. You guys live an exciting life."

"Was the girl with the neck tattoo about so high —" I indicated a height a couple of inches shorter than me, "—with short, peroxide hair? And was the tattoo a snake?"

The farmer drew his thick eyebrows together. "Yeah. The description fits."

"Do you know her?" Beth demanded.

I nodded. "I think so. Do you remember the woman in the red coat who was angling for an introduction to Con Ryder?"

"She shoved her card in my pocket." My sister pulled a face. "I'm not likely to forget *that* encounter."

"Tracey was on the island with several of her coworkers. One of them fits Paddy's description of the girl with the tattoo, and one of the guys they were with is on Liam's list of witnesses. It would make sense if Siobhan were with Barry when he saw the Santas go into the bank." I shifted my attention back to the farmer. "Do you remember anything else that struck you as odd?"

"Apart from six eejits in Santa outfits?" Paddy curled his lip. "No."

"Six?" Beth and I exclaimed in unison, our attention fixed on the farmer.

"Are you sure?" I demanded, my pulse picking up the pace. "There were only five Santas in the bank. Liam never mentioned a sixth when I spoke to him. Who took your statement?"

"Some young fool from the mainland. Garda Walsh, I think he called himself."

"Did you mention seeing six people in costumes?"

"He didn't ask me for a number." Paddy sounded belligerent. "How was I to know it was relevant?"

The farmer's assessment of Garda Walsh as a young fool was spot on. The guy needed a crash course in Witness Questioning 101. "Did you see the sixth Santa go inside the bank?"

"I wasn't interested in Santas," the man muttered. "All I wanted was to escape the crowd and have my pint of Guinness."

How could such a taciturn and bad-tempered specimen of manhood have two women at loggerheads over him? "Think, Paddy. What happened to the last Santa? Did you see him go into the bank, or did he go somewhere else?"

The man mumbled words under his breath that I was sure were uncomplimentary. "I don't know. Maybe one of them went around the back."

"Do you mean around the back of the bank?" I demanded. "As in the lane between the back of the bank and the fish factory?"

The farmer grunted. "Yeah. That direction."

My mind reeled. If the gang still had a sixth member, was Jasper not one of them after all? Had his role in the operation been confined to the counterfeit goods racket? Frankly, this scenario made more sense. In spite of dying in a Santa costume, I couldn't picture Jasper Ramsbottom holding up a bank. Maybe the gang's getaway driver had served a different purpose for the Whisper Island job. With no possibility of driving through the town after the robbery, perhaps the sixth gang member had hidden the cash in suitcases while his comrades changed out of their costumes. That would help explain how they'd gotten away before Lenny and I had reached the lane. I had to let Liam know the police needed to look for six people, not five.

"Thanks for talking to us, Paddy."

The man glowered at his unwanted guests. "I suppose you'll be wanting a cup of tea."

"No thanks." I slipped my notebook and pen back into my purse. "We need to make tracks."

His relief at getting rid of us was palpable. "Okay, then. I'll be seeing you."

"Hopefully in a parallel universe," Beth whispered as we made our way back to my car. "You weren't exaggerating about Paddy."

"Nope. He's a curmudgeonly old fart." I opened my door and slid behind the wheel. Within seconds, I'd gunned the engine, and we were off.

"Where to now?" My sister asked when we were back on the coast road.

"First up, we have two elderly ladies to visit. Mrs. Miles is a farmer's widow and lives twenty minutes from Paddy's place. Her sister-in-law is staying with her for the holidays. Apparently, they both saw the Santas enter the bank, but were even more vague on the details than Paddy was. I doubt we'll get more out of them than Sile Conlan did, but we can try."

"Where do we need to head after Mrs. Miles and her sister-in-law?"

I grimaced. "Nowhere I want to go. Melanie Greer is the next name on the witness list."

Beth whistled. "Ouch. Isn't she the one Paul cheated on you with?"

"Yeah, but I don't hold it against them." Not anymore, at any rate. "Melanie and I were never destined to be best buddies. She and Paul run the Whisper Island Hotel."

My sister grinned. "I didn't think I'd say this, but staying with you is turning out to be fun."

24

Mrs. Miles and her sister-in-law plied us with tea and gossip and shed no new light on the events of yesterday afternoon. They were lovely ladies, if forgetful and partially deaf, but the visit was a waste of time. Several stodgy shortbread biscuits later, Beth and I made our escape. Our next port of call was the Whisper Island Hotel.

"Please tell me Melanie won't force us to drink tea," my sister said in a mournful tone as we drove through the hotel's gates. "That black concoction Mrs. Miles served us was strong enough to fuel a car."

"The older islanders don't approve of weak tea, and they're even less tolerant of drinks containing coffee." I grinned at Beth's expression of horror. "Don't worry. Melanie can't stand me. I doubt we'll be offered a drink. If we are, she has a decent coffee machine in her office."

"I didn't see any sign of Paul when I was staying at the hotel," my sister mused. "Does he still work there?"

I snorted with laughter. "Allegedly. He's the manager, but Melanie has taken charge over the last year. Everyone who works there knows to go to her."

"So you guys are still at daggers drawn?"

I eased my foot from the gas pedal and pulled into the hotel's parking lot. "I wouldn't go that far. We'll never be friends, but we've reached an understanding of sorts."

In the year that I'd lived on Whisper Island, I'd had a reason to interact with Melanie during several of my investigations. The first involved the murder of her mother, which I'd solved and apprehended the culprit. Since then, we hadn't become friends, exactly, but we'd learned to tolerate one another. Her daughter's friendship with Hannah had helped to bridge the gap between us over the summer, but my glimpse at another side to Melanie disappeared as soon as Hannah left the island. Now that the girls were reunited, I was curious to see if Melanie's attitude toward me would soften. I'd never be the woman's number one fan, but she was a good mother, even to a daughter who reminded me of myself at that age.

Beth and I got out of the car and crossed the courtyard to the short flight of steps that led up to the hotel entrance. A smart doorman dressed in a top hat and tails greeted us when we entered the lobby. The Whisper Island Hotel was a five-star establishment, complete with spa facilities, a golf course, and an award-winning restaurant for which one of Lenny's brothers was the head chef. Although I'd worked here undercover for a few weeks during the spring, the hotel wasn't a place that I frequently visited. The restaurant, while delicious, was way out of my price range.

"Melanie's at the reception desk." My sister nodded her head in the direction of the polished wooden reception desk.

Sure enough, Melanie Greer was issuing orders to one of her minions, and consulting a printed list in her hand. She glanced up when we approach the desk, and her mouth tightened at the sight of me. She addressed my sister first. "Hello, Eliza. Nice to see you again. I hear you'll be joining us on Christmas Day."

"My whole family will, actually." Beth gave Melanie her most winning smile. "Con wants to meet my Irish relatives."

"How lovely." Melanie slid her gaze to me. "Hello, Maggie. I've been expecting you."

I raised an eyebrow. "You have?"

The other woman cast me a sardonic look. "I'm sure your boyfriend told you I saw the bank robbers yesterday. I figured you'd come sniffing around for information."

"Congratulations. You win the jackpot." I nodded in the direction of her office. "Seeing as we're cutting to the chase, can we go somewhere private to talk?"

Melanie smirked and finished giving instructions

to the receptionist before leading my sister and me into the office that was officially her husband's but in reality her domain.

Beth and I sank onto the plush leather chairs opposite Melanie's desk. Our host gestured toward the Italian coffee machine in the corner. "Can I offer you a cup of coffee?"

It was on the tip of my tongue to refuse, but my sister's acceptance of the offer of a latte was enthusiastic, so I relented. "An espresso, please."

After she'd served the coffees, Melanie took a seat. "I doubt I can tell you anything you don't already know. I was outside the bank at the time the robbers went in, but I was with my youngest child, and he was kicking up a fuss. I recall seeing several guys wearing Santa Claus costumes, but I was distracted, and I didn't pay that much attention."

I took a sip from my espresso before posing my first question. It was good. The changes Melanie had made to the manager's office were positive. "You say you saw several guys. How many, exactly?"

Melanie scrunched up her perfect forehead and considered my question. "There were five of them. No, six."

"Are you sure about the number?"

She nodded in a decisive fashion. "There were six Santas, but one of them left the others and went down the lane behind the bank."

This tallied with Paddy's statement. "You referred to the Santas as guys. Are you sure they were men?"

Melanie shook her head. "I used guys in the general context. I have no idea what gender they were. I assume the tallest ones were male, but it's hard to tell what people look like under padded suits and masks. I'm sorry I can't be more help. I like Joseph McCarthy. I'm sorry that he has to deal with the stress of a bank robbery right before the holidays."

"Did anything else strike you as out of the ordinary?" Beth asked, echoing a question I'd posed at Paddy Driscoll's farm.

"No," the hotel manager said. "If it had, I'd have included it in my statement to the police."

"You say you were with your kids. Did any of them see the Santas?"

"Just the youngest was with me," Melanie corrected. "Paul took our oldest son to Galway for the day, and my father-in-law went to the Cave of Sorrows with the twins. Damien is too small to give a statement. Anyway, he was too busy throwing a tantrum to notice what was going on around him."

I drained my espresso cup and placed it on the edge of the desk. "Thanks for the coffee and your time. I realize this is a busy time of year for you."

She smiled, the first proper smile she displayed since we'd been in the hotel. "I don't mind being busy. I like the holiday season, and so do the kids. Hannah's in the pool with Caoimhe and my mother-in-law at the moment. When my shift ends, we'll bake mince pies together."

"Sounds like fun."

I stood, and my sister followed my example. We shook hands with Melanie and said goodbye.

"I hear your pal Lenny will be dressing up as Santa for tomorrow's pageant," Melanie said when we reached the door of her office. "I can't believe Philomena asked him."

I shrugged, refusing to rise to the bait. Melanie would like nothing more than for me to show my fangs. "He has the costume," I said, keeping my voice neutral, "and Lenny's pretty good with kids."

"That's hardly surprising." The other woman's mouth curved into a sneer. "His maturity level is on par with a child's."

I started to give Melanie a piece of my mind, but my sister broke in before the fight had a chance to escalate. "I'm supposed to meet Mr. Ryder for dinner this evening. It doesn't make sense to go back to Maggie's place first. Do you have an opening at the beauty salon for a facial?"

Never one to miss an opportunity to make money, Melanie reverted to her professional demeanor. "I'll check our bookings right away, but I'm sure we can squeeze you in."

The receptionist, a brunette in her thirties, glanced up when we approach the desk. "I have a message for you, Ms. Donati."

Beth brightened at being addressed by her stage name. "Oh, yes? Who's it from?"

The receptionist consulted a sticky note. "Mr. Ryder called. He and Mr. Vaglietti won't be back until late tonight and have to cancel dinner. He said that you could go ahead and have dinner in the restaurant if you wanted and put it on his tab."

My sister's face fell. "I don't feel like eating on my own. What are your plans, Maggie? Do you want to join me?"

"Sorry, but no can do. I need to get back to my place." Her forlorn expression tugged at the heartstrings I didn't know I had. Maybe Beth was a good actress after all. "Oh, all right. You can tag along if you like."

"Thank you. Eating alone in a restaurant is awful."

I exchanged an amused glance with Melanie. "I can think of worse fates. Carl Logan's cooking makes up for a lot."

"I take it you won't be needing that facial appointment?" Melanie's sardonic gaze fixed on my sister.

"Not today," Beth said breezily. "I'm going to hang with my sister."

If I hadn't known my sister's enthusiasm for my company was only down to her lack of desire to be alone, I might have been flattered. "Come on then." I glanced at my watch. "I need to get going."

We trudged back to my car, navigating a path through the blanket of snow that had fallen since we'd entered the hotel.

"It's really starting to come down now," my sister remarked as we got into the car. "Do you think it'll stick? I've never experienced a white Christmas before."

Neither had I. Given the circumstances, I'd happily skip a snowy Christmas this year. "Conducting an investigation in the snow won't be fun."

"Perhaps not, but we could build a snowman."

Beth's childlike enthusiasm brought a smile to my lips. Before I could list the inconveniences of living in a remote cottage in a part of the island that rarely saw a snow plow, a figure strode onto the road without looking.

I slammed on the brakes to avoid a collision and sat on my horn. "Are you crazy?"

The woman who'd stepped in front of my car spun around, and our eyes met through the windshield window. Recognition hit me like a punch to the throat. I rolled down my window. "Siobhan? What are you doing here?"

She flushed, her reddening skin drawing attention to the snake tattoo on her neck, and shoved her large, gloveless hands into her jacket pockets. "Sorry, Maggie. I wasn't paying attention to where I was going."

"No problem. I'm surprised to see you still on the island. I thought you'd gone back to Galway yesterday.

"No. Derek treated me to a night at the hotel." Siobhan glowed with pride. "He even booked me a massage."

I recalled the neckless biker in the vacation

photos Siobhan had shown me at Dennehy's. A night at a five-star hotel and a massage at its award-winning spa seemed expensive for a guy who was out of work. At least, I'd assumed Derek was unemployed because Siobhan had been vague about what her boyfriend did for a living. "That's sweet," I said diplomatically. "Did the others stay overnight on the island, too?"

She shook her head. "No. Tracey and Barry caught the last ferry home."

"Hey, did you hear about the bank robbery?" I kept my tone breezy and casual. "My boyfriend said Barry had to give a witness statement."

"Oh, yeah? Wow." Her surprise came a second too late to be convincing. Siobhan was not destined to score a role in Tracey's movie.

"You didn't happen to see guys running around in Santa costumes near the bank? I'd imagine they were hard to miss."

"Uh, maybe." Her flush was back in force, the redness stretching all the way to the roots of her short, peroxide hair. "I might have seen a guy in a costume."

The woman's discomfort at my questions was screamingly apparent, but I pressed her all the same. I needed her to clarify a point. "Just the *one* guy?"

"Yeah." Her assertion held conviction. "He didn't go into the bank, though. I saw him disappear into a lane. Maybe he had nothing to do with the robbery. A lot of people are wandering around dressed as Santa these days."

"A lot" was an exaggeration, but I let it slide. "Could be. Are you heading home later?"

"Huh?" Siobhan rapid-blinked, and hesitated before responding. "Yeah. I just need to finish packing." She ran a hand over her woolen hat and her face clouded in confusion, as though she'd forgotten she was wearing it and was expecting to feel hair underneath her fingers. "I'd better get back."

"Sure." I smiled at her and started to roll up my window. "Have a good Christmas, Siobhan."

"You, too, Maggie."

I kept an eye on Siobhan in the rear view mirror after I'd pulled away. She stood still, staring after my car. "That was weird."

"I'll say," Beth said. "Why was she lying?"

I snuck her a curious look before I returned my attention to the road. "What made you think she was lying?"

"The whole thing about needing to pack. It's nearly six o'clock. Even if she and this Derek person were planning to leave the island on an evening ferry, they should have checked out by ten this morning. The hotel will keep cases for guests after checkout time, but Siobhan would have needed to pack her case beforehand."

"Well spotted," I said, reluctantly impressed. "Maybe we'll make a detective out of you after all. Did you notice anything else strange?"

My sister considered my question for a minute and then shook her head. "What did I miss?"

"Siobhan was walking away from the hotel, not toward it. No way was she planning to go back and pack a case."

Beth sucked in a breath. "Of course. Why did she lie to you? Was she telling the truth about only seeing one Santa?"

"I'm not sure. I believe her when she said she saw one of them enter the lane behind the bank, but I don't know if she was telling the truth about not noticing the others. The only reason for her to lie to us is if she knows something about the robbery." We drove through the hotel gates, and I swung the Yaris onto the road that led back to my cottage, pressing my foot down and coaxing the car to perform a half-hearted acceleration. "I need to talk to Liam and Lenny. I'd like to know more about Siobhan's boyfriend."

My sister bounced in her seat. "Do you think he's involved in the robbery?"

"I don't know. Apart from Siobhan acting shifty, we don't have a lot to go on. From things she's said, Derek is flash with the cash but doesn't appear to have a discernible source of income. He's worth checking out."

Beth sighed. "I never thought I'd say this, but I'm glad Con and Luke stood me up. I don't want to miss a second of your investigation."

"Trust me, life on Whisper Island isn't always this exciting. Frankly, I'm looking forward to peace and quiet in the new year."

My sister regarded me with a shrewd expression. "No way. You love the excitement. You'd go crazy if you were stuck trailing cheating spouses all the time."

"You might have a point," I conceded at the same moment my stomach rumbled. "You hungry?"

She nodded. "I could eat."

"Awesome. Let's go back to my place and eat Chinese. Solving crimes can wait a while."

25

When we reached Shamrock Cottages, I slowed the vehicle and drove through the open gates. Lenny lounged on the bench in front of my house, chatting to Jennifer. A large food box sat between them, and Bran lay at their feet. In anticipation of the Chinese, my mouth began to water. I pulled into my parking space and cut the engine.

"I didn't realize you'd invited visitors," Beth said in a stiff tone. "I don't want to intrude."

Gah. In my preoccupation with all I'd learned today, I'd forgotten to mention the brainstorming dinner to my sister. "Look, I don't want a fight. You're welcome to have dinner with us, but we arranged to meet to discuss the case. We're going to need time alone after we eat."

"You want me to hide out in my room?" Beth bristled. "I'm not a gossip, Maggie."

This was true. My sister was shallow and sometimes bitchy, but I couldn't recall her spreading rumors.

"Besides," she added, "I was with you when you talked to your list of witnesses. I might remember something you forgot to write down."

I doubted that, but I didn't want to hurt her feelings. "Okay, but I'm serious about you keeping quiet about anything we discuss. This is real life, not a situation you can milk for your acting career."

"You don't want me blabbing to Con and Luke." Beth slid out of the car and closed the passenger door. "I get it. But can I make a suggestion?"

A wary sensation settled on my shoulders. "Sure."

"Can I participate? As an outsider, I might have an observation you guys won't think of. And if I go into my room or the living room, I'm going to hear every word you say anyway."

"I'll see what Liam says," I said noncommittally. She had a point. The interior walls of my cottage were thin and didn't exactly lend themselves to privacy. If Beth was going to eavesdrop, intentionally or not, she might as well sit at the table with the rest of us.

Lenny unfurled his skinny body from the bench and stood. "Yo, ladies. How's it going? Liam's hopped under his shower, Maggie." He patted the dog on the head. "I guess taking Bran for a run wore him out."

From Lenny's animated expression, he had news. Hopefully, Liam did, too. I turned to Jennifer.

"Thanks for picking up the food. Is it okay if my sister joins us?"

"Sure." Jennifer smiled at Beth. "It'll be nice to talk to you in a non-dramatic situation."

"Yeah. I'm still freaked out after yesterday." My sister shuddered as if to illustrate the point.

I unlocked my front door and we all trooped inside. Five minutes later, a freshly showered Liam arrived, and we set up camp at my kitchen table. My boyfriend helped me to serve the Chinese food that Jennifer had brought with her, and I warmed up a pot of my non-alcoholic Cherry Apple Punch.

"Beth wants to sit in on our meeting," I murmured under my breath, "and I can't think of an excuse to get rid of her."

"As far as I'm concerned, she can stay. I'm not bringing up any gory details or anything that could derail the investigation if shared." His mouth quirked in amusement. "Besides, if we don't tell her, she'll pull a Hannah and eavesdrop."

I laughed. "Probably. I'll try to be discreet, but I want us to come up with actionable ideas. I hate the idea of waiting around for the police to haul in Lenny and me for yet another round of questioning."

Liam dropped a kiss on my cheek. "It'll be okay, Maggie. Gavin's a good cop, and Craddock has a strong reputation."

"I wish they'd hurry up and catch the killers soon."

He raised an eyebrow. "You're still convinced one of the Santas murdered Cara and Jasper?"

"Yeah. It's the only thing that makes sense."

"Oy, you two," Lenny yelled from the table. "Stop yapping and get over here. I'm starving."

"So am I," Beth said, eyeing the containers of Chinese food with interest. "I feel like I haven't eaten in days."

"That's what you get for picking at your food," I said. "Screw the movie role. You've got to eat."

When everyone was seated and had a plate of food and a mug of punch, I addressed the group. "Thanks for coming, everyone. After Sergeant O'Shea's unwelcome intrusion this morning, and Inspector Craddock's unexpected visit to the island, I thought it was time we put together an action plan. I'm not willing to sit around and wait for the police to pin the crimes on Lenny and me."

"To be fair," Liam interjected, "I don't think that's their intention. Craddock is an unpleasant fellow, but he's an honest police officer, and he'll want to arrest the right people."

"Why is he convinced that Lenny and I are connected to the Santa gang?" I demanded. "Because that's the impression I'm getting. If we were involved with the bank robbers, we'd hardly share the information about the costume serial numbers with police."

"You know how it goes, Maggie," Jennifer said. "Some criminals love to get involved in the police investigation. We believe you and Lenny are innocent, but Craddock sees your connection to the two murder victims, and you were both present at a bank robbery commissioned by the gang he suspects killed Cara Mackey and Jasper Ramsbottom."

I swallowed a forkful of food. "Let's take turns in filling one another in on what we discovered today. I'll go first."

I provided them with a summary of my visits to Paddy, Mrs. Miles, and the Whisper Island Hotel, and finished with a detailed account of my strange meeting with Siobhan.

"So there were six Santas." My boyfriend scribbled a note on the piece of paper next to his plate. "And one waited in the lane behind the bank to assist the others to make a quick getaway with the loot."

"That's my guess."

"Did you speak to that Barry guy you worked with?" Lenny asked. "Wasn't he on your list of people to question?"

"I tried, but his phone went straight to voicemail. I left a message. Hopefully, he'll call me this evening." I turned to Liam. " What do we know about Cara? Has your brother shared any information with you about her?"

My boyfriend hesitated for a moment. "It goes without saying that anything we discuss goes no further, right?" He looked around the table. "We're all agreed on that?"

Everyone murmured their assent, and Beth leaned forward, her avid curiosity palpable.

"Okay, here's what I know." Liam leaned back in his seat. "Contrary to Maggie's assumption, Gavin hasn't shared many details about his investigation with me. However, I did some digging in our database, and called in a few favors from friends on the force."

I took a sip of my punch and leaned forward, eager to learn more. "What did you find out?"

"Cara Mackey was a known con woman and a convicted shoplifter. She allegedly had a relationship with Jasper Ramsbottom, but I don't know if that was still going on at the time she died. What everyone agrees on is that while Cara was involved in plenty of illegal activities, there's no record of her ever being party to violence."

"What about Jasper?" I asked. "Did he have a criminal record?"

Liam shook his head. "He was questioned about a few of the scams that Cara was involved in, but the police couldn't pin anything on him. He might not have been a criminal mastermind, but he was a slippery fellow all the same."

"What about the Evan guy Maggie and I saw on the surveillance footage?" Lenny asked. "The police must've caught up with him by now."

"Oh, I haven't had a chance to talk to you about that," I said. "When Craddock spoke to me this morning, he said that Evan admits to being a paid accessory to the missing cash, but denies more involvement."

"Do we believe him?" Jennifer asked.

I shrugged. "Nothing links him with the counterfeit goods scam or the Santas. And if Evan's involvement was just to help Cara and Jasper steal money from the store," I added, "there's no reason to assume he had anything to do with the gang. From the conversation Jasper had with the masked guys during our stakeout, it was clear Jasper and Cara's cash grab wasn't part of their plans."

"You saw the masked men at the department store," Liam remarked, "and you saw the robbers in the Santa costumes. Did they look similar to you?"

I pulled a face. "I've considered that, but I can't say. The leader of the Santa gang certainly had a similar swagger to the Del guy who threatened Jasper, but the padding under their costumes made it difficult to be sure. What do you think, Lenny?"

"Same as you," my friend said. "I've gone back over the scenario in the store, but I can't even say if the masked guy called Del was the leader of the Santas. That Santa made an effort to change his voice to a sort of growl in the bank."

"Was his accent similar to Del's?" Jennifer asked. "Did they both come from around here?"

Lenny tugged on his straggly goatee and contemplated her question. "I'd say both the leader of the Santas and Del were probably from the Galway area."

"Is that the guy who held me at gunpoint?" Beth demanded. "When you catch up with him, I want to give him a piece of my mind."

"I don't think that's wise," I said dryly, "although I

appreciate the sentiment." I turned back to Liam. "Has your brother mentioned tracking down Del?"

He shook his head. "They're still looking."

"What about you, Lenny? You said you were going to look for people named Del around the Galway area."

"I've done a thorough search for everyone called Del, Dale, and Derek. Unfortunately, that gives me a long list to work with, and I haven't had a chance to narrow it down yet."

"Derek?" Beth and I chorused.

Lenny blinked at us, taken aback. "Well, yeah."

"Why are you looking for people named Derek?" I demanded. "I can see why you'd check for Dale in case we misheard, but I don't see how you came up with Derek as an option."

"Maybe it's not common in the U.S., but Del is a nickname for Derek," Liam explained. "It's more usual in the U.K., but it's used here as well."

"Del is short for Derek?" I drew in a breath. "Siobhan's boyfriend is named Derek. That's why Beth and I were so surprised when you mentioned the name."

Liam jerked to attention. "Siobhan who works at Dennehy's?"

"Yes," Beth said, her excitement rising. "And Siobhan told Maggie that she and Derek spent the night at the Whisper Island Hotel."

Liam leaped to his feet, sliding his phone from his pocket in the process. "I'll call the station and get them to watch the ferry. Maybe Siobhan and Derek are still on the island. If not, my brother and Craddock can look for them in Galway. Did you see Derek when you met the Dennehy's crowd outside the Movie Theater Café?"

"No, but Siobhan she mentioned their plans to meet him down by the harbor."

"Do you know his surname?" Lenny asked, pulling his laptop out of his backpack.

"No, but Siobhan's name is Prescott. Maybe you can find him through her social media profiles."

Several tense minutes later, Lenny looked up from his laptop screen, a beam on his bony face. "I've got it. Siobhan's boyfriend is called Derek Michael Riordan."

"You're a genius." I scribbled the name down on a piece of paper and showed it to Liam, who was still on the phone to Gavin.

While Liam spoke to his brother, I warmed up more punch and Beth and Jennifer cleared the table. Lenny had located a box of Christmas chocolates, and I refilled everyone's punch mug.

Bran, sensing the presence of more food, slunk into the kitchen, a hopeful expression on his face.

"Can I give him a doggy biscuit?" Beth's eyes grew round as saucers. "He likes when I do that."

I suppressed a smile. My sister loved being adored. Part of the thrill of feeding Bran treats was reaping the rewards of his enthusiasm. "All right," I said, "but just one."

"I know I wasn't much help, but today has been fascinating." Beth reached for the chocolate box and selected a coconut-covered truffle.

"I hope the information helps crack the case," I said, noting the wistful tone of my voice. If our brainstorming session helped to catch the Santas, I'd be glad, but I had to admit I was disappointed to be on the sidelines while the police were in on the action.

I was on my second chocolate when Liam returned to the kitchen, a broad grin on his face. "Derek Riordan is on Gavin's list of people to question. Riordan has previous convictions for home invasion and the armed robbery of a petrol station, but until today, the police had nothing to link him with Jasper Ramsbottom or Dennehy's department store. They're on their way to bring him in for questioning."

"Oh, awesome." I high-fived my friends. "Good job, guys. By the way, does this other case have anything to do with a strangulation? Your brother and Craddock acted mighty strange when I asked them if Cara was the only strangulation victim they'd encountered recently."

"Yes, as a matter of fact. A docks worker was found strangled in his work hut a few weeks back. The only clue the police found was fibers that match the Santa costumes that Lenny's costume place makes.

"Wow." Beth looked impressed. "You're good at this, Maggie."

"You were pretty good to notice the discrepancies in what Siobhan told us," I pointed out.

"Will Gavin keep us updated?" Jennifer asked.

"Yes, if he finds Derek. Sile and Sergeant O'Shea are in charge of looking for him on the island. With Hannah staying overnight at the Greers' house, I said I'd help." Liam's eyes met mine. "We'll want to talk to Siobhan as well. Do you think she's involved?"

"I don't know. She was acting shifty today, but I don't recall noticing that before. She was moody and taciturn, but my coworkers said she's always like that."

"Before I head—" my boyfriend glanced at his watch, "—Gavin said you and Lenny were allowed back into his brother's apartment to get the rest of your stuff. You'll need to collect your phones and laptops from his station."

Lenny perked up at this news. "Awesome. I feel naked without all my gear. Want to head over tomorrow, Maggie?"

"Don't you need to stick around and dress up as Santa for my aunt's pageant?" I teased.

My friend shuddered. "Yeah, but she doesn't need me until four o'clock. If we catch a morning ferry, we'll be back in plenty of time."

"Why don't you check the timetable and let me know when we should meet?"

Lenny nodded. "Sounds good."

"I'd better get going. I'll keep you updated when I get a chance." Liam kissed me on the cheek and ruffled my hair. "Later, Miss Maggie."

"I should get home and wrap holiday presents,"

Jennifer said, standing up from her chair. "Do you need a lift, Lenny?"

"Would you mind? Granddad dropped me over here earlier."

"No problem," the lawyer said, then turned to me. "In case I don't see you before then, will you let me know the time for Christmas dinner?"

"Sure. I'll call you as soon as Beth's director dude confirms the time."

After our guests had left, Beth lingered in the hallway. She twisted a lock of hair and shot me a questioning glance. "I guess I'll go read in my room."

I shifted my weight from one leg to the other. "Uh, yeah. I guess I'll do the same."

Beth paused for a moment. "Okay, then." She opened the guest room door, and Mavis and my other two cats shot in before her.

After the guest room door closed behind my sister, I stood in the hallway for a long time, Bran by my side. Should I knock and ask her if she wanted to watch a movie? Maybe offer her one of my holiday cocktails? I hovered indecisively for several minutes before finally going into my room and resigning myself to a restless night.

26

I set my clock for early the following morning. Lenny and I had arranged to meet at Carraig Harbour in time to catch the eight-thirty ferry to Galway, and I needed to take Bran out for a walk before I left.

The instant I emerged from my bedroom dressed in my winter running clothes, Bran leaped out of his basket and bounded over to me, whining. I leaned down and scratched his ears. "Time for our run, buddy?"

He barked in approval and tugged at the leash that was hanging on a hook by the door.

I laughed. "You know how this works, don't you, boy?"

"Can I come with you guys?"

I whirled around at the sound of my sister's voice. "Hey, Beth. You're up early."

"Since I started running with Luke, I've gotten

used to waking earlier. So can I come with you? I need to burn off those chocolates from last night."

Eyeing Beth's enviably slim figure, I doubted a couple of chocolates would make any difference, but refusing her request would be rude. "Fine by me, but Bran and I like to run fast."

She jutted her jaw. "I can do fast. I've been training with Luke, and he runs ultramarathons."

"Okay," I said with a shrug. "But you'd better hurry. I need to get back in time to catch the eight o'clock ferry."

By the time Beth had changed into her running gear, Bran was ecstatic to get going.

"Whoa," I said when I stepped outside. "I didn't expect this much snow."

White flakes fluttered down on us in a light snow-fall, but covering on the ground was noticeably higher than it had been yesterday.

"Can we run in this?" My sister regarded the snow dubiously. "I don't want to fall on my face."

"We can take it slow and see how we go," I suggested. "If you don't feel comfortable, we can always turn back."

Beth held her nose high. "I'm no coward. Come on. I'll race you."

The road outside Shamrock Cottages was thick with snow. Thank goodness I had the option of walking to catch the ferry from Carraig Harbour. I hadn't taken a lot of stuff with me to Galway, so there wasn't much for me to collect from Lenny's brother's apartment. If I took a large backpack, and a carrier bag for my laptop, I should have enough space for everything.

I pointed right and Beth followed my cue. "This is one of my favorite running routes. We'll cross a few fields and then go through a small wood."

"Sounds lovely."

While we ran, it was easy to forget my grievances with my sister and enjoy the shared experience of running outdoors.

"You're pretty fit," Beth said when we stopped to catch our breath after a particularly challenging hill.

I laughed. "Don't sound so surprised."

"I didn't mean it like that. I like jogging, but I usually do it on a treadmill. Luke's the one who loves to run outdoors."

I took a long drink from my water bottle. "What's the deal with you and Luke? Are you serious about him?"

To my surprise, my sister's cheeks turned pink. "I don't know. I mean, maybe? I'm not sure how he feels about me."

I smothered a laugh. "He looked pretty smitten when I saw you two together the other day."

Her face lit up. "Do you think so? It's so hard to tell with guys sometimes, especially the strong silent type like Luke."

"Do you go running with him often?"

"Depends on where we are. Over the last few months, I've been followed by paparazzi. I can't go anywhere looking less than perfect. Photos you see of celebs running with their trainers are staged, you know."

"That doesn't surprise me, but it reinforces my belief that it's no life for me."

"I knew what I was getting into when I started the channel," Beth said. "I couldn't be sure it would be a success, but that was the goal. And fame has its advantages. I have more money than I ever dreamed of, and I'm getting to visit places I never dreamed I'd see."

"But do you really get to see them? Or is it just one hotel room after another?"

"It's a lot of hotel rooms, sure, but I've done shoots in the desert and other far-flung places. Where possible, I've tried to add on time for vacation. But of course, it doesn't always work."

"I'd hate to be recognized everywhere I went," I said, turning my gaze to the blissfully deserted landscape. "I like my privacy."

"But aren't you recognized all the time living in such a small place?" Beth asked. "Everyone seems to know you."

Was it my imagination, or did she sound wistful? Why would my sister yearn for a simpler life like mine? She'd always wanted fame, and now she had it. "I guess most people know me by now. The population's not exactly huge, and my private investigation agency is a novelty." I paused. "Plus I have my stellar reputation as a dead-body magnet."

This made my sister laugh. It was probably the first time in many years that I'd heard her utter anything other than the fake titter that drove me crazy.

Bran barked at us, impatient to get moving again. Beth and I settled into a slow run that left us with enough breath to talk.

"So how does your blogging venture work?" I asked.

"Strictly speaking, I'm what's known as a vlogger. I have a YouTube channel, and I review makeup products and do tutorials for people interested in learning how to copy catwalk looks."

"I guess going to beauty school paid off, after all."

"Yeah. I would've been happy to work as a makeup artist on fashion shows or for a movie studio, but it's a hard industry to break into. I started my channel as a side hustle while I was working at Sephora."

"If you earn enough money over the next couple of years to retire, would you do it?"

Beth screwed up her nose. "And do what every day? I need a purpose. I don't have kids, and I probably never will. I don't want to sit around twiddling my thumbs for the rest of my life. If I get the money together, I'll work on launching my makeup brand."

Talking to my sister about our respective goals felt surreal. Until she'd brought up the topic of launching her own makeup brand, it had never occurred to me that Beth had ambitions beyond painting her face. But then, how well did I know my sister? We hadn't spoken more than a few words to each other in years, and before that, we had a strained relationship that didn't lend itself to sharing confidences.

"What about you? Are you happy on Whisper Island? You seem to have settled down here. No regrets about moving?"

"Absolutely none," I said with conviction. "Moving here was the best decision I've ever made, and opening my agency was the second best. It sounds strange to say, but I feel at home here in a way that I never did in San Francisco."

"I get that," Beth said. "I feel more at home in an anonymous hotel room than I ever did at Mom and Dad's house."

In spite of my strained relationship with my parents, this revelation surprised me. "But you were always their favorite."

"Being the favorite child isn't all it's cracked up to be," she said, wrinkling her nose. "They put a lot of pressure on me to succeed because I wasn't pursuing a career they'd mapped out for their children. I felt that if I didn't make it big, it would all have been for nothing. I envied you because you didn't have that same level of pressure."

"That's so not true," I protested. "Mom and Dad started talking about my police career before I could talk. They assumed I'd follow their footsteps, and that included rising in the ranks like Mom."

"And making a suitable marriage," Beth said softly. "For what it's worth, I never liked Joe."

"You're not the first person to tell me that. I just wish people had said it before I married him."

Beth smiled. "Would you have listened? You were proud of marrying a guy Mom approved of. She saw it as a way for you to get ahead in the police department."

"I know. But I've never been great at taking orders or at kissing butt. In my experience, both are requirements for promotion."

"Whereas my job requirements are to eat as little as possible, drink as much as possible—but only if it's water—and schmooze with online stars whether or not we have anything in common. Trust me, hanging with celebs, in real life or online, isn't all it's cracked up to be. The competition is fierce, and you're only as good as your last month's stats."

"Are you serious about wanting to be an actress?" I asked. "Like, do you enjoy the process of standing in front of the camera and pretending to be someone else?"

Beth laughed. "What do you think I do for my video tutorials? That's performance art, too. Even if I'm having a lousy day, I have to pretend I'm on top of the world and engage with my fans. I don't know if I'll enjoy working on the movie, but it's another way to get my name out there. Who knows? Maybe the movie will lead to more roles. It's worth a shot."

"I hope it works out for you." To my surprise, I

meant it. I didn't hate my sister. I never had. I just didn't understand her, and I wrestled with my feelings of jealousy and resentment. I recognized those emotions for what they were, but it didn't make it any easier to get past them.

"If acting doesn't work out, I'll fast forward my plan to launch my brand."

I pointed at the cottage ahead of us. "You want to turn back? Were almost at Noreen's house."

My sister nodded. "Okay. But only if I can race you."

"It's a deal. Ready, set, go."

We took off. Our progress was hampered by the snow, but the resistance under our feet only served to motivate us to push on. By the time we reached the gates of Shamrock Cottages, we were both breathing hard. I beat my sister to my door by a second, and Bran congratulated us both with enthusiastic licks.

Beth bent down to pet him. "He's a sweet dog. I'd love to get a puppy, but it wouldn't be fair. I'm not home enough."

I unlocked the door, and we went into my cottage. I glanced at my watch. "Is it okay if I hit the shower first? I need to hurry."

My sister glanced up from untying the laces of her running shoes. "Go for it. I'm at a loose end until nine. Con and Luke are collecting me, and we're going to discuss the movie script over coffee."

I showered and dressed fast. While I was drying my hair in my room, my sister took her shower. She emerged from the bathroom in a haze of fog just as I was pulling on my winter coat. "Here's the hairdryer in case you need one that's compatible with Irish voltage," I handed her the appliance.

"Thanks, Maggie. I got a text from Con. It seems Philomena persuaded him to go to her pageant this evening, so I guess I'll see you there."

I laughed. "You'll get to see Lenny wear his beloved padded suit under his Santa costume. He's been looking forward to trying that out."

My phone buzzed with an incoming call. Frowning, I glanced at the display. "Hey, Liam. What's up?"

"Hi, Maggie. I'm at the station. The Greers have agreed to keep Hannah with them until the pageant. Apparently, your aunt has found her a small, last-minute role to play. Hannah's thrilled."

"Sweet." That was just like Philomena. When Julie got around to having babies, her mother would make an awesome grandmother.

"But I'm not calling about the pageant." His voice had sobered. "Gavin and Craddock got a tip that Derek Riordan and his brothers returned to the house they share in the early hours of the morning. One of the brothers, Danny, got careless. We found his fingerprint on the Dumpster in the lane behind the bank, and we assume Derek's three brothers are members of the Santa gang. The police are about to storm their house and arrest them."

"Wow. Good work, Liam."

"Thank *you*. You and Lenny gave us a name to

work with. Anyway, I just wanted to let you know before you head to Galway."

"I appreciate it. I'll see you later." I blew him a kiss down the phone and disconnected.

I slipped my phone into my coat pocket and put on my hat, scarf, and gloves.

"Before you go, can you show me where you keep your coffee grinder?" my sister asked from her doorway. "I meant to ask you yesterday, but I forgot."

"Sure. It's in the cabinet next to the fridge, middle shelf."

"Thanks." My sister disappeared into the kitchen. A moment later, she emitted an ear-piercing scream.

I dropped my purse and raced into the room. "What's the matter?"

Wordlessly, my sister pointed at the window that overlooked my small backyard. Sunrise was making a feeble attempt to penetrate the heavy clouds, and an eerie blue light illuminated the snow-covered yard. But the sight that met my eyes was eerier still. Propped up on a garden chair, several stab wounds in his chest, sat the lifeless body of Derek Riordan.

27

I swore under my breath. So much for Gavin and Inspector Craddock's house siege.

"He's dead," my sister wailed, pointing at the corpse in my backyard.

"Looks like it."

I squeezed my eyes shut. Seriously, why did these things always happen to me? Why couldn't someone else find dead bodies all the time? Okay, time to put a period on my self-pity party. Lingering wouldn't make my next task any more pleasant.

I opened my eyes and squared my shoulders. "I'd better check him for a pulse. The cops like that kind of thing, even if the victim was a murdering scumbag."

"What?" Beth's jaw descended. "Do you know this guy?"

"Yeah. You do, too." I paused in front of the

backdoor and regarded my sister. "The dead dude is Derek Riordan."

"The man who held a gun to my head?" Her voice rose to a crescendo.

"Probably the man who held a gun to your head," I amended, "but it's a very high likelihood that they're one and the same."

After I'd replaced my warm gloves with a pair of my ever-present disposables, I slid shoe covers over my boots. Once I had my makeshift detection kit at the ready, I stepped outside into my snow-covered yard. The white flakes were falling fast, heavier now than they had been during our run. With one snow plow to service the entire island, and my side of the island a low priority, I had no idea how emergency services would make it through.

I hunkered down in front of the chair and examined the corpse. The dead man's white face was frozen in an expression of horrified disbelief. Whoever had killed Riordan had taken the guy by surprise. Gingerly, I touched his cold flesh and felt for a pulse, but I didn't need a medical degree to know that rigor was well advanced.

Neither my sister nor I had gone into the kitchen before our showers, and we'd had no reason to go out to the yard. Judging by the condition of his body, Riordan had been killed before Beth and I woke up this morning. Why was the man at my place during the early hours of the morning? Had he planned to hurt me? And who had killed him?

Taking care not to move the body, I studied him from every angle. His attacker had stabbed him multiple times in the chest and abdomen. From the direction of the blows, it looked as if his killer had struck while Riordan was sitting, and there were no signs of defensive injuries. This presented two possible scenarios: either Riordan had known and trusted his killer, or he'd been taken by surprise.

I slipped off one of my gloves and retrieved my phone from my pocket. Liam's number went straight to voicemail, so I tried the number for the station.

When the unwelcome voice grunted down the line, my stomach sank. "Whisper Island Garda Station. Sergeant O'Shea speaking."

"This is Maggie Doyle. I'd like to speak to Sergeant Reynolds."

A long silence. "Sergeant Reynolds is *working*, Ms. Doyle. In case you've forgotten, we have a bank robbery to investigate."

"I know, but—"

"Stop wasting taxpayers' money with your social calls." The lazy lump disconnected, leaving me to a chorus of static beeping.

For the second time that morning, I swore, not caring if anyone heard my colorful language. "That man is an idiot," I muttered and dialed the station's number for the second time. It rang and rang. My fingers tightened around the phone, anger rising in my chest. The fool was refusing to take my call. After the twentieth ring, I gave up.

I'd contact Noreen and ask her to pass on the message to the station, but first I'd snap a few shots of the victim. Given my recent past, I'd be the prime suspect, and possibly Beth, too. Any evidence I could gather before the cops arrived might help my case.

The back door creaked opened. "Have you called the police?" My sister stood in the doorway. Her fair hair hung past her shoulders, still wet from the shower.

"I tried to." I moved toward the door and went back indoors.

Beth wrapped her bathrobe around her slim body and shivered. "How do you stand it?" This is the first time I've seen a dead body, and it's a murder victim, too."

"I don't think you ever get used to it, but you learn to deal. There's no point in freaking out." I closed the door behind me. "You'd better get dressed. No point in catching a cold."

"Okay. I don't want to look like this when the police stop by. The police might have journalists in tow, and I can't afford to be photographed looking like this."

She held her hands over her perfect face. Frankly, my sister looked better just out of the shower than most of the rest of us did with a face full of makeup.

As I reached for my phone to call Noreen, it began to ring. Frowning, I checked the display. I hit Connect. "Hey, Lenny. Good thing you called. Something's come up. I can't make it to Galway today."

"I know that tone of voice," my friend said excitedly. "You found another body, didn't you?"

"Beth found him, actually, but yes. There is a corpse."

"Who is it this time? Anyone I know?"

"Dude, don't sound so enthusiastic. Believe it or not, I'm not thrilled by this unexpected turn of events." I glanced through the window at the partially frozen body. "And you kind of know him. It's Derek Riordan, a.k.a. Del."

"No way," Lenny breathed. "How'd he kick the bucket?"

"He had it kicked for him—forcibly. Multiple stab wounds to the chest and abdomen."

"That'll do it," my friend said sagely. "Did you call the guards?"

"Yeah, but that buffoon hung up on me, and I can't get hold of Liam. Can you try the station's number for me? I was about to call Noreen to see if she'd do it for me."

"Sure thing, but the weather is making my phone unreliable. I was glad I got through to you. Want me to pack your stuff, too?"

"Isn't your grandfather dropping you off at the harbor? How will you carry your stuff and mine?" The original idea was to take my car over to Galway on the ferry, but both the weather and Dead Del had put the brakes on that plan.

"We came by tractor." Lenny delivered this statement as if transportation by tractor was perfectly normal.

I stifled a laugh. "Probably the only way to get through the snow."

"Yeah. I'll take as much stuff as I can carry from Jake's place, and we can get the rest after the holidays. Sound good?"

"Yes. Thanks, Lenny."

Static crackled over the line. "You're breaking up. I'll call you as soon as I reach the station."

A moment after I'd disconnected, my sister reappeared from her bedroom. She'd dressed, dried her hair, and applied perfect makeup. I had no idea how she managed to transform herself in the amount of time it took me to do up my shoelaces.

"Is there any news?"

"Nope. Lenny's trying to call the police station on my behalf." My friend's number flashed on my phone's display. "That's him now. Hey, Lenny. Did you get through?"

"Sorry, Maggie. There's no reply."

I glanced out at the corpse propped up in one of my yard chairs. "I don't think I can drive to the station in this weather."

"Want to walk down to the harbor? Seeing as it's an emergency, we can ask the ferry captain to make a detour and drop us at Smuggler's Cove."

"That's not a bad idea." I checked my watch. "If I hurry, I'll make it before eight."

"Okay. See you in a sec."

I shoved my phone into my pocket and grabbed my purse. "I'm meeting Lenny at the ferry after all. We'll ask the captain to take us to Smuggler's Cove."

My sister's eyes darted toward the window. "You can't leave me here alone."

I sighed. "If you want to come with us, you'll need to hurry. I'm going to have to run through the snow as it is."

Beth flashed me a dazzling smile. "Give me five, and I'll be ready."

OUR CUNNING PLAN TO persuade the ferry captain to make an unscheduled detour went south the moment we stepped on board.

"I don't recognize any of the crew," I whispered to Lenny as we walked up the ramp and onto the ferry.

"Yeah. Neither do I," my friend replied. "A lot of people are sick with the flu at the moment."

I looked around. So far, we were the only passengers. And unless someone showed up within the next few minutes, it would be just us on the crew for the trip over to the mainland.

"Does it matter if you don't know any of these people?" Beth demanded impatiently—and loudly. "We have a murder to report. The crew will have to make a stop at Smuggler's Cove."

"Excuse me," I said to a young man wearing a ferry company uniform, who was shouting orders to a coworker on the other side of the boat. "I'd like to speak to the captain."

"Why? He has a boat to sail." The young man joined his friend, and they hoisted the ramp back on board the ferry.

"I need to discuss a serious matter with him." I followed the crew members as they walked back and forth getting the ferry ready to leave the harbor.

The guy I'd first addressed gave an impatient sigh. "I'll ask him, but he'll want you to wait until we've cast off."

The ferry shuddered into life, and we began our journey across the sea. "This is an emergency," I insisted. "We need to get to the police station in Smuggler's Cove. Please ask your captain to make a detour."

The young man laughed. "Good luck with that. Our captain doesn't make a detour for anyone."

I was wasting precious seconds arguing with this man, and the ferry was leaving Whisper Island behind. If we wanted to make it Smuggler's Cove, the captain needed to turn around soon.

Ignoring the protests of the crew members, I shoved my way past them and ran to the bridge. I yanked open the door and burst inside. The captain reared back in alarm at this unexpected intrusion. "What the——"

"You need to make a detour," I said breathlessly. "We have to get to the police station in Smuggler's

Cove, and we couldn't drive through the snow. Please. This is an emergency."

"Not my problem," the captain growled. "You can contact the police when you get to Galway."

"I have a dead body sitting in my garden," I snapped. "I need to report a murder."

The man snorted. "Did Frank put you up to this?"

"What? I don't know anyone called Frank. Now can you please turn the boat around and sail for Smuggler's Cove?"

The man shook his head. "No way. I'm not allowed to make detours unless there's a medical emergency."

"A man is dead. Doesn't that count as a medical emergency?"

"If he's dead," the captain retorted, "then he'll still be dead when you get to Galway. Now go away and let me do my job."

In frustration, I pulled my phone out of my pocket. A few swipes later, I shoved a photograph of Dead Del in the captain's face. "The guy's not looking his best, but you get the picture. Multiple stab wounds, lots of blood."

The man recoiled, his face a tableau of horror. "Where did you get that picture? The internet? What sort of sick individual are you?"

"Right now, I'm an individual who's sick of you. I have a frozen dead guy sitting on one of my yard chairs. I have a police sergeant who won't take my calls. And now you're refusing to take me to the nearest police station."

The young guy I'd first asked for help peered at the photograph on my phone. "Even if this is genuine, it makes more sense to wait until you get to Galway to report just at this stage. We will be there in thirty minutes."

I blew out my cheeks. "Will you at least contact the police on my behalf and ask them to meet me when the ferry docks?"

The captain was slowly recovering his composure. "All right. I'll call them, but I want you to stay away from me."

"With pleasure."

I stomped back to Lenny and Beth. My sister was frowning at her phone. She looked up at my approach. "Lenny gave me the station's number, but there's no reply."

"Useless buffoon," I muttered. "O'Shea, not you, Lenny."

"Look on the bright side," my friend said cheerfully. "The district superintendent will have to take you seriously when you make a complaint against O'Shea. Maybe he'll finally get rid of the old fool and leave Liam in charge."

"We can always hope."

We sank into a gloomy silence for the duration of the journey. When we docked in Galway, Inspector Craddock and Gavin Reynolds were waiting for us. The captain emerged from the bridge and glared at me. "I hope you're not going to waste their time now."

"I wouldn't dream of it," I retorted. "And thanks for nothing."

I stomped down the ramp, my mood growing worse with every step. The sight of Inspector Craddock's hostile face had that effect.

"Wait up, Maggie." Lenny ran down the ramp and caught up with me. "They're going to want to talk to you at the station. Can you collect my tech gear as well as yours? I'll go to Jake's apartment and pack our stuff."

"Okay. I'll call you when we're finished, but it might take a while."

He checked the time. "I need to be back on the island for your aunt's pageant. That means catching the three o'clock ferry."

"It's only nine now. We'll make it." My voice sounded more optimistic than I felt. I had no idea how long Craddock and Gavin would keep us at the station, but I was determined not to let my holiday plans be derailed by Del, dead or alive.

t five minutes to three, Gavin pulled up in front of the ferry. "If you run, you'll make it."

Beth and I needed no further encouragement. We tumbled out of the squad car. "Have a good Christmas," I called. "See you on New Year's Eve."

We waved to him and sprinted down the pier to the ferry.

When we clambered up the ramp, Lenny was already on board, pacing impatiently. He pounced on us the instant he saw us. "Man, I thought you wouldn't get here on time."

"We almost didn't." I shivered in the strong sea breeze and wrapped my scarf around my neck. "Want to go inside and we'll fill you in?"

"Yeah. The captain said we could have free drinks." Lenny grinned. "I think he's feeling guilty for casting you in the role of a madwoman."

I laughed. "His expression when I showed him the photo of Dead Del was fabulous. I'll cherish the memory."

"Ugh." My sister shuddered. "The whole situation gives me the creeps. That was my first time in a police station in an official capacity. I don't know how you two can stand hanging out in those places."

"We don't hang out there for fun," I said, descending the stairs to the ferry's small café. "Lenny and I only go near police stations when we're involved in an investigation."

"Which is often." My friend gestured for us to sit. "What will you have?"

I requested an espresso and Beth opted for a cappuccino. While Lenny placed our order, I scanned my surroundings. In contrast to this morning, the ferry was crowded. For anyone who wanted to reach Whisper Island before Christmas, this was one of the last ferries due to cross.

A minute later, Lenny returned with our coffees. The brown liquid tasted even worse than it looked, but at least it was warm. I cradled my cup in my hands, relishing the heat against my cold skin.

"Come on, ladies. Don't leave me in suspense." Lenny looked from Beth to me. "What happened at the station? Did you learn anything new?"

In the noise of the café, no one would overhear us.

"The good news is we're not suspects," I began. "Inspector Craddock and Gavin's early morning siege wasn't a waste. They didn't get Del, but they were able to arrest his brothers. One of the brothers went to pieces and confessed his role in the robberies in Galway and on Whisper Island, and confirmed that Derek was using Dennehy's as part of a counterfeit goods racket. They all deny any involvement in the three murders."

"The police are pretty certain that Del killed the first two victims, right?" Beth looked at me for confirmation.

"That's correct. The question is: who killed Del?"

"Siobhan?" Lenny suggested. "Maybe she found out about the murders and killed him in a fit of rage."

I shook my head. "I don't think so. Siobhan caught the last ferry to Galway yesterday evening. She must have left soon after Beth and I saw her in the hotel grounds. By that point, the police were looking for Del and met her off the ferry. Depending on what the pathologist says, it's unlikely Siobhan could have killed him. She spent the night at the station in Galway, answering questions, and Gavin got the impression that she was genuinely devastated when he told her Derek was dead."

"Did she reveal anything interesting?" Lenny asked. "Like, did she know her boyfriend was a killer and bank robber?"

"She claims she only found out about it yesterday because she caught Derek sneaking part of the loot into her suitcase," Beth supplied, her face animated. "She'd heard about the bank robbery and put two and two together. When Maggie and I saw her, she'd just had a fight with him about it and stormed off to clear her head. Siobhan says Derek was alive when she left him."

"To sum up, Derek a.k.a. Del murdered Jasper and Ms. Butt Bleach, and he was the guy who held a gun to Beth's head." I added another sugar to my coffee to make it palatable. "Three of his brothers were among the bank robbers, and the police suspect two of their friends were also involved."

"The night of our stakeout, Del and Jasper made it pretty clear that neither of them was the gang's leader." Lenny's brow creased. "Did the talkative brother mention who was in charge?"

I shook my head. "He claims he didn't know. Del got orders directly from the gang's mastermind, and he passed them on to the rest of the group."

My friend eyed me shrewdly. "Did you ever get through to your pal, Barry?"

"Not yet, and I know what you're thinking." I pulled a face. "The thought crossed my mind, too. Barry has the brains to plan a complex criminal operation, but I don't know that he has the temperament."

"Just because you like him doesn't mean he didn't do it," Beth pointed out. "His nice guy persona could be an act."

"Speaking of acting——" Lenny pulled a colorful flyer from his jacket pocket, "——I found this at Jake's place. It's probably nothing, but I thought I'd ask you, just in case."

I took the flyer from him and examined it. It advertised a performance of Oscar Wilde's *The Importance of Being Earnest*. "Where did you find this?"

"The police searched the rubbish in the kitchen, but kindly left it to stink up the place." Lenny wrinkled his nose as if in remembrance of the stench. "When I tied up the bag to take it outside, this flyer fell out. I only kept it because it struck me as odd. If you wanted to go to the theater, why would you have a flyer for a play that had already finished its run?"

I took another look at the flyer. And sucked in a breath. "This play was put on by Tracey's acting group."

"The one who accosted me with her business card?" Beth asked in a bone-dry tone.

"Yes." I ran a finger down the list of performers. Unsurprisingly, Tracey had played Gwendolen, one of the main female roles in the play. A stirring of excitement tickled my stomach. Finally, I had a lead. "The Eyre Square Players. I'm going to look up the group online."

I located my phone in my purse and checked the site for Tracey's acting group. I swiped through photos of recent plays they'd put on. My former coworker featured prominently, frequently taking the starring role. I found the photos from November's production of *The Importance of Being Earnest* and scrolled to the bottom of the list of people involved in the play.

At the sight of one name, my heart lurched.

"Look at this." I jabbed a finger at the screen. "Cara Mackey was Lady Bracknell's understudy."

"Ms. Butt Bleach was part of Tracey's acting group?" Lenny whistled. "Didn't you say Tracey was around when Ms. Butt Bleach approached you at Dennehy's?"

"Yes, she was, although she disappeared pretty fast." My mouth hardened. "And she never mentioned she knew Cara."

"Will you tell the police?" Beth demanded. "You said Tracey lives in Galway, right?"

"Correct, and I'll send Gavin a text right away. Siobhan didn't mention anything about Tracey spending the night on Whisper Island, so we can assume she went home on Friday evening."

"Once you contact him, you're officially on vacation," my sister said. "Seriously, Maggie. It's in the police's hands now."

"Your sister hates not being part of the action." Lenny grinned at me. "Right, boss?"

I stuck my tongue out at him. "Yeah, but I know when to call it quits. We have no excuse to go back to Galway, and Gavin wouldn't let us tag along even if we did."

"No, he wouldn't." My friend sounded wistful.

"We'll have to rely on your Santa Claus impression to distract us." I cast him a sly smile. "And you get to try out your padded suit."

Lenny's thin face lit up at the mention of his beloved padded suit. "That's the only part I'm looking forward to. I got the XXL size, so I'm gonna be huge."

Catching my sister's bemused expression, I added, "On Whisper Island, we take our entertainment wherever we find it. Murder victims, bank robberies, Lenny in a costume…we're not fussy."

Beth laughed. "Con and Luke will be there. If Lenny impresses Con with his performance, he might cast him in his movie."

"No way. I'm sticking to private investigation. Actors only get to pretend to go on stakeouts. We get the real deal."

A kaleidoscope of images from our various disastrous stakeouts flashed through my mind. "That we do." I raised my coffee cup. "Congratulations to my fellow sleuths. Hopefully, Gavin will contact us with news of an arrest before Lenny sweats to death in his padded suit."

29

T he town hall was located in an old building near the Smuggler's Cove library. Philomena and her helpers had hung tinsel and festive garlands from every conceivable space, and a huge Christmas tree dominated the center of the stage. The hall was packed with islanders of all ages. I spotted the Two Gerries and The Spinsters from the Movie Theater Café, as well as Noreen and her friend, Sister Pauline. Lenny's pharmacist friend, Mack, waved to us from his perch in the back row, and I spent the first few minutes after my arrival fielding questions about my latest dead body.

After a garrulous elderly lady released me from her clutches, Beth laid a manicured hand on my arm. "Is it okay if I sit with Con and Luke? They saved me a place."

"Sure. Go for it." I dodged curious neighbors and made it to the seat Liam had saved for me.

When I slid in beside him, he kissed me on the lips, his rough cheek tickling my soft skin. "I hear you've had a busy day."

"No thanks to your esteemed fellow officer." I scowled at the thought of the work-shy buffoon who'd refused to take my call. "It'll give me great pleasure to file a formal report against him."

"I've already filed one," Liam said easily. "The district superintendent needs to hear your side of the story, but Sile overheard O'Shea refusing to listen to you, and letting the phone ring when you tried to call back. As of this evening, O'Shea is on administrative leave."

"Wow. I didn't expect things to move that fast."

My boyfriend's smile broadened. "Put it this way: if he were a cat, he'd have used up all of his nine lives by now. The superintendent is sick of the Whisper Island Garda Station getting a bad reputation because of O'Shea's incompetence."

"Once your brother and Craddock catch up with Tracey, all of this will be over." I leaned against Liam, and noticed him stiffen. "Oh, I'm sorry. I didn't think. Do you have any news on Robyn's stalker."

"None so far. Robyn contacted me this afternoon. We've decided to enroll Hannah in the island school, at least provisionally."

I blinked. "How does Hannah feel about that?"

"I haven't mentioned it to her yet. I need to find a sitter first. Melanie Greer mentioned the possibility of Hannah coming to their house after school, if their childminder is okay with taking on an extra kid."

"That would be good for Caoimhe, too. She's not the most sociable of kids, and Hannah brings her out of her shell."

"Before I forget, I borrowed your car. When we were finished examining Riordan's body, my squad car refused to start, and I had your set of spare keys."

"No problem. How did you get through the snow?"

He grinned. "I'm afraid I pulled rank. I asked the snow plow driver to clear the coast road so the police could get through. We did have a murder to investigate, even if it just so happened to have occurred next door."

"Speaking of the police, did one of your fellow officers have anything to do with Lenny's strange behavior in the Dumpster? He acted mighty weird when Sile showed up. Come to think of it, he always does."

Liam winked at me. "I'm saying nothing. You'll have to ask Lenny about that."

A dramatic drumroll and flickering lights indicated the start of the pageant. The curtain rose, and we were treated to ninety minutes of singing and dancing children, including Hannah, who'd been assigned the role of an elf.

Lenny didn't make his grand entrance until the end of the play. He lumbered onto the stage in a massive padded suit that made him look five hundred pounds. "Ho, ho, ho. Merry Christmas, everyone."

The children cheered and clambered around Santa, waiting for their present. With the exception of the youngest Greer child, who took exception to a fellow reindeer, the performance went off without a hitch.

Until my sister screamed.

Beth's shriek filled the hall, making heads swivel and eyes strain to see what had prompted her outburst. Liam and I joined the rest of the audience in trying to discover the source of my sister's distress, but we drew a blank until Lenny let out a yowl from the stage. "Tracey," he roared, lurching forward and hurling himself off the stage.

My friend was not the agilest person at the best of times, and wearing an XXL padded suit under his costume did not help matters. Instead of landing in the aisle in front of the stage, Lenny's maneuver sent him flying into the audience. People shrieked as my friend crowd surfed over several rows of seats, losing his fake beard and a cheek stuffer in the process.

Before Lenny had time to free himself from the spectators, I was on my feet, running toward my sister.

"What happened?" I demanded when I reached her.

Wordlessly, she pointed to the back of the hall. I whirled around to see Tracey holding a knife to Con Ryder's chest. At that moment, the lights came on. Tracey blinked, her eyes adjusting to the light. She pressed the weapon closer against Ryder's chest. "Nobody move," she snarled, "or I'll knife him."

If my guess was correct, she'd already knifed one man today. She wouldn't hesitate to stab another.

My breath froze when Liam stepped forward. "Please, Tracey. Let him go and talk to me. We can sort this out."

She sneered at him. "I doubt that. The only person I want to talk to is Ryder. Now everyone, stand back, and let me leave."

Aware of the knife to Ryder's throat, a horrified silence hovered over the room. The moment Tracey and her hostage were out the door, I was in motion. Ignoring Liam's shout of protest, I took off at a sprint.

Outside the town hall, Tracey almost mowed me down as she roared past in a BMW that looked very like the Greers' car. Without hesitating, I ran into the parking lot and found my car. I slid behind the wheel. The passenger door opened and Liam leaped in, barking instructions into his phone.

I'd just gunned the engine when the back door opened an enormous Santa squeezed into the back. "You're not leaving me behind," Lenny wheezed, pulling his body forward onto the seat.

"Can you fit?" I demanded, noticing the padded butt that was protruding from the open door.

"Almost." He made a huge effort to pull himself into the car, but it was no good.

"Get out," Liam yelled. "We have to go after them."

Lenny huffed and puffed before turning a sheepish face to us. "I think it's a Pooh Bear situation. I can't get in, and I can't get out."

Liam let out a string of uncomplimentary phrases, while I failed to stifle my laughter.

"Just drive, Maggie," Lenny said. "I'll be fine."

I wasn't convinced, but we didn't have time to quibble. I took off, and we sped out the gate, although "sped" was an exaggeration. With the snow and ice, we couldn't go fast, but the poor driving conditions also meant that Tracey wasn't driving at full speed, either.

By the time we reached the end of the town and the start of the coast road, Lenny had succeeded in pulling the rest of himself into the car by shedding his padded behind and throwing it out onto the road. "There she goes," he said mournfully, regarding the discarded piece of costume. "And I only got to wear her once."

"She? Since when did a costume have a gender?" Liam demanded, still grumpy over the delay Lenny had caused us.

"When this is all over, I'll buy you a replacement." I eased the car over the snow-covered road and dared to press down on the gas.

"There she is." Liam pointed through the windshield at the car lights in front of us.

The BMW slid all over the road, perilously close

to the cliff edge. My heart was in my throat as I braked and pulled in to the side of the road farthest from the cliff. Tracey's car continued swerving from side to side, first left, then right, then left again.

"They're going to go over the cliff," Liam said in a tone so calm it chilled my soul. "And there's nothing we can do to stop them."

But the BMW didn't go over the edge. Instead, it lurched to the right and landed in the snow-filled ditch. I was out of my car in an instant, Liam right behind me. "Stay back, Maggie. I don't want you to get—"

A bullet zipped through the air and hit Liam in the leg. With a cry of surprise, he went down. Con Ryder crawled out of the passenger side of the BMW, keeping low. Tracey leaped out from behind the car and fired another shot with her revolver.

I slid over to Liam. "Where did she get you?"

"It's a graze. I'll be okay. Just hurts like the devil."

He tried to stand, but stumbled. A third bullet whizzed past, narrowly missing my ear. "Tracey only has three bullets left," I whispered, "and she's a lousy shot. Let's persuade her to get rid of them, and then take her down."

"I can help with that," Lenny whispered, crawling toward us. He'd landed in the snow outside the back of the car. I suspected his efforts to run had been hampered by a combination of ice and his costume.

"I don't think that's a good idea," Liam said dryly. "Leave this to Maggie and me."

"Seriously, Lenny," I urged. "Stay down. Whatever Tracey's goal was with her crime empire, it's come crashing down on her. She's manic and she's desperate. I don't want you to get hurt."

A bullet whizzed past. This time, it did graze my ear. Before I had time to react, Liam threw himself on top of me, pressing me down into the snow a second before another bullet hit the side of my car and shattered the window.

"Only one bullet left," he whispered, his warm breath tickling my good ear. "Stay down, Maggie. I can't lose you."

"That woman is insane." Con Ryder had crawled over to join us, keeping his head low. Some people clam up when they're spooked. Others develop verbal diarrhea. Ryder appeared to fall into the second category. "She kidnapped me because she wants me to make her film. Can you believe she said she organized bank robberies to finance it?"

"I do believe it," I said. "She's several bales short of a load."

"I can't make a film with a crazy person. I mean, I deal with crazy every day, but Hollywood crazy, you know? Diva demands and temper tantrums, not knives to my throat."

"Yes," I said soothingly. "Now keep your voice down. She still has one more bullet."

"Not for much longer," a voice beside me said.

To my horror, Lenny let out a guttural roar and charged at Tracey. He reached into his enormous pants and pulled out his second padded buttock. Before Tracey had a chance to fire her revolver for the last time, Lenny hurled his buttock at her, hitting her in the face. Tracey discharged a shot just as my friend threw his padded stomach at her. The bullet went through the material in an explosion of foam. Tracey began coughing and flailing, desperate for air. She fell to her knees, grasping at her throat.

I got to my feet, and Liam staggered to his. "Should we save her?"

"There are laws against letting someone choke to death without trying to help them," Liam said, dead-pan. "Unfortunately, I'm supposed to see that justice is done, and that involves keeping her alive."

"I can move faster than you," I said, already in motion. "Get the cuffs ready, and I'll try to clear her airway."

I grasped my former coworker under the arms and performed the Heimlich maneuver, not caring if I broke her ribs in the process. On my third attempt, Tracey hacked up a piece of foam and collapsed on the ground, gasping. Liam was on her in an instant and had her cuffed and in the back of my Yaris before she'd recovered the use of her vocal chords.

The rest of Christmas Eve passed in a blur of police statements, groveling thanks from Con Ryder, and Lenny embellishing the wonders of his padded suit. By the time I drove Liam, Hannah, and Beth back to Shamrock Cottages, it was already past midnight and officially Christmas Day.

When we piled out of the car, Hannah rubbed her sleepy eyes. "I'm too tired to open my presents."

Her father laughed and ruffled her hair. "That's good because I'm too tired to stay awake and take pictures."

Liam unlocked his cottage and Hannah went inside, after wishing all of us a yawned Goodnight.

Beth hovered on the doorstep of my cottage, and opened her mouth as if to say something. She closed it without uttering a word, and instead came over and hugged me.

I was so stunned by this act of affection that it took me a moment to react. "Wow," I said, once I'd recovered my wits. "What did I do to deserve more than an air kiss?"

This made my sister laugh. "Thanks for letting me stay over the holidays, Maggie. It's been fun, in a weird kind of way."

"Fun, Whisper Island-style," I drawled. "Stabbings, shootings, and crazy costumes."

"Pretty much. I can't wait to see what happens next." She smiled and stood back. "Night, guys. I'll leave you two lovebirds to your own devices."

After Beth had disappeared into my cottage, Liam pulled me into his arms and gave me a kiss that my grandmother's old-school romance novels would have described as "crushing." When he finally let me go, he brushed a stray curl from my cheek. "Merry Christmas, Maggie. May this be the first of many we celebrate together."

"And may all the others remain murder-free," I added with a grin.

He trailed kisses down my cheek. "Let's not get carried away, Miss Maggie. A dead body or two is part of your charm."

THE END

A NOTE FROM ZARA

• Thanks for reading **Rebel Without a Claus**. I hope you enjoyed Maggie's fourth adventure on Whisper Island! If you liked the sound of the non-alcoholic Cherry Apple Punch Maggie made in the story, turn the page for the recipe!

• Maggie and her friends will be back in the spring for more murder and mayhem in **Some Like It Shot.**

Happy Reading!

Zara xx

Join my mailing list and get news, giveaways, and a FREE Movie Club Mystery serial! Join Maggie and her friends as they solve the mystery in *To Hatch a Thief*. http://zarakeane.com/newsletter2

•I also have **an active reader group**, **The Ballybeg Belles**, where I chat, share snippets of upcoming stories, and host members only giveaways. I hope to join you for a virtual pint very soon!

Would you like to try Maggie's recipe for the Cherry Apple Punch cocktails that she served in **Rebel Without a Claus**? Here's the recipe!

CHERRY APPLE PUNCH

- 2 cups (475ml) orange juice
- 2 cups (475ml) apple juice
- ½ cup (120ml) cherry juice
- 2 (475ml) cups water
- 2 cinnamon sticks
- 10 whole cloves
- 2 whole star anise
- 5 bags hibiscus tea
- Honey or agave syrup to taste

1. Put all the ingredients (except for the honey and tea) in a large pot and bring to the boil.
2. Reduce the heat, cover and simmer for 15 minutes.
3. Add the tea bags and let them steep, covered, for 10 minutes.
4. Remove the tea bags and add honey or agave syrup to taste.
5. Reheat the punch until hot.

Maggie's tip: If you don't like honey or agave, choose the sweetener of your choice.

ALSO BY ZARA KEANE

MOVIE CLUB MYSTERIES—Cozy Mystery

Dial P For Poison

To Hatch a Thief (novella)

The Postman Always Dies Twice

How to Murder a Millionaire

The 39 Cupcakes

Rebel Without a Claus

Some Like It Shot (Spring 2018)

BALLYBEG SERIES—Contemporary Romance

Love and Shenanigans

Love and Blarney

Love and Leprechauns

Love and Mistletoe

Love and Shamrocks

BALLYBEG BAD BOYS—Romantic Suspense

Her Treasure Hunter Ex

The Rock Star's Secret Baby

The Navy SEAL's Holiday Fling

Bodyguard by Day, Ex-Husband by Night

The Navy SEAL's Accidental Wife

DUBLIN MAFIA—Romantic Suspense

Final Target

Kiss Shot

Bullet Point (2018)

ABOUT ZARA KEANE

USA Today bestselling author Zara Keane grew up in Dublin, Ireland, but spent her summers in a small town very similar to the fictitious Whisper Island and Ballybeg.

She currently lives in Switzerland with her family. When she's not writing or wrestling small people, she drinks far too much coffee, and tries—with occasional success—to resist the siren call of Swiss chocolate.

Zara has an active reader group, **The Ballybeg Belles**, where she chats, shares snippets of upcoming stories, and hosts members-only giveaways. She hopes to join you for a virtual pint very soon!

zarakeane.com

REBEL WITHOUT A CLAUS

Copyright © 2017 by Sarah Tanner

Published 2017 by Beaverstone Press GmbH (LLC)

This book is a work of fiction. The names, characters, places, and incidents are products of the writer's imagination or have been used fictitiously. Any resemblance to persons, living or dead, actual events, locales, or organizations is entirely coincidental

EBOOK ISBN: 978-3-906245-55-3

PRINT ISBN: 978-3-906245-56-0